Praise for the Daytime Mysteries

LOVE YOU MADLY

"Oh joy! Linda Palmer has another winner with this outstanding series." —*Rendezvous*

"A fantastic addition to this series. Full of insider dish on everything from New York co-ops to Daytime dramas, it zips along at a brisk pace . . . This is the rare book in which the main character and her world are every bit as intriguing as the mystery she finds herself embroiled in." —*Romantic Times*

"Entertaining . . . a complex story with unexpected twists and turns." —*MyShelf.com*

"A slice of pure escapism, a modern cozy set in the world of television." —*ReviewingTheEvidence.com*

LOVE HER TO DEATH

"Morgan is a wonderful character . . . strong, intelligent, and witty . . . The author clearly knows her way around Daytime TV and conveys the inner workings of a network with assurance. The mystery takes several interesting twists and will keep readers guessing." —*The Romance Reader's Connection*

"The heroine can be summed up in one word: spunky . . . Rich in characterizations and action . . . Linda Palmer proves with this fine cozy that she has what it takes to reach the top of her profession." —*The Best Reviews*

continued . . .

LOVE IS MURDER

Daytime Mysteries by Linda Palmer

LOVE IS MURDER
LOVE HER TO DEATH
LOVE YOU MADLY
KISS OF DEATH

kiss of death

linda palmer

BERKLEY PRIME CRIME, NEW YORK

THE BERKLEY PUBLISHING GROUP
Published by the Penguin Group
Penguin Group (USA) Inc.
375 Hudson Street, New York, New York 10014, USA
Penguin Group (Canada), 90 Eglinton Avenue East, Suite 700, Toronto, Ontario M4P 2Y3, Canada
(a division of Pearson Penguin Canada Inc.)
Penguin Books Ltd., 80 Strand, London WC2R 0RL, England
Penguin Group Ireland, 25 St. Stephen's Green, Dublin 2, Ireland (a division of Penguin Books Ltd.)
Penguin Group (Australia), 250 Camberwell Road, Camberwell, Victoria 3124, Australia
(a division of Pearson Australia Group Pty. Ltd.)
Penguin Books India Pvt. Ltd., 11 Community Centre, Panchsheel Park, New Delhi—110 017, India
Penguin Group (NZ), 67 Apollo Drive, Mairangi Bay, Auckland 1311, New Zealand
(a division of Pearson New Zealand Ltd.)
Penguin Books (South Africa) (Pty.) Ltd., 24 Sturdee Avenue, Rosebank, Johannesburg 2196,
South Africa

Penguin Books Ltd., Registered Offices: 80 Strand, London WC2R 0RL, England

This is a work of fiction. Names, characters, places, and incidents either are the product of the author's imagination or are used fictitiously, and any resemblance to actual persons, living or dead, business establishments, events, or locales is entirely coincidental. The publisher does not have any control over and does not assume any responsibility for author or third-party websites or their content.

KISS OF DEATH

A Berkley Prime Crime Book / published by arrangement with the author

PRINTING HISTORY
Berkley Prime Crime mass-market edition / May 2007

Copyright © 2007 by Linda Palmer.
Cover art by Haydn Cornner.
Cover design by Lesley Worrell.

ISBN: 978-0-425-21582-1

BERKLEY ® PRIME CRIME
Berkley Prime Crime Books are published by The Berkley Publishing Group,
a division of Penguin Group (USA) Inc.,
375 Hudson Street, New York, New York 10014.
The name BERKLEY PRIME CRIME and the BERKLEY PRIME CRIME design are trademarks belonging to Penguin Group (USA) Inc.

PRINTED IN THE UNITED STATES OF AMERICA

10   9   8   7   6   5   4   3   2   1

To D. Constantine Conte

I AM GRATEFUL . . .

To Claire Carmichael (aka mystery novelist Claire Mc-Nab), a marvelous writer and the world's most generous instructor. Thank you for turning a screenwriter into a novelist.

To Norman Knight: my real-life "knight" (and the uncrowned "Prince of Latvia").

To Morton Janklow and Rebecca Gradinger: you are more than brilliant agents, you are gladiators. Thank you for everything.

To Kate Seaver, gifted editor. Thank you for your suggestions that made the manuscript better. It's a joy to work with you.

To a wonderful group of "test readers," all so talented in your individual ways. Your early reactions are a tremendous help: Carole Moore Adams, Hilda Ashley, Dr. Rachel Oriel Berg, Christie Burton, Rosanne Kalil Bush, Carol Anne Crow, Ira Fistell, Richard Fredricks, Judy Tathwell Hahn, Nancy Koppang, Kay Partney Lautman, Susan Magnuson, Mari Marks, Jaclyn Carmichael Palmer, Dean Parker, Corrine Tatoul, and Kim LaDelpha Tocco. "Morgan" and I thank you.

To Rosanne and Buddy Bush, who took me to Cucina's and to The Main Street News in Palm Beach, Florida, to show me where "Walter Maysfield" would have his daily breakfasts and buy his out-of-town newspapers.

To Christie Burton and Susan Magnuson for convincing me that "Nancy" deserved a better man.

To Bruce Thompson, my friend and the computer "man of steel."

To Richard Fredricks, who ignited the idea of writing a mystery series.

To Wayne Thompson of Colonial Heights, Virginia, who is the inspiration for "Chet."

And to Berry Gordy, always and forever.

Chapter 1

BETTY KRAFT, THE assistant I shared with my co-executive producer, Tommy Zenos, burst into our office, waving a sheaf of papers. Her corona of gray curls bouncing like Ping-Pong balls, Betty exclaimed, "Morgan, what the hell did the writers do to Evan Duran?"

I was busy revising the taping schedule of *Love of My Life*, the Daytime drama for which I was also the head writer, because one of our actors had just shattered his right knee in a skateboarding accident.

On Tommy's side of our antique English partners' desk, his plump fingers broke off a substantial piece of a Cadbury's Fruit and Nut bar and popped it into his mouth while he shuffled through photos of child actors. Puzzled, Tommy looked up at Betty. "Who's Evan Duran?"

That name was vaguely familiar, but I couldn't quite place it. "Is there a problem?" I asked Betty.

"You bet your Emmy!" Betty was close enough for me to see that the pages she gripped were reports printed out from the network's *Love of My Life* chat room. "The soap channel's running old episodes," she said. "Some viewers noticed that the Evan Duran character went upstairs to take a nap—ten years ago—and never came back down again."

"It's not our fault," Tommy protested. "Morgan and I have only been with the show for five years."

"But you two are in the captain's chairs now," Betty said. "And fans are making jokes about the character's ten-year nap."

"Jokes?" Tommy blanched. "Morgan—think of something! Ridicule hurts a show. We could lose viewers!"

That worried me, too. The Global Broadcasting Network owned *Love of My Life*. If our audience share declined, Tommy and I could be replaced. In television, whoever is in control of a show when ratings fall gets the blame. I wanted to stay on *Love* to protect the characters and the storylines I had created. New head writers have a tendency to take shows in what they tout as "a fresh direction." The results could be disastrous, with beloved characters damaged and the hard-won trust of the audience betrayed.

Tommy's fear was different from mine. If he lost this job he might have to go to work for his father, Alexander Zenos. Zenos père had created three other popular daytime TV dramas, but he was a notorious tyrant, and Tommy was terrified of him.

I got up and crossed over to the wall behind Tommy where I'd pinned up our character graph. I'd begun making it the first week I was hired as an associate writer. Betty followed me.

Constructed of poster paper, the graph was two feet high and four feet long, and diagrammed the biological and emotional connections of all the continuing characters.

Using manicure scissors, I had cut small photos of the actors into the shape of Christmas tree ornaments, and hung them from the various branches of the multifamily, three-generation story. If a part had to be recast, I pasted the new actor's photo over the previous actor's image.

Betty studied the photos and said to me, "You're as pretty as any of the girls on the show. I've wondered why you didn't become an actress."

Compliments about my looks had always made me uncomfortable. "There are a lot of things I can't do, and one of them is act." I tapped a picture on a low branch, about two feet from the beginning of the graph. "Here he is—Evan Duran. He's Sylvia's younger brother. Duran was her maiden name, before she became Mrs. Hansen, Mrs. Truscott, and Mrs. Marks."

Betty grinned. "Hansen, Truscott, and Marks—sounds like she caught a whole law firm."

"She's been on the show for twenty years," Tommy said. "Erica Kane had five husbands by the time she'd been on *All My Children* for twenty years."

Back at my desk, I pulled out the character bio file and found the folder marked "Evan Duran." Scanning the pages, I said, "He started in his teens as a rock singer, then he joined the marines, went overseas, had some bad experiences—but the head writer at that time never specified exactly what happened to him. When Evan left the marines and came back to Greendale, he went to medical school . . . then his story just *stops*."

Betty cocked her head quizzically. "What does that mean?"

"That his story wasn't brought to a conclusion," Tommy said. "He wasn't killed, or sent away into a Witness Protection Program—something like that."

"It looks as though my predecessor forgot about him," I said.

Betty's narrow lips curved in a skeptical smile. "Just forgot? I wonder if that really was the reason."

Perhaps because she'd been a psychiatric nurse before she left that profession and joined the bizarre world of

Daytime drama, Betty was one of the sharpest observers of people I'd ever met. I asked her what she was thinking.

"That actor might have messed himself up on drugs or booze," she said.

Tommy grimaced. "We've been through that a couple of times. Not fun."

"I'm going to find out the truth," I said. "This could be a fabulous opportunity for the show. Fans love it when a familiar actor comes back in his original role. It'll be great publicity."

Tommy started to bite his thumbnail, but caught himself and instead took three packs of Reese's Peanut Butter Cups from the chocolate stash in the top drawer of his desk. He offered candy to Betty and me, but we declined.

Tommy tore open a package. "You've got thirty-two contract players to create stories for now. That's already a ton of work. Maybe the actor's dead," he said hopefully.

I shook my head. "We would have heard if anyone who'd been on the show passed away. Actors' obituaries always include their credits . . . Betty, look up the name of the actor who played Evan Duran and see if you can find out where he is now."

"Will do," Betty said crisply. She hurried out of the office on her mission.

Tommy finished one peanut butter cup and started another. "How are you going to explain the ten-year nap?"

I'd already been thinking about that. "Assuming that Betty can find him and that he's able to work, a couple of weeks before he appears on-screen I'll have characters start talking about him. His sister, Sylvia, will mention that after medical school he did his internship and residency in some other state—then he's been doing humanitarian work out of the country, but now he's coming back to Greendale."

"With some awful tropical disease?"

"No disease," I said firmly. Not to discourage Tommy's attempt at creativity, I added, "Maybe in a year or so.

Whether or not it's fatal depends on whether or not he's popular again with the fans."

Now that the problem was established as mine and not Tommy's, he expelled a deep sigh of relief. He picked up the pile of photos he'd been looking through before Betty came in and shook his head in frustration. "I don't know why anybody bothers to take pictures of kid actors. They look different five minutes after their head shots are printed." He tossed the glossies into the wastebasket beneath the desk. "We've got to find a ten-year-old girl to play Gareth's daughter. How 'bout if I have Casting schedule some kids for us to see tomorrow morning?"

"Tomorrow's fine."

In another few minutes I'd finished rearranging the taping schedule and gathered the papers together to give them to Betty for distribution to the actors, to our revolving "wheel" of four directors, and to the technical staff.

Taking my shoulder bag from the coat tree by the office door, I said, "I have an appointment downtown. See you after lunch."

Tommy was instantly curious. With a teasing glint in his eyes, he asked, "You sneaking off to have a romantic lunch with one of the men in your life? Which one—the cop or the crime writer? Or is there somebody new?"

Trying to sound casual, I said, "It's not as exciting as a rendezvous. Just some personal business—nothing to do with the show. I'll keep my cell phone on, in case you need to reach me before I get back."

I hurried out of the office without giving Tommy time to ask anything else. Much as I liked Tommy, I didn't want him, or anyone else, to know that I was on my way to hire a private detective.

Chapter 2

THE GLOBAL BROADCASTING Network building, where Tommy and I have our office and where *Love of My Life* is taped Monday through Friday, is located on Central Park West between Sixty-fourth and Sixty-fifth streets in New York City, not far from one of our competitors, the American Broadcasting Company. As always during weekdays, there was a moderate amount of pedestrian traffic on the sidewalk, but vehicle traffic was heavy. When I have time, and Manhattan is not being pounded with rain or snow, I like to walk, but even though it was a fine day in mid-May, I didn't have time to hike the five miles to my destination. I hailed an empty cab headed south, climbed in, and gave the driver an address on MacDougal Street in Greenwich Village.

During the ride downtown, I thought about the question Tommy had asked, whether I was going to meet Homicide Detective Matt Phoenix or writer Chet Thompson who was also a psychologist whose specialty was criminal behavior.

I'd met both of them seven months ago as a result of the murder of Damon Radford, who was then the network's head of Daytime. Many people detested Damon the Demon, and there were very few genuine mourners at his funeral, but I shot to the top of the long suspect list when I discovered—to my shock—that he had left me eight million dollars in his will. There was no way I could explain satisfactorily why a man I had continually rebuffed and insulted would leave me so much as a bus token, let alone what my friend Nancy Cummings called "F-you money."

The first thing I did was repay Nancy what she had loaned me for the down payment on my third-floor co-op in the Dakota. Next, I paid off the mortgage so I would actually own the first real home I'd ever had. Now, this afternoon, I intended to put to use some more of my unexpected inheritance.

Familiar sights of Manhattan flashed by the taxi's windows, but they barely registered. What I was about to do filled my stomach with the fluttering of nervous anticipation. And dread. By no means was I sure I was doing the right thing. A voice inside my head urged me to tell the cab driver to turn around and take me back to the office. But that was what I called "the voice of good sense," and I had never listened to it.

ROBERT NOVELLO PRIVATE Investigations is located on the ground floor of a nineteenth-century, four-story apartment building on MacDougal Street. It's half a block from the house in which Louisa May Alcott created *Little Women*, and a short walk to the club where Edgar Allan Poe wrote "The Raven." I knew those sites, and others in what I called "Literary Old New York," because I'd explored them eagerly when I first came to the city as an eighteen-year-old freshman at Columbia.

I pressed the bell labeled "Novello, 1B." After

identifying myself, and being buzzed in, I hurried down the hallway.

Bobby stood in his doorway, and greeted me with an exaggerated Groucho Marx leer. "Heh, heh, heh—come into my lair, young woman."

I gave his extended hand a friendly squeeze. Although his grip was gentle, his arms and shoulders were corded with muscles. His hands were strong—toughened through years of martial arts. I'd seen Bobby in an exhibition a few weeks ago, when he split a cement block in half with a single blow from one of those hands.

With his lively hazel eyes and the rose-gold hair that cascaded over a high forehead to curl just above his eyebrows, Bobby was one of the best-looking men I knew. But his handsome face was not what most people noticed first. Bobby is a Little Person, a dwarf standing four feet tall. His torso is as broad as that of a man of so-called normal height, but his legs are abnormally short.

I liked coming downtown to Bobby's home office. No matter what problem was worrying me, I always smiled with pleasure at the sight of Bobby's beloved exotic birds in their huge, antique cages. The musical trills and cheeps of what poet James Thomson called these "merry minstrels of the morn" seemed to rise in greeting to me.

Stepping aside to let me enter, he said in his melodic tenor, "When are you going to ditch those other guys and fall for me?"

"There's an insurmountable obstacle, Bobby." I lowered my voice to a whisper. "I have a . . . *c-a-t*."

Bobby performed the comic flinch he does at any mention of what he refers to as "the *c* word."

I saluted Bobby's feathered friends. "Hi, guys." A flash of brilliant red caught my attention. It was mostly crimson, but with touches of yellow and blue: a magnificent macaw, uncaged, and shifting from one foot to the other on a T-bar stand behind Bobby's desk.

"Well, there's a new face," I said. As though in response, the macaw squawked at me.

"I named him Archie, in honor of Nero Wolfe's Archie Goodwin."

Gesturing for me to sit in his red leather client's chair, Bobby stepped on an antique footstool and from there settled into the wing chair behind his desk. With the lemon yellow couch to my left, and the red leather chair positioned next to a table that was perfect for writing a check, Bobby had replicated the home office of Nero Wolfe in those Rex Stout mystery novels. And, like Wolfe for his clients, Bobby had done excellent work for me when I'd hired him previously.

Watching me with studied casualness, Bobby asked, "What can I do for you this time, pretty lady?"

"I want you to find a missing child," I said. "A girl. I don't care how much you have to spend."

Bobby grinned. "Music to my ears, but I'm on a case that's going to take another two or three weeks to wrap up. Will that time frame be a problem for you?"

I was almost relieved. "No. Finish what you're doing."

"Good." Bobby took a fresh notebook from the top drawer, opened it to the first page, and selected a pen from the collection standing in the red and white *Love of My Life* coffee mug I had given him a few months earlier, when I discovered he was a fan of our show. Pen in hand, Bobby asked, "What's the child's date of birth?"

"I don't know precisely."

Bobby shrugged. "No big deal. Where was she born?"

"I don't know."

"What's her name?

I shook my head. "Sorry."

Bobby laid the pen across the blank page in his notebook, planted his elbows on the desk, leaned forward, and asked, "Did you have a baby and give it up for adoption and now you want to find her?"

"No, that's not it." Until this moment, I hadn't been entirely sure I'd be able to tell Bobby the truth. Making the appointment to see him was a big first step. Now I was about to take a bigger one. "The child is *me*. I want you to find out who I am."

Chapter 3

A SUDDEN WAVE of nausea hit me. My throat closed up. I felt the bitter taste of bile rise into my throat and fought it back down.

Bobby whistled softly. "Wow. Even you people who look like you've got perfect lives can be carrying around some heavy baggage." I saw sympathy in his eyes. "Tell me about it."

I took a calming breath and plunged. "I don't know where I was born, who or what my parents were, or exactly how old I am. Twenty-four years ago I was found on a road outside a place called Downsville, West Virginia. A doctor there said I was approximately six years old."

"Were you alone when you were found?"

"I was in the back of a van . . ."

The image of a face I'd spent years trying to forget suddenly flashed into my mind, and a new wave of nausea struck.

Something must have shown in my face because Bobby

leaned forward, frowning in concern. "Morgan, are you okay?"

The queasiness passed, replaced by the cold steel of resolve. Just for a moment I had been that helpless child. *Never again.*

"I'm not helpless anymore," I said aloud. My voice sounded hard, but I needed to be hard if I was going to go through with my plan.

Bobby looked startled by my non sequitur, but he let me continue at my own pace, in my own way. With effort, I softened my voice to what I hoped was its normal tone. "Before we go into . . . that . . . I want to tell you about the person who found me."

Recalling one of my few happy childhood memories, I was able to smile. "He smelled like *coffee*," I said. "Maybe that's why I like coffee so much. His hair was gray, he wore glasses, and his face was round and red. His body was round, too, like a Santa Claus. He had a big gray mustache—really big, out to the sides and down over his top lip. His uniform shirt was so tight I thought the middle button was going to pop off. I kept staring at that button, but somehow it held."

"You said 'uniform.' Was he a cop?"

"A sheriff. Sheriff Maysfield."

"First name?"

"I don't remember. There's a lot I don't remember about . . . back then."

"Take it slow. Tell me what you can."

I made myself dredge up everything I could remember about my time as a prisoner, and about the monster in the van . . .

WHEN I FINISHED, I felt limp, exhausted.

Bobby's hands were balled into fists; his knuckles were white. "If I'd been your husband, I'd have wanted to find the creep and kill him."

I shook my head. "He never knew. I met Ian Tyler near the end of my sophomore year. He was a famous wildlife photographer who came to lecture. Instant love for both of us. We were married a week after we met, and I flew off to Africa with him. He taught me to use his cameras, so I could work with him. It was wonderful. During almost six years together, he told me practically his whole life story. The few questions he asked about me, I managed to deflect. I guess he thought an inexperienced girl of nineteen wouldn't have anything interesting to tell."

"He was wrong," Bobby said wryly.

"Don't think badly of him, please. I wasn't ready to talk about it, so I was careful not to volunteer anything that would have invited questions."

"I have a question about going to Africa: How did you get a passport? You'd have needed a birth certificate."

"When they couldn't find anyone who was looking for me, the sheriff went to a judge who created a birth certificate. He said it was something they did for 'foundlings.' I used it to get a passport as soon as I came to New York. One of my dreams was to travel, and I wanted to be ready."

Bobby nodded thoughtfully. "When you hired me the first time, I did a little research on you. I know you're a widow—your husband died in Kenya. A car accident."

"Our Land Rover blew a tire, and we went crashing down into a dry riverbed full of rocks. Ian was killed. I escaped with just a broken wrist, and managed to make my way to a game warden's station . . ." Determined not to let that old cloak of sadness settle over me, I shook it off. "While I was out of the country with Ian, I'd kept in touch by e-mail with my best friend, Nancy Cummings. You've met Nancy, haven't you?"

Bobby nodded. "The lawyer who looks like a swimsuit model."

More than one man had described Nancy in similar terms. If she heard that, I knew it would make her cringe.

I ignored it and went on. "I told Nancy I didn't want to stay in Africa without Ian. We'd been living *his* life, but all of a sudden I had to make a life of my own. She persuaded me to come back to New York and stay with her until I figured out what to do. With less than two years of college, and only the usual student part-time jobs, I didn't even know where to begin."

Amused, Bobby said, "You certainly found yourself a challenging new career."

"Pure luck. Nancy saw an article in *TV Guide* that said Global Broadcasting was looking for people to train as Daytime drama writers. They wanted what they called 'fresh voices.' Novelists or journalists or playwrights were invited to send in writing samples. Nancy talked me into submitting a play I'd written when I was a theater major. She'd kept a copy of it."

Afraid this story was getting to be as long as *Gone With the Wind*, I fast-forwarded to the end. "They liked the dialogue. The head writer of *Love of My Life* hired me to work with him."

Bobby was about to ask a question when my cell phone rang. The I.D. on the face told me the call was from my assistant, Betty Kraft.

"I'm sorry. I have to answer this, but I'll make it quick."

"Take your time." He settled back to gaze at his birds.

"Hi, Betty. Is there a problem?"

"Not at the moment," she said in her brisk, competent voice. "Jay Garwood is the actor who played Evan Duran. I Googled him. Not much information. No website. No acting credits since he was on our show."

"Do you know where he is?"

"AFTRA gave me the name of his old agent. Garwood was dropped from the client list, but the agent said he ran into him a couple of months ago, working as a bartender at Sauce for the Goose down on West Fourth, just above Seventh Avenue South. I checked—he's on days this week."

"Great work, Betty. Thanks. Now, would you call Archives and get us copies of his last few episodes?"

"They're already on your desk."

Once more, Betty had anticipated me. Tommy, who adored her—and needed the mothering she gave him—liked to say that beneath her steel-gray hair she had a steel-trap mind. "You're awesome," I told her. "What would we ever do without you?"

I heard Betty's dry chuckle. "Pray you never have to find out. Anything else?"

"You'll probably think of it before I do," I said with an appreciative laugh.

When I disconnected, Bobby asked, "Who else have you told about . . . your situation?"

"No one. Not even Nancy. All she knows is that I don't have any family, and that I lived in a Catholic boarding school until I won the scholarship that took me to Columbia. Columbia's where Nancy and I met."

"You remember the name of the town, and the sheriff," Bobby said. "Did you ever make any inquiries yourself?"

"No, for the same reason lawyers shouldn't represent themselves, because they're emotionally involved. I've tried to forget about that time, but I can't. I need answers."

"Last year I found a client's birth mother for him, but he didn't like what he learned. She wasn't anything like his fantasy," Bobby said. "Sometimes it's better to leave things alone. You've got a great job, and friends—a good life now."

Vehement, I shook my head. "I have to find out where I came from, and how I ended up in that van . . . I don't know any more about myself than anybody knows about a collarless animal they find and take home. Some nights I've looked at Magic and wondered what happened to his mother. Did he have any brothers or sisters? If he did, what happened to them? Where was he before Matt found him on the street, hungry and homeless? Not knowing . . . I think that may be why I fell in love with a man twice my age and abandoned my own dreams, why I went halfway around the globe with Ian, to follow *his*. Maybe it's why both Matt and Chet accuse me of not letting them really get to know me. When enough people say the same thing, it's time to listen."

Bobby was watching me carefully. "I get it. Okay, I admit you've got a good reason for this. Now tell me: What's the rest of the job?"

Caught. "You're right. There is a little more." I fought to keep my voice even, my manner cool. "The person who kept me in the van—I want to know whatever you can find out about him."

Bobby picked up his pen again. "Name?"

"All I know is . . . he made me call him 'Daddy.' " I almost gagged, but I controlled the reflex, and managed to force terrible visions back into the dark place where they lived.

I gripped the arms of Bobby's red leather client's chair. "Look, in addition to your own fee and expenses, I'm authorizing you to spend whatever you need to get information. I don't care what it costs."

"Money's a useful investigative tool," Bobby said. "It tends to loosen tongues. Suppose I find out what you want to know. *Then* what?"

"Your job's over."

"But what are *you* going to do?"

"I don't know," I said. But that was only partially true.

Bobby must be a good poker player; I couldn't tell what he was thinking.

Finally, he said, "Okay. Let's start with part one of the job and see where it takes us." He indicated the shoulder bag beside my chair. "Do you have a hairbrush in there?"

"Yes."

"Let me see it."

I took my emergency hair-taming tool out and handed it across the desk.

"You've got a good, healthy mane," he said. Carefully, he removed several strands from the bristles. "This is what I need—some hair that includes the roots."

"You're going to have it tested to get my DNA profile."

"If I turn up a potential blood relative for you, we'll be ready to compare so we can know for sure."

Bobby wrapped the strands around one index finger and placed them in a manila envelope he took from his desk. It was the same kind of envelope I'd seen Matt Phoenix and his partner, G. G. Flynn, use when they gathered evidence at a crime scene. An apt analogy, I supposed; my childhood was a crime scene.

Bobby wrote something on the flap and sealed the envelope. He put his notebook away and climbed down from his chair. "You need nourishment. I'll make us some lunch."

I managed a smile. "You can *cook*? Or am I being foolishly optimistic?"

"I make omelets," he said with pride. He started toward his kitchen. As I got up to follow, he added casually, "This lady I'm seeing taught me how."

Lady? I realized Bobby had been keeping a secret of his own!

Chapter 4

I FOLLOWED BOBBY into his compact yellow and white kitchen. Lined up against the back wall were a refrigerator, gas stove, stainless steel double sink, and a ceramic tile counter on which rested a microwave oven, toaster, juice-maker, TV set, and metal canisters labeled, with whimsical artistic flourishes, "For the Birds." Everything was immaculate.

A sudden breeze and the sound of flapping startled me, until I realized Archie had followed us into the kitchen. He flew directly to a T-bar perch in the corner of the window that faced onto Bobby's small back garden.

I saw two men in overalls working out there. One was unfurling a huge roll of chicken wire, while the other was packing thick layers of dirt against the brick wall that enclosed the garden.

"What's going on?" I asked.

Bobby looked past me and nodded, a pleased expression on his face. "I'm having a wall of clay put up. Macaws eat clay—it's important for their digestive systems. When it's finished, a chicken wire roof will go up over the garden. I'll have an outside aviary, so all the birdies who want to fly around outdoors will have a safe place to do it."

Bobby gestured for me to sit at the breakfast table next to the window. I noticed it had already been set for two. The napkins were cloth, not paper. I was pretty sure that Bobby's cloth napkins were due to a woman's influence.

Bobby extracted a mixing bowl—one of a matched set—and a new-looking omelet pan from a cabinet beneath the counter.

"So," I teased, "you've just been toying with me. Tell me about your lady. Is this serious?"

Bobby's cheeks turned pink with embarrassment, but he was grinning as he took eggs and milk and cheese out of the refrigerator.

"Could be. Maybe," he said. "Her name's Gail, and she's a Broadway dancer—she's in that new revival of *Chorus Line*. When she's not working, she loves to cook. Even makes her own pasta."

"Where did you meet her?"

Bobby's grin widened. "In the basement laundry room—her apartment's on the fourth floor. She's something special."

"And she has very good taste in men," I said with affection.

Bobby's color deepened. Pretending to ignore me, he moved his kitchen footstool into place in front of the stove, stepped up, and focused on making our lunch.

The cheese omelets were excellent. "My compliments to your teacher," I said.

"I want you to meet her, Morgan. Maybe you and Chet—or you and somebody—and Gail and I can go out together some night, when her show's dark."

"I'd like that," I said sincerely.

When we finished eating and were washing the dishes,

I asked, "Have you heard of a bar called 'Sauce for the Goose'?"

"I've been there. It's a neighborhood pub on West Fourth."

"An actor who used to be on our show tends bar there. I need to take a look at him, and maybe talk to him about coming back."

"I'll go with you," he said, putting the last dried plate in his china cabinet.

"Do you have time? I know you're on another case."

"I've got a couple of hours, until a report I'm waiting for comes in," he said.

SAUCE FOR THE Goose was less than half a mile from Bobby's house, a pleasant stroll on this beautiful spring day. Although of short stature, Bobby had a vigorous stride; I didn't have to shorten my own to accommodate him.

Within a few minutes we'd reached a two-story brick building that had dark green canvas awnings shading front windows made of beveled glass. The words SAUCE FOR THE GOOSE were written in white script on the green canopy above the entrance.

Bobby opened the door and stepped back for me to precede him.

Inside the bar it was pleasantly cool and dim. Coming from the afternoon brightness, my eyes needed a few seconds to adjust to the sudden reduction of light.

The building's walls and windows were thick enough to muffle most of the street noises. I was so accustomed to New York's routine din—the soundtrack of the city—that now I only noticed it in its absence.

Two elderly men and a middle-aged woman sat drinking at three separate tables, seemingly lost in their separate thoughts. At the far end of the bar two men in their thirties sat together, drinking and watching a baseball game on the TV set suspended from the ceiling. I knew what Bobby and I were doing here, but I wondered about the other customers. What kind of lives did they have outside Sauce for the Goose?

We took stools at the opposite end of bar from the ball game.

No bartender was visible. Indicating the swinging door behind the bar, between long rows of shelves that held bottles and glasses, Bobby said, "He must be in the back. Want me to go look?"

"No. He's bound to come out sometime."

An impish glint twinkled in Bobby's eyes. "Unless he's lying back there in a pool of blood and a bullet hole in his head, in which case you'll be right in the middle of another murder investigation. That'll make your devoted homicide detective go ballistic—no pun intended."

"Matt Phoenix is not *my* homicide detective. We're not going out together any longer."

To close the door on that subject, I turned away from Bobby to examine my surroundings. A sign on the north wall read GREAT GEESE OF THE WORLD. Below it, the surface was plastered with photographs: Mother Goose, Grey Goose Vodka, Goose Island Beer Company, The Goose Girl (with a framed copy of the Edna St. Vincent Millay poem called "The Goose-Girl" beside her), the young Anthony Edwards in his role of Tom Cruise's best friend, "Goose" in *Top Gun*.

Next to Edwards was a picture of the plane I recognized as a Howard Hughes invention: the *Spruce Goose*. He'd intended it to be a great American asset in World War II because it was designed to carry 750 fighting troops in full gear, and a couple of Sherman tanks. Unfortunately, construction on the immense wooden flying boat wasn't completed until several years after the war was over.

Below the plane were photos of beautiful actresses of the 1930s, '40s, and '50s—the "flock" of women who were rumored to have been more than friends to Hughes.

The door behind the bar swung open, and a man in a white shirt with the sleeves rolled up and a bar towel slung over his shoulder came through it.

He had a bushy beard and was a good ten years older than the picture of Jay Garwood on the *Love of My Life* chart at the office, but his straight nose with its high bridge was similar to that of the man I was here to see. When he came toward us, and stood beneath one of the recessed lights behind the bar, I saw a crescent-shaped scar just above his right eyebrow. I'd seen the same scar in our picture of Jay Garwood.

Garwood greeted Bobby with a nod of recognition. "Hey, Bud." His gaze went from my face to my chest, and stayed there. With an insolent sneer, he said, "Another beautiful broad. You little guys must do something special in the sack."

"Cut that kind of talk," Bobby snapped. "This lady's my friend."

Garwood leaned on the bar and said smoothly, "Just kidding. I didn't mean to offend."

"You want to go?" Bobby asked me.

"Not yet."

"Bad joke. I had a rough night, but that's no excuse—I was out of line." Garwood sounded sincere and extended his hand. Bobby was gracious and took it. They shook and Garwood turned to me. "I apologize."

I nodded. "Accepted. Let's forget it."

"What'll you have?" Garwood asked us.

"A diet anything," I said.

"Make it two."

Garwood set tall glasses on the bar in front of us and poured two soft drinks from a large plastic bottle. Into one glass he put a plastic spear with a cherry and a piece of pineapple on it. He handed me that glass, gave Bobby plain soda, and began to polish a tray full of glasses.

Even though I was sure of the answer, I asked, "Are you Jay Garwood?"

He stopped polishing. "Who wants to know?"

"I'm Morgan Tyler. I work on *Love of My Life*."

Garwood's lips curled in a sneer. "What do you play on that piece of crap? A nun who can't keep her vows? An oversexed neurosurgeon? Or maybe a lawyer-by-day, hooker-by-night?"

"You're digging your grave with your big mouth," Bobby warned.

I shook my head at Bobby. "It's all right." To Garwood, I said, "I'm the head writer and co-executive producer. I came down here to meet you, and *perhaps* discuss your coming back to the show. But if you think the show is so bad—"

Garwood did a lightning-quick change. "That was just another stupid joke. *Love* was a great show! Still is."

"You don't watch," I said, "or you would have known I'm not on it."

Garwood made another instant course correction. Now playing aw-shucks embarrassed, he stared down at his hands and said softly, "You're right. I don't turn it on. After I was let go, it just hurt too much to see everybody else working." He looked up and gave me soulful. "I couldn't get any other acting jobs. Casting directors all said I was too identified with Evan Duran. After a while, I couldn't get any auditions at all. Prime-time shows didn't want me because I'd been branded with the scarlet letter *S*—soaps. And movies—forget it! When I couldn't keep up the payments on the house in Great Neck, my wife called me a loser. She took our little girl and divorced me."

"Things have changed in ten years," I said. "Actors on Daytime get a lot more respect now."

"Did you mean it, about wanting me back?"

"Yes. Come to the studio tomorrow morning and we'll talk specifics."

A happy smile lighted his face. Fingering his beard, he said, "I'll shave, and have my hair styled."

"No! Keep the beard. I have an idea about you getting shaved—on the show." Mentally, I was picturing having a female character shave him, in a scene that could be both poignant and sensual.

The ringing of a cell phone interrupted my thoughts. Automatically, Bobby patted his jacket pocket and Jay Garwood reached for the phone clipped to his belt.

"It's *my* phone," I said, fishing it out of my shoulder bag. A glance at the faceplate identified the caller as Nancy Cummings.

"Morgan, I really need to talk to you." I heard anguish in her voice. "Something's happened."

Chapter 5

MY CAB TURNED off Central Park West and slowed to a stop in front of One West Seventy-second Street, the Dakota. Much of the movie *Rosemary's Baby* was filmed in this late nineteenth-century Gothic apartment building. It's also the setting for Jack Finney's popular time-travel novel, *Time and Again*. To some who pass by, this address is a curiosity, or a Manhattan landmark, but to me it's home.

Nancy Cummings, tall and elegant in a navy blue linen summer suit, with shoulder-length hair the color of champagne, waited for me in front of the stone archway entrance. She was listening intently to Ralph, the Dakota's day security man, who stood in front of his phone booth–size shelter. Ralph spotted me and hurried over to open the taxi's rear door.

"Hi, Mrs. Tyler. Your friend's here."

"Thanks, Ralph." I greeted Nancy, surveyed her fashion-magazine-cover outfit, and said, "You're the only person who can wear linen without it getting wrinkled. Don't you ever sit down?"

Ignoring my lighthearted remark, Nancy squeezed my hand and whispered urgently, "Arnold lied to me!"

"What? What happened?"

"Shhhh. I'll tell you when we get upstairs." With her perfect posture and controlled movements, she appeared calm, but I heard the tension in her voice.

We started for the entrance into the courtyard when Ralph called, "You want me to get your mail, Mrs. Tyler?"

I paused in midstride. "Did a messenger bring a package from my office?"

"No, ma'am."

"Then leave the mail; I'll come down for it later."

"Yes, ma'am. I'll keep an eye out for your messenger." With a salute, Ralph retreated to his post.

Nancy and I hurried past the courtyard's big round fountain with its profusion of sculpted calla lilies, to the entrance to my wing of the building. Inside, our heels clicked on the marble floor that led to the ornately carved staircase.

My co-op is on the third floor. I always take the stairs, but Nancy usually prefers the luxury of the vintage wood-paneled elevator. Today she was too impatient for that, and followed me so closely I had to accelerate my pace.

The moment I unlocked my front door, I heard the welcome sound of soft little paws running down the hallway toward us. I dropped to my knees just as my green-eyed, all-black cat made a graceful leap into my arms and started to purr.

I rubbed the top of his silky head. "Hello, Magic. I'm home early."

Nancy leaned over to give him a few affectionate strokes. "Hi, little sweetie." She straightened up, said, "Let's make some coffee while I get my head together," and headed for the kitchen.

While Mr. Coffee did its brewing thing and Nancy set mugs and accessories on the table, I changed Magic's water and opened a fresh can of Natural Balance salmon for him. "What was Ralph telling you that was so absorbing?"

"He was explaining how he handicaps horses for betting at the racetrack."

It was the last answer I expected. "How in the world did that subject come up?"

Nancy gestured to her satchel handbag. A magazine called *Young Rider* was sticking out of it.

"Oh, Ralph must have thought you were interested in horses," I said, adding with a smile, "instead of in a young rider's father."

In reply, Nancy yanked the magazine out of her bag, and threw it into the kitchen trashcan. The sound startled Magic, who looked up from his dish in alarm.

Nancy was immediately contrite. Reaching out to give him a gentle rub under his chin, she said softly, "Oh, Magic, I'm sorry. I didn't mean to frighten you. Forgive me?"

He went back to eating with his usual healthy appetite.

"I don't know what's the matter with me," Nancy said. "I haven't thrown anything in anger since I was ten."

I filled the two mugs with coffee and joined her at the kitchen table. "Are you ready to tell me what happened?" She nodded. "Is this about Didi?" I asked, referring to the twelve-year-old daughter of the divorced criminal lawyer Nancy loved, the girl who was a champion rider.

Nancy uncharacteristically loaded her mug of black coffee with three spoons of sugar. "Do you have any of Penny's carrot cake left?"

I shook my head. "I had it for breakfast."

"Just as well. I'm mad enough to kill—I don't want to get fat, too."

Two swallows of sweet coffee later, I heard the story. "Arnold called me this morning and said he'd come down with a cold and he was going to stay home in bed today to knock it out. He said he'd call me tonight. I was worried about him because his housekeeper's off visiting her daughter this week, so at one o'clock I picked up a big jar of his favorite chicken matzo ball soup and went to his apartment. But Arnold wasn't sick—and he wasn't alone."

My heart constricted with fear for Nancy. Arnold Rose was the first man with whom she had ever been completely in love.

"*Veronica* was there," Nancy said. She pronounced the name as though it tasted like poison on her tongue.

"Who?"

"His ex-wife, Didi's mother. Didi was there, too," Nancy added. "I wouldn't have minded Didi—but she and her mother were moving in with Arnold!"

"With Arnold? But you said they were moving back to New York this month, and he was finding them an apartment somewhere."

"*Somewhere* turned out to be in Arnold's building. He never told me that." Nancy's voice was full of pain, and anger. "Then today I discover that they're actually going to be living with him. At least until their apartment is ready—and it's on the floor below!"

Tears glistened in Nancy's eyes. I reached for her hand and held it comfortingly.

"When I showed up unexpectedly, he looked guiltier than one of his criminal clients. Morgan—he wasn't that nervous when we were waiting for the jury to come back in a murder one case!"

"Arnold is in love with you," I said. "If Didi and her mother are staying with him for a couple of days—even if they're going to be living in the same building, that's probably so he can see Didi a lot. You said yourself that you wanted him to be close to his daughter. I'm sure this arrangement is just a matter of convenience, for Didi's sake."

"If it's so innocent, why did he lie to me?"

"Because even men as smart as Arnold can be stupid about women. What's the wicked witch from Boston like?"

"She's one of those petite, porcelain-doll types." Nancy's tone was biting. "Shorter than Arnold, which means she can wear high heels with him while I can't. She was all superficial charm, but she treated me like *office help*! When Arnold introduced us, she looked for a moment as though she'd never heard my name, then she pretended to remember it and said in a sticky-sweet voice, 'Oh, yes—Nancy. You're Arnold's secretary, or do you call yourselves *assistants* now?'"

"Ouch! What did you say to that?"

"Nothing—for once in my life, I was nonplussed. Arnold told her I was an attorney—and his *friend*. He actually used the word 'friend'! She made a big show of apologizing for what she called her 'natural mistake' because I'd come to the apartment with chicken soup. I swear, Morgan, I wanted to hit her over the head with the jar!"

"Veronica and Arnold are divorced," I reminded Nancy.

"Some divorced couples get back together," Nancy said. "I never asked Arnold why they broke up, or who left who. It didn't seem important."

The phone connected to the Dakota's reception desk rang. I got up and crossed to the instrument mounted on the wall.

It was Chet Thompson. "Honey, I'm downstairs." I heard urgency in his voice. "May I come up?"

Now what? "Of course."

"A messenger just delivered a package for you. Want me to bring it?"

"Yes, please." Replacing the receiver, I told Nancy I was worried. "Chet's here, but he never just drops by without calling first."

"This must be your day for friends in crisis," she said ruefully. "He's gorgeous, but not a pretty boy. He's accomplished, rich, and straight, and he's tall enough so I could wear high heels with him. I'm surprised some woman hasn't snatched him up already."

"Maybe because he doesn't stay in one place long enough."

The front bell rang. "My Lord," Nancy said, "he must have taken the steps three at a time."

As soon as I opened the door, Chet Thompson stepped inside and drew me into his arms. The box he carried pressed against my back.

His kiss was warm and deep, full of desire, but not a "let's make love" kind of kiss. When we came up for air, I said, "You're breaking our date tomorrow night because you're going out of town."

Chet stared at me in amazement. "You could tell that from how I kissed you?"

He handed me the box he'd brought up from the reception desk. A glance told me it was the old Jay Garwood tapes I'd asked Betty to send over to the apartment.

"I'm tempted to let you think I can read minds—or, rather, lips," I said, "but the truth is when I opened the door I glimpsed a suitcase in the hall."

He chuckled, but I saw lines of anxiety etched deep in his face.

"Nancy's here," I said. "Come into the kitchen and have coffee with us. Do you want something to eat?"

He shook his head. "No time. Cab's waiting downstairs to take me to the airport. My father's had a heart attack."

"Oh, no!" I grasped Chet's hand in sympathy.

"It's serious. Dad's in a hospital in El Mirage, Arizona. My mother's with him, but I want to be there for anything I can do."

"Of course. Will you call, and tell me how he is?"

"The minute I know anything. I'll come back as soon as I can, but I'm not sure just when that'll be." In a teasing tone, he added, "You're not going to run off and marry anybody while I'm gone, are you?"

"Not a chance." *That's the only thing in my life I'm absolutely sure about.* "I'll pray for your dad," I said. "Fly safely." We kissed again, and said goodbye.

When I returned to the kitchen, I told Nancy what had happened.

"Oh, I'm so sorry. I hope his dad's going to be all right." From the concerned expression on her face, I thought she might still be grieving the loss of her own beloved father several years ago.

Hoping to lift her spirits, I waved the box of tapes and said, "How about dinner and a movie?"

NANCY AND I watched Jay Garwood's scenes from ten years earlier on the TV in the den, lounging in club chairs. Our feet were up on the big, shared ottoman, trays of Chinese takeout in our laps.

Magic nestled between us on the ottoman. He was watching the TV in his sphinx position: front paws curled under, facing the action on the screen. Soon as one scene was over, I used the remote to fast-forward to Garwood's next appearance.

"He's playing a nice guy here," I said, "but I saw a flash of *bad guy* in the bar this afternoon. That's a quality I can use. We need another troublemaker for the Cody-and-Amber storyline."

Turning to Nancy, I realized she hadn't been paying attention to me; she was still stewing about Arnold's ex-wife.

"*Veronica* must have made at least one trip to the plastic surgeon," Nancy said. "A nose like hers has never occurred in nature!"

Chapter 6

I WAS ABOUT to leave for the office when Chet called from Arizona. It was eight A.M. my time, two hours earlier for him.

"Dad made it through the night," he said. "The doctor's optimistic, but he warned Mom and me it'll be awhile before we can be sure he's going to be okay. I'm encouraged because Drake Memorial's cardiac unit has the best reputation in the state."

"Is there anything I can send you? Or your mother?"

"No, but thanks. You can keep the prayers coming."

"You've got it," I said.

"What's going on in your nutty world?"

Chet laughed when I told him about discovering we had a character who lay down for a nap ten years earlier and vanished from the story. "Betty found the original actor, so we're going to work him back in. And this morning Tommy and I are auditioning child actors."

On his end of the line Chet groaned. "A couple years

ago I had dinner with a woman I thought might be interesting. In the middle of the appetizer course she told me her profession was managing her six-year-old son's *career*. That date lasted about twenty-five minutes before I sent her home in a cab."

In the background, I heard a woman's voice. Chet turned away from the phone for a moment. When he came back he said, "Honey, they're going to let us visit Dad in the ICU. I'll call you tomorrow."

After we said goodbye, I thought about our conversation. His father, Richard Thompson, a decorated former P.O.W., was the man Chet admired most in the world.

Magic sauntered into the room with that "it's time to pet me" look in his big green eyes. He rubbed the top of his head and his shoulder against my ankle. I picked him up and cuddled him. When he was finally satisfied, I set him down.

Glancing at the clock, I calculated the amount of time Chet would have been allowed to stay in the ICU, and called Chet on his cell phone. He answered on the second ring, and sounded pleased when he heard my voice.

"Chet, would you like me to come to El Mirage for a couple of days, to keep you company at the hospital?"

"*Of course* I would!" His enthusiasm erased any concern that I might not be welcome. "I've wanted you to meet my folks. Can you really get away?" I heard his self-deprecating chuckle. "I must sound demented."

"No more than usual," I joked. "If it's convenient, I can be there late this afternoon, your time."

"That would be great!"

"Don't think about meeting me. I'll get the first cab out of the airport."

Chet gave me the address of Drake Memorial Hospital. As soon as we said goodbye, I dialed Nancy's number.

"I'm going to El Mirage, Arizona, for a couple of days, to be with Chet, while he's waiting to find out about his father's condition."

"That's good," she said. "I remember when he flew all the way from The Hague to make sure you were safe, and how he rushed to Las Vegas when you were missing."

"Can you do me a favor? Penny's so busy getting ready for the taping of her first TV show I don't want to ask her to take Magic. Would you keep him for me until I come back on Saturday?"

"I have a better idea. I'll stay at your place. That way the little prince doesn't have to be in a strange environment. And it'll do Arnold good to wonder where I am."

WHAT WITH PACKING a carry-on duffel bag with clothes and other items I'd need for the trip to Arizona, writing out instructions about Magic's care—including the name and number of his veterinarian—calling Betty and asking her to have the company's travel agent book my round-trip airline reservations, saying goodbye to my four-legged room-mate, and leaving my spare key at the reception desk for Nancy, I didn't get to the office until nearly ten o'clock.

Carrying my duffel and a tote bag, I got off the elevator on the twenty-sixth floor to face an unusual sight: a double row of folding chairs on which sat the twelve little girls that the casting people had called in to be interviewed by Tommy and me. With each of them was an adult woman, presumably the mother. Some of the children and adults were whispering to each other, creating a soft rustle that sounded like the tide stroking a shoreline. Several women were fussing with the little girls' hair and clothes.

As I made my way around the chairs, the whisperers fell silent. I sensed the group watching me. They were probably wondering who I was, if I was somebody *important*.

I turned to smile at the children and their chaperones, and greeted Betty Kraft at her desk outside the office I shared with Tommy. "Your ticket confirmations are just coming through from the travel agent," she said. "Where are you going to stay in Arizona?"

"At whatever hotel or motel is closest to the hospital in El Mirage. When I get there, I'll let you know. If you need me, I have my cell."

Betty handed me a sealed envelope. "I drew five hundred dollars cash for you."

"Oh, Betty, thank you! I forgot about cash."

"Figured you would," she said with a smile. "I've arranged for a car to take you to the airport and pick you up when you come back."

"Thank you, again!"

Easing the airline ticket information out of the printer, she asked, "Do you have credit cards with you?"

I patted my tote. "Right here. Oh, I almost forgot. Sometime this morning Jay Garwood is coming—"

"He got here at nine o'clock. I introduced him around," she said.

"What was your impression of him?"

She hesitated for a moment before answering. "He's *hungry*," she said. "Company manners. Too early to tell what he's really like."

On his side of our partners' desk, Tommy was nervously eating an apple fritter from a donut box in front of him. He offered the box to me, but I shook my head. "No thanks. I had breakfast."

"So did I, but we've got to talk to *children*, so I need fortification." Tommy swallowed a few bites as I sat down and stowed my duffel and tote under the desk. He finished the fritter and put the box in a deep drawer. The act reminded me of one of those old movies where the private eye keeps a bottle of whiskey in his desk.

Wiping his hands on a paper napkin, Tommy said, "The casting people canvassed the kid actor agencies and preinterviewed about fifty little girls until they narrowed the list down to those outside."

I buzzed Betty and asked her to send the girls in one at a time. "Alone, please—no adults. We want the child to be as natural as possible, without the stress of a parent hovering or coaching."

As each child came into our office, we had her sit in the visitor's chair Tommy had positioned so that it faced both of us.

The first eight girls we saw resembled the actor who played Gareth enough so that they might possibly be his daughter. To get an idea of their personalities, we chatted with them, and then had them read a few lines from the script. Some talented performers did poorly at cold readings, but then came alive in front of a camera. We had them read mainly to see how they handled the challenge, because in addition to connecting with the camera, we need performers who can listen and take direction.

The moment the ninth child came into the office we could see that her coloring was wrong for the part. She had an interesting, offbeat quality—which is how she must have survived the screening process—but I didn't think the audience would believe that she was the daughter of actor Parker Nolan, who played Gareth.

I could tell by the glance Tommy shot at me that he felt the same way.

"Your name is Monica?" I asked, looking at the list in my hand.

"Yes." Her voice was little more than a whisper. She handed me her photograph with her few professional credits fixed to the back.

"I'm afraid this isn't going to be the right role for you, Monica," I said gently. *I hate this part of the job! Please, dear God, don't let her cry.* "We'll keep your picture, and call you when another part comes up."

Monica's head bobbed up and down, bravely accepting rejection.

As soon as she left, I told Tommy, "I feel like a monster."

"Me, too, and I didn't even have to tell her," he said.

Betty rushed in. Her face was white.

"Monica's mother just slapped her across the face, right in front of me, because she wasn't in here as long as the other girls were!"

I felt as though *I'd* been slapped, and my reaction was rage. I jumped up and yanked the door open. Betty followed me. Typically, Tommy, who hated confrontations, stayed behind.

We caught up with Monica and her mother at the elevator. A red mark still burned on the little girl's cheek.

Forcing myself to smile, I looked down at Monica. "Sweetie, I know I told you that *this* part isn't right for you, but you impressed us so much we just thought of another role you can play. Betty, would you take Monica over to Craft Services and get her some juice, or milk—whatever she wants."

Betty took Monica by the hand and led the girl away.

Monica's mother was practically giddy with delight. "How exciting! What kind of a part are you giving—"

No longer able to conceal my fury, I backed Monica's mother against the wall between the elevators. I kept my voice low, but my tone was icy. "I know hundreds of people in this business," I hissed. "If you *ever* lay a hand on that child again I promise you I'll hear about it. I'll turn you in to child protective services, and you'll lose your little captive meal ticket."

She began to sputter and defend herself, but I cut her off. "There is no excuse for what you did, and I swear to God I'll make sure you never do it again." Of course, I was bluffing, but I could see I'd frightened her so I pressed the advantage. "I have your address. To make sure you don't hurt that child again, I'm going to have you *monitored*."

That was a real whopper of a lie, but she was shaking, too cowed to realize that I didn't have any such power. Time to change tactics, before she recovered her wits. I took a step back, and in a more pleasant manner, I said, "Go to our studio cafe down on the tenth floor and have a cup of coffee. My assistant will bring Monica down in a little while. Order lunch for the two of you, and sign my name to the check."

Of the final three girls we saw, number eleven was the one Tommy and I immediately agreed would be perfect to play Gareth's daughter. We interviewed the final girl out of courtesy, but made sure she stayed with us as long as had the others. Later today, Tommy would tell our head of casting to call the selected child's agency and make the deal to hire her.

Betty stuck her head in the door. "Security is on the line. Didi Rose and her mother are at the desk downstairs. Didi said you invited her to come to the studio."

Not a message I wanted to hear. "I said she could visit the show *sometime*."

"Well, she's here now," Betty said.

Chapter 7

FOR NANCY'S SAKE, to help make things pleasant with the daughter of the man she loved, I put on my "welcome" expression and met Didi and the former Mrs. Rose at the elevator.

Mother and daughter were the same height, about five feet three, but Didi's build was slim and strong; her mother's body was more delicate. I couldn't picture Veronica Rose doing anything more athletic than shopping.

Didi rushed up as soon as she saw me. "Will I meet Cody? Is he here today?"

"You're in luck." I glanced at the wall clock. "He'll be taping a scene in a little while. You can watch, if you want to."

"Oh, I do!" She was practically jumping up and down with excitement. "This is so cool!"

With her glossy chocolate brown hair, big brown eyes, and heart-shaped face, twelve-year-old Didi Rose was showing unmistakable signs of the grown-up beauty she would become.

Politely, I extended my hand to her mother, who was watching me with a calculating expression in her eyes.

"I'm Morgan Tyler. Mrs. Rose?"

"Call me Veronica." She spoke so softly I had to lean forward to hear her. "It was so nice of you to invite us to your studio."

"I'm delighted to have you here," I lied. "Didi impressed me with her comments about the show."

"I knew Cody's last girlfriend was a phony," Didi said proudly.

"Don't brag, darling."

Didi's voice was natural and enthusiastic; her inflections ran all up and down the tonal scale. In sharp contrast, her mother's voice was almost a whisper. I imagined Veronica practicing that breathy, little-girl quality, for the seductive effect it had on some men.

Arnold's ex-wife flashed a smile that revealed two rows of sparkling white teeth, but not a hint of warmth. "You must be busy, doing . . . what you do. If you'll just have someone show Didi what she wants to see, we won't have to trouble you."

I introduced our guests to Betty, and asked her to give them a tour of the studio.

"Didi especially wants to meet Link," I said, referring to actor Link Ramsey who played Cody. "When Link's taping, they can watch from the control room."

Betty led Arnold's daughter and his ex-wife toward Studio 36, where Link would be blocking the scene he'd tape later.

Our office was empty, but I saw Tommy had stuck a note to my monitor. "Gone for a massage. Don't forget to come back from Arizona," it said. I was glad to have the privacy. There was a lot of work to be done in reintroducing Evan Duran to the audience.

Privacy lasted for ten minutes. There was a knock on the door, followed immediately by the entrance of Veronica Rose. Alone.

"I hope I'm not disturbing you—Morgan, isn't it?"

As if she didn't know. "Yes, it's Morgan. I am very busy, but what can I do for you?"

Uninvited, Veronica perched on the edge of the visitor's chair closest to my desk and said, "I want to do something for *you*, or rather, for someone else. Didi says you're friends with that tall girl who works in my husband's office."

I kept a grip on my temper. "You're referring to Nancy Cummings? She's a highly regarded corporate attorney."

She dismissed that with a wave of one perfectly manicured hand. With a jab of apprehension, I noticed that Veronica wore a diamond engagement and wedding ring combination on the third finger of her left hand.

"I'm afraid Nancy's going to be terribly hurt," she said. "Perhaps, for her own good, you could have a little talk with her."

I didn't say anything, but Veronica didn't need encouragement to go on.

"Your friend seems to have a serious crush on Arnold. It's happened to quite a few girls who've worked in the office. Arnold enjoys the attention. He's only human, after all. But now I've moved back to New York."

"Aren't you two divorced?"

"I *left* Arnold. He's never really gotten over me. I'm unfinished business, you see. And we have a child we both adore. That's a bond between us that no other woman will ever break."

"You shouldn't be talking to me about this."

Having planted her little bomb, Veronica got up. "I'm merely trying to save your friend some pain. Arnold has led vulnerable young women on before." She flashed a smile with those unnaturally white teeth and glided out of the office.

Arnold's ex was as transparent as a freshly washed window. I knew she expected me to tell Nancy what she'd said. Her game was to stir up trouble, but I wasn't going to play.

Then, suddenly, I wondered: Was there any truth to what Veronica had said? I didn't want there to be, because if there were then Nancy would be in for terrible heartbreak.

No! I refused to believe Veronica because I'd spent time with Nancy and Arnold, and never saw anything that made me doubt he loved Nancy. And I knew how much she loved him. Arnold's ex-wife probably regretted their divorce and wanted him back. I was sure her phony sympathy—trying to get me to "warn" Nancy, was just an act of manipulation.

Putting Veronica Rose out of my mind for the next two hours, I concentrated on writing dialogue inserts for scenes that would be taped the following week. Characters would talk about Evan Duran, establishing him in the minds of the audience, before he appeared on-screen in scenes he would begin taping in two weeks. A lot of rewriting was needed, but the publicity of bringing back an original actor from earlier days would be valuable.

I'd have to create Garwood's first few scenes myself. It would be quicker than explaining to the associate writers on the staff what I had in mind. Future scripts would be assigned to others, after Garwood was on the *Love of My Life* canvas. By then the writing staff would have had a chance to study the actor, to catch his rhythms, and they'd know the story I had in mind for the Evan Duran character.

I was printing out the inserts when Betty came in. "You've got to leave for the airport."

"I know." I removed the last of the pages and handed them to her. "Would you put these inserts into the revised scripts—I've indicated the particular episode numbers at the top of each page—and then distribute them?"

Betty glanced at the sheets and nodded.

"How did it go with our visitors?" I asked.

A half smile curved Betty's lips. "Little Didi reminds me of an old joke about a man who didn't know the meaning of the word 'tact.'"

"What did she do?"

"She told Jay Garwood—about his beard—that he looked like he was wearing a squirrel on his face."

"That's awful, but it's funny. How did he take it?"

"He laughed, but I think he was trying to impress Mrs. Rose with what a good sport he was."

"What do you think of Didi's mother?"

Betty grimaced. "She's one of those greedy women who've got to have every man in the room wanting her. Link didn't pay any attention to her display of charm, but when she gave Jay Garwood a blast of it, Jay looked at her like he was a hungry dog and she was a sirloin steak."

I stuffed two white legal pads and a handful of my favorite pens into my tote bag; they were the materials I'd need for writing on the plane to Arizona. "He didn't do or say anything inappropriate, I hope."

Betty shook her head. "Perfect gentleman. Anyway, I think she was just practicing on the poor guy."

I looked up from gathering pages of story notes. "What do you mean?"

"She's a bitch," Betty said.

Smiling in silent agreement, I left for the airport, to lend support to Chet.

Chapter 8

AS IT TURNED out, visiting Chet had not been one of my better ideas. The "Law of Unintended Consequences" struck again. Forty-eight hours after I landed in Arizona, I was back again at John F. Kennedy International Airport.

I was surprised to see Nancy, instead of a network chauffeur, waiting for me on the sidewalk.

"I had Betty cancel the studio limo," she said. "I wanted to pick you up."

My immediate reaction was that I was very glad to see her; I needed to talk about what had happened with Chet. But then cold tingles of fear shot up my spine. *Why* was she here? Had something bad happened?

Nancy must have seen worry on my face because she quickly assured me, "Magic is fine. And nobody's been murdered while you were gone. Come on, my car's in the garage over there."

When we reached her little blue Mercedes two-seater, I said, "You haven't asked me if I had sex with Chet."

"Don't need to. You haven't." Nancy unlocked the car door.

"You're right. At any moment his father might have gone into cardiac arrest. That's not a romantic atmosphere." I opened the passenger door, tossed my duffel into the compartment behind the seats, and climbed in. "Besides, we slept in the hospital's guest quarters, where I shared a room with Chet's mother."

Nancy buckled herself in behind the wheel, but didn't turn on the ignition. "So you still don't know whether or not Chet snores, but you know if his mother does."

"She's a sweet woman," I said. "I liked her." For just a moment, I thought my voice was going to crack, but I got a grip. Not quick enough, though.

"What's wrong?" Nancy asked. "Did Chet do something to knock himself off your romantic radar?"

I didn't answer directly. Instead, I told her about Doctor Teddy.

"In the hospital's gift shop I found this big, stuffed bear about three feet tall. It was wearing a doctor's scrubs, and even had a little stethoscope around its neck. Mr. Thompson was still in the ICU, but Chet and his mother got a big laugh out of it. When it looked as though Mr. Thompson was stable, and it would be safe for us to leave him for a little while, Chet took the bear and we went to the therapy room in the Children's Wing. Chet introduced it to the kids as 'Dr. Teddy,' and proceeded to do a ventriloquist act with it."

Nancy gaped at me. "Chet can do *ventriloquism*?"

I laughed. "No, he's terrible—probably the worst ventriloquist in the free world. But the kids were crazy about him. And I saw something . . . Chet adores kids."

Sensing what was coming, Nancy reached over and squeezed my fingers in sympathy. "Did you tell him?"

"That I can't have children? I had to. For nearly two days, I'd seen how close he is to his family, how much he loves his mother and father. Chet's brother is a doctor in the Navy. Married, two small children. He's stationed in Guam, but he's on his way back to Arizona on special leave to be with his dad. Chet showed me pictures of his niece and nephew—he carries them in his wallet . . . When we were alone for a little while this morning, I knew I had to tell him."

"What did he say?"

I shrugged. "The comforting things you'd expect. He said doctors make mistakes about that all the time. I told him this *wasn't* a mistake. I'm really not able to have children."

I was silent. Nancy waited quietly until I was ready to go on. "Chet made a joke, or tried to. He said if we ever managed to spend enough time together to get to that point, at least we wouldn't have to use birth control."

Nancy frowned. "That's not funny."

"He realized it, and apologized immediately. He kissed me, and told me that if two people really come to love each other, it won't matter."

"He's a good guy," Nancy said.

"Yes, he is."

"How did you two leave things?"

"We'll get to know each other better, and see what happens. But it *does* matter to him, Nance. That's the simple truth." Eager to get off the subject, I asked, "How are you and Arnold? Did he wonder where you were this weekend?"

Nancy's lips narrowed into a grim line. "He never called to find out." Seething with anger, she turned the key in the ignition with uncharacteristic force.

To lighten the mood in the car, I said "On the way back from Arizona, I thought of a stunt Link can pull on Penny's TV show tomorrow. I called him from the plane, and he's willing." When I told Nancy what he was going to do, it got a genuine laugh out of her.

"Did you tell Penny?" she asked.

I shook my head. "She should be just as surprised as the audience."

Nancy was dubious, but she agreed. "TV is your field, not mine. Besides, I'd rather worry about what Penny's going to do tomorrow, than what Arnold might be doing *tonight.*"

Chapter 9

THREE MONTHS AGO, Nancy made a deal for one of her corporate clients to purchase—at a bargain price—the Better Living Channel, a struggling cable network.

Shortly after the papers were signed, and knowing that the new owner, Mickey Jordan, was desperate to come up with shows that could attract viewers, Nancy told him about our friend, Penny Cavanaugh, who's an absolute wonder at cooking and decorating. Nancy described her as "Martha Stewart for normal people."

When Jordan met Penny, he challenged her to "be creative" using just whatever she could find in Nancy's office. A few minutes later she presented him with a bouquet of edible rosebuds that she'd made from some pink foil and a handful of the Hershey's Chocolate Kisses on Nancy's desk. The fact that Penny's also very attractive didn't hurt.

Deciding to gamble on giving Penny a TV show, Jordan hired an experienced producer to work with her in planning the segments. After weeks of meetings, creative decisions, recipe testing, and assembling a tech crew, the first of the daily *Penny Wise* half hours was about to be taped.

Nancy and I arrived forty-five minutes early at the squat, gray, no-frills structure on Ninth Avenue and West Eighteenth Street where the cable network tapes those of its shows originating in Manhattan. A small black sign on the door identifying it as the BETTER LIVING CHANNEL differentiated the building from its equally undistinguished neighbors.

We gave our names to the elderly security guard at the entrance. He squinted at his clipboard, clutched in hands that weren't altogether steady, finally found us on the guest list, and let us in.

Originally a warehouse, the interior of the building was all on one level, but soared two stories high. Powerful lights needed for taping a TV show hung from a web of pipes above the *Penny Wise* set. The lights were being tested and adjusted by two gaffers on a scaffold.

The set consisted of a large working kitchen that looked remarkably like the one in Penny's home. A few feet to one side, there was a dining room area with a rectangular table and four matching chairs. It was separated from the kitchen by a waist-high room divider, on top of which sat a row of indoor plants.

Theater seats, arranged in four graduated rows, faced the set. Today's show would be taped in front of an invited audience. For future broadcasts the audience would consist of people who'd written to the channel for free tickets.

At the outer edge of the set, a stunning black woman was directing placement of two big cameras that would be used for the show. Her dark hair, cut in a sleek pageboy, emphasized her large eyes and high cheekbones.

Glancing up, the woman saw Nancy, gave a welcoming wave, and came over to where we were standing. After the two of them exchanged warm greetings, Nancy said, "Morgan Tyler, this is Iris Fuller. Iris is the show's producer."

I extended my hand. "It's nice to meet you."

The other woman's grip was firm and confident. I liked her poise, and guessed that she inspired confidence in those who worked with her.

"Morgan produces *Love of My Life*," Nancy said.

"*Co*-produces," I corrected quickly. "I share the heat."

"Lucky you," Iris said with a rueful smile. "On this gig the buck stops with me. The good part is that I get to boss everybody around."

"How do you like working with Penny?" I asked.

Iris laughed and fingered the belt around her slender waist. "Penny's a doll, but if I'm not careful, she's going to make me fat. And, Morgan, thanks for lending Link Ramsey to be our first 'guest cooker.'" Her lips curved into a slightly wicked expression. "He *almost* makes me wish that I wasn't happily married."

Needing to follow producer-to-producer protocol, I told Iris, "Subject to your approval, Link wants to surprise Penny with a comedy bit."

When I described his little stunt, she laughed out loud. "Go for it. I'll make sure one camera stays on Link and the other on Penny for her reaction."

Something in the rigging above us drew Iris's attention. She called up to the gaffers, "Hey, guys—that spot's in the wrong place." Turning back to Nancy and me, she said, "I gotta take care of this."

"Is it okay to find Penny and Brandi and wish them luck?" Nancy asked.

"Sure. They're in the little makeup room behind the set." With a jaunty thumbs-up, Iris Fuller went off to deal with repositioning the lights.

THE BETTER LIVING Channel's makeup room was the size of a walk-in closet. Penny sat in a straight-back chair, with her eyes closed, facing a theatrical mirror ringed with lightbulbs that cast a strong, even illumination. A towel covered her thick, brown hair and a collar of paper towels protected her dress from makeup stains.

Applying paint and powder to Penny's face was Brandi Flynn, wife of Detective First Grade G. G. Flynn, Matt Phoenix's partner at the Twentieth Precinct. Brandi's hair, which was a color she called *I Love Lucy* red, was piled on top of her head, creating the effect of an exploding fireball. Today, in her capacity as Penny's on-air kitchen assistant, she was dressed in a comparatively modest green blouse and black slacks. I say "comparatively" because while the blouse's neckline was high, Brandi's breasts were bountiful, and her slacks were as tight as a gymnast's skin.

Anyone but Brandi Flynn would have looked like a hooker in the outfits she wore, but with her sweet face and the kindness in her eyes, the effect was benignly outlandish rather than crude.

Brandi glanced up from her work when we came in. "Hi, gals. Isn't this exciting?"

Penny opened her eyes and greeted us with a nervous smile. "Can you believe it? This is actually happening! I didn't sleep at all last night, worrying that I'd forget everything I'm supposed to do."

I gave her ice-cold fingers an encouraging squeeze. "It'll be easy. Think of it as being at home, cooking and talking."

Brandi turned her attention from Penny, leaned in close to the mirror, and gave her own lashes another swipe with the mascara wand. "Iris told me they wouldn't have a makeup artist," she said, "so I brought my stuff from home. Do you believe it—Penny doesn't even *own* makeup! She's like you, Morgan, she never wears anything but lipstick and mascara. For me, that would be like running down Fifth Avenue naked!"

Removing the towel from Penny's head, Brandi presented her to us with a flourish. "Doesn't she look *gorgeous*?"

Hastening to add, "Not that you don't always look nice, Pen."
Brandi gave Penny's lustrous brown hair a few strokes with a
brush.

"You're beautiful," I told Penny sincerely. Nancy
echoed the sentiment with a nod.

"Thank you, but I really don't care how I look. I've been
praying I don't set fire to the kitchen, in front of all those
people!"

AT THE SCHEDULED time, invited guests filed in and took
their seats. Per Penny's request, Nancy and I sat in the center of the front row. I'd told Penny that with those powerful
TV lights in her face, she wouldn't be able to see us, because the audience would be in darkness. Still, she'd said it
would make her feel better just to know we were close by.

Link Ramsey, *Love of My Life*'s romantic rogue hero,
arrived only a few minutes before the show was to begin.
Although he was one of the most disciplined and reliable
actors I knew—fully prepared and never late—he always
looked as though he'd just awakened. And the sleepy twinkle in his dark chocolate eyes suggested that he hadn't
been in bed alone.

Iris Fuller introduced herself to Link, they whispered
together briefly, and she ushered him backstage. Just before the security guard closed the outside door, I glimpsed
the figure of a young man wearing a white shirt and black
slacks, carrying something over his arm, slip into the studio and disappear behind the set.

Iris Fuller came out onstage, introduced herself as the
producer, and welcomed us to the first show of the Better
Living Channel's new series, *Penny Wise*. When she said
that Link Ramsey, star of *Love of My Life*, was going to be
Penny Cavanaugh's guest, the audience broke into sponta-
neous and prolonged applause.

Audience lights dimmed and the *Penny Wise* theme

began to play over the sound system. It faded down as Penny came out into the kitchen set, introduced herself and Brandi, and explained that today:

"We're going to make a *turkey dinner*. Practically everybody loves turkey, but for some reason we only have it on Thanksgiving Day. There's no reason we can't have it any time of the year—and it's so easy to do! Now, to help us demonstrate how really simple it is to cook, please welcome a man who says he's never even scrambled an egg: one of television's most popular actors, Link Ramsey!"

Link came into the kitchen set on a wave of vigorous applause.

He smiled at Penny, and at the audience, then fingered his casual sweater with embarrassment. "Gee, Pen, I'm sorry. I planned to be dressed appropriately for you, but my dry cleaning . . . Oh, here it is!" Link gave someone off-stage a big "come in" gesture, and onto the set hurried the young man carrying what I could see now was a dry cleaner's bag. "It's about time," Link said, tearing off the plastic covering to reveal a chef's outfit. As he kept talking about the problem of getting dry cleaning delivered on time, Link proceeded to strip off his clothes—down to his shorts!—and put on the chef's white slacks and jacket.

The audience roared with laughter, Brandi giggled, and Penny stared—her mouth open in speechless shock. The expression on her face, as she tried to look anywhere *except* at Link undressing, was so funny that only a trained actress could have pulled that off on purpose.

In a few seconds, Link was completely outfitted. As though nothing unusual had just gone on, he began asking Penny about cooking a turkey.

Thanks to good camera work, the viewers would see Brandi putting together a simple apple, bread, and sautéed sweet onion stuffing at one end of the work counter, while at the other end Penny was showing Link how to prepare the turkey by sprinkling the cavity with salt and pepper.

Next, under Penny's direction, Link rubbed the turkey all over with butter.

"That's perfect, Link!" Penny moved down the counter to check the stuffing, gave it a quick taste test, and smiled with approval at Brandi. To her guest cooker, Penny said, "Link, would you bring the turkey down here? We'll fill it with Brandi's delicious stuffing."

Link picked up the turkey with both hands—and then something happened that absolutely had *not* been planned. The twenty-pound turkey slipped out of Link's grasp and fell with a colossal *splat!* onto the floor in the middle of the set.

The audience gasped in shock! Brandi's hands flew to her mouth in horror! The camera operators gawked. Link, genuinely mortified—he wasn't acting now—muttered apologies.

Only Penny remained unruffled. In a calm but deliberately *firm* voice, Penny said, "There's nothing to worry about. Not a thing. Brandi—just pick the turkey up, take it into the kitchen backstage, and bring out the *other* turkey."

I bit into my fist to keep from laughing, but I needn't have bothered to hide my amusement. The rest of the audience whooped with delight, as they realized that Penny was really telling Brandi to duck out of sight, brush it off, and bring back the *same* turkey.

"I can cross Penny off my list of people to worry about," Nancy whispered.

AFTER THE TAPING, working my way through the crowd of guests to congratulate Penny, I glanced around to see if a particular someone had come to the show.

Penny guessed what I was thinking. "Matt isn't here," she said softly. "Brandi and I were so nervous, we asked Matt and G. G. not to come to this first show."

"That's was probably a smart thing to do," I said, hiding my disappointment.

"I know you two aren't seeing each other right now," Penny said. "Matt told me how he feels about you having more money than he has. That's positively . . . antediluvian!"

It's also ironic, I thought ruefully. I went from having no men in my life after Ian died, to suddenly, just a few months ago, having two men courting me. Then there's a third man—mysterious Nico Andreades, who, by any rational gauge, is completely wrong for me. Nico is somewhere out in the mist, and I'll probably never see him again. So, with Chet wanting children, and Matt wanting me, but not my money, I'm effectively back to having no man again.

Considering the assignment I gave Bobby Novello, it's probably just as well that I'm alone.

Chapter 10

FOR THE NEXT month, events at *Love of My Life* were reasonably calm—that is to say we didn't have more than one case of hysteria per week. Jay Garwood had turned out to be a team player, and seemed to be getting along with his fellow actors. At least I wasn't hearing any complaints.

Judging from the e-mails that were pouring in, Penny's new TV show was doing well. The Better Living Channel had begun with a discouragingly small number of viewers, but *Penny Wise* was getting good publicity. A service that charted viewer numbers showed that more and more people were watching the Better Living Channel. I joked to Penny that she was doing for Better Living what *The Sopranos* had done for HBO, and without whacking anybody.

Chet remained in Arizona with his father, and the news from there was good; Richard Thompson was getting stronger every day. Chet had been able to spend time with his brother before Commander David Thompson had had to return to Guam.

There had been a subtle change in my relationship with Chet. From calling me once or twice every day, our phone conversations had dwindled to twice a week. The words were still warm—our affection for each other was real—but I knew that my not being able to have children mattered to Chet. I understood. It was an obstacle—difficult, perhaps impossible, to get past.

Concentrating on work, I had written a small part for Monica, the girl whose mother slapped her. She'd play a friend of the child we picked to be Gareth's daughter.

Betty came into my office while Tommy and I were watching the video of that episode. Noticing Monica on the screen, Betty leaned on the desk to watch it with us.

"She's not pretty, but she's got an interesting quality," Tommy said.

"Having an unusual look can be better than just being pretty," I said. "We see hundreds of young girls with those model perfect features, and it's sometimes hard to tell them apart."

When the episode concluded, Tommy turned off the set. He stood up and stretched, working a kink out of his shoulder. "I've got a lunch date at Twenty-One," he said. "You two want me to bring you back anything?"

I shook my head. "No thanks."

"I brought lunch," Betty said.

Tommy left the office, but Betty lingered. I saw her gazing at the blank TV screen, a troubled expression on her face.

"Betty? What's the matter?"

She made a "hmmm" sound before she answered. "I wonder if by giving little Monica that part you're really helping her."

That surprised me. "I'm hoping her mother will treat her better."

"What happens when we can't use her anymore?"

"She'll have a good reel to show other producers." But

as I said that, I began to wonder if I might be giving Monica false hope. What if she couldn't get any other jobs? That hadn't occurred to me.

Betty was watching me, as though she was reading my mind. "I've seen you take in strays," she said, "like your cat, like Jay Garwood, and the stunt double who was killed a few months ago. Now this little girl with the rotten mother. You can't protect everyone, Morgan. Sometimes strays turn on the people who try to save them." As though making an effort to shake off her dark attitude, she forced a smile. "Maybe I should go back on the antidepressants."

Her mood worried me. "Are you all right, Betty?"

"I probably just need to get laid," she joked. As she was leaving, she paused at the door and said, "I didn't mean that you should worry about little Magic turning on you. He's an angel in fur. Generally speaking—at least in my experience—animals are more trustworthy than people."

WHILE AT THE studio things were proceeding smoothly, Nancy wasn't doing so well. Usually the calmest and most rational person in any group, by her own admission she had lost her cool in a confrontation the day before with Veronica Rose.

"I ran into her in our conference room," Nancy said. "She was waiting for Arnold. They were going to have lunch with Didi, after Didi's riding lesson. We were alone, and Veronica used the opportunity to taunt me about how close she and Arnold are."

"What do you mean?"

Nancy made a kind of "grrrrr" sound expressing her anger and frustration, then mimicked Veronica's breathy, little-girl tone: " 'Arnold is soooo sweet. Last night, after Didi was asleep, he lighted a fire in his bedroom fireplace, and scattered pillows in front of it. We lay down on the floor, on that bed of pillows—just like we used to do when we were first married. As a surprise, Arnold brought home a tin of my favorite caviar, Beluga—that's the *real* caviar, the black kind. We drank champagne, and we fed spoonfuls of caviar to each other.' "

My reaction was, "Yuck!"

In her natural voice, Nancy said, "The scene on the floor with the pillows and the champagne—that was just too much! In the back of my brain, I knew she was trying to provoke me, but she pushed the right buttons. I'm ashamed to admit I lost my temper. I told Veronica I thought her little game was disgusting and pathetic. I was really giving it to her—and at that moment, Arnold came into the room! It made me look terrible because all he heard was me attacking poor little Veronica. To say the least, he was not pleased. We were supposed to go to the ballet tonight, but he just broke our date with the flimsiest excuse."

Because Nancy was in love with him, I had done my best to like Arnold, and I'd succeeded for months, as long as he was treating Nancy well. But lately, I'd begun to wish that he wasn't the man she wanted to marry. He was brilliant and successful, and he used to behave as though Nancy was the love of his life, but ever since Veronica Rose had come back to New York, I'd glimpsed coldness in Arnold I hadn't seen before, and it made me uneasy for Nancy.

"Here's an idea," I said. "A revival of *School for Wives* opened last week off-Broadway. It's the Richard Wilbur translation. If you'll come with me, I'll get us tickets for tonight. Shouldn't be a problem for a Wednesday performance."

"There'll probably be plenty of seats." Nancy said wryly. "You're the only Richard Wilbur fanatic I've ever met."

"He's my favorite living poet, and he writes the absolute best translations of Moliérè."

"Okay, okay. I surrender," she said.

That night Nancy and I laughed loudly at the play's hilarious rhyming dialogue. For two hours we forgot our own concerns. The next afternoon, Thursday, Bobby Novello called. It had been four weeks since our meeting.

"I found your Sheriff Maysfield!"

Chapter 11

MY CONTINENTAL AIRLINES flight left Newark, New Jersey, at 7:40 Friday morning, landing on time at Palm Beach International Airport, in West Palm Beach, a little before eleven A.M. Bobby had tracked Sheriff Maysfield to his retirement home in this Florida city.

The airport, a huge, modern structure, stretched over four levels. Bobby, greeting me with a cheerful grin, met me at the Continental arrival gate on Concourse B. "You got a baggage check?"

"I just brought this duffel," I said. In spite of my insisting that the bag wasn't heavy, Bobby took it from me and started toward the exit.

I followed him through a two-story concession mall that ran the length of the building. Against an immense wall of windows there was comfortable lounge seating for those who wanted to watch takeoffs and landings. Surprised that there weren't more people in the airport, I said, "I expected to fight my way through a mob."

"It's mostly the locals who stay in Florida during the summer. Winter tourists and the kids on spring break have gone home."

I understood why they'd left when we stepped out of the temperature-controlled terminal and a blast of hot air struck me. I felt my scalp bead with perspiration and my hair lose the hot roller–created waves.

"Whew!"

"They say it's not the heat, it's the humidity," Bobby said ruefully. "But this is no worse than Manhattan in August. At least here the air is clean."

It *was* clean, much cleaner than what I was used to breathing, and a soft breeze, although hot, slightly lessened the impact of the temperature.

Sweat was trickling down my skull, but I felt more comfortable as soon as I slipped out of my blazer. I was glad I'd worn a cotton blouse instead of silk, a khaki skirt, and strappy sandals instead of my usual jeans and ankle boots. As soon as I had the chance, I'd get rid of the panty hose.

Bobby waved toward a light blue car parked in the line of taxis. "I couldn't rent a vehicle fitted with hand controls," he said, "so I hired us a car and driver."

"Good idea." Because of his short legs, Bobby wasn't able to operate a standard automobile.

The driver of the blue car responded to Bobby's signal by pulling out around the taxis. I saw a dark-haired man behind the wheel. Bobby said, rapid-fire, "His name is Emilio, he's originally from Cuba, he owns a limo company with eight employees—but I didn't want to call attention with a limo, so he's driving his personal Caddy. He's married, has three daughters in college, he loves America, and he hates Fidel Castro. Don't ask him how he is, or he'll tell you about his knee-replacement surgery."

I laughed. "And how long have you been here?"

"Since yesterday."

Emilio nosed the car diagonally against the curb in front

of us, effectively creating a parking space where there was none. He stepped out so easily that I guessed his knee surgery had been a complete success. Bobby introduced us. Emilio bowed gallantly and took my duffel to stow in the trunk.

"I got us two nice rooms at a Marriott," Bobby told me. "Want to go to the hotel first?"

I shook my head. A combination of excitement and apprehension had suddenly made it difficult to speak.

Emilio opened the rear passenger door. Bobby climbed in beside me and told Emilio, "We're going back to that address on Flagler Drive."

As soon as Emilio got behind the wheel, we took off down a beautifully landscaped road bracketed by dark water that sparkled in the sunlight. Bobby said, "That's called Crystal Lake, even though it's no bigger than a pond."

"It's is the prettiest route into and out of an airport I've ever seen."

From the front seat, Emilio said, "Thank you, Miss." In the rearview mirror I saw him beaming as though he'd personally excavated the little artificial lake and filled it with water.

Emilio's car was a vintage Cadillac, perfectly maintained. The air-conditioning was sweet relief from Florida's steamy heat. I settled back against a rear seat as soft as glove leather.

"This is a beautiful car, Emilio," I said.

Another big smile. "Thank you, Miss. We are at your *dis*-pose."

THE RIDE FROM the airport took about fifteen minutes, during which Bobby chatted with Emilio about all the celebrities who had made south Florida their home because there was no state income tax. That discussion segued into one about the possibility of the Marlins winning a pennant.

Grateful to Bobby for the wall of sound he was creating, I tried to use the privacy to sort through my tangled emotions, but it was hard to think clearly. Ready or not, the time had come to face something I'd spent more than twenty years trying to forget.

Emilio turned the Cadillac onto Flagler Drive, a quiet residential street lined with handsome private homes. Some were Spanish-style, with red tile roofs, and framed with lush swags of red or purple bougainvillea. Others were low modern ranch houses, with an occasional Cape Cod as a kind of architectural punctuation. Further along Flagler, facing a large, curving lake, was a procession of apartment buildings and condos, a mixture of the modest and the elegant.

At the corner of Flagler Drive and Tenth Street, Emilio slowed the car and stopped in front of a two-story multiple-family dwelling. It wasn't a new structure, but it was freshly painted: cream stucco, dark green shutters framing the windows, green front door. On either side of the entrance, shiny green hibiscus bushes exploded with scarlet blooms the size of salad plates.

I absorbed those details almost subliminally, because my attention was fixed on a portly, gray-haired man sitting reading a newspaper in one of a pair of canvas chairs in the middle of the shallow lawn. A red and yellow beach umbrella shaded him from the sun. At his feet were several other newspapers. A wrought iron table at his elbow held a big plastic travel mug.

The man glanced up when he heard the car. There, separated by a pane of glass, a sidewalk, a dozen feet of grass, and twenty-four years, I was looking at the face of the man who had saved my life. Digging my nails into the palms of my hands, I willed myself not to cry. I sat frozen until I realized that Emilio had come around and opened the rear door.

The man on the lawn stood up when he saw me get out

of the car. The newspaper slipped from his hands. I stared at him, taking in every detail. The same bright eyes behind the owlish glasses, the same wild, bristling mustache, the same powerful shoulders and the Santa Claus belly that looked as though they were parts of two separate human beings. He was grayer now, but I would have known him anywhere.

As he came toward me almost tentatively, I remembered that slow, cautious gait.

He said, "Little Miss Morgan, all grown up . . ." The rasp in his voice told me he was trying to hold on to his emotions, too. The years fell away and without thinking, I threw my arms around him in a bear hug. He still smelled like coffee . . . I felt tears sliding down my cheeks.

Chapter 12

WE WERE SITTING at Walter Maysfield's kitchen table, eating bowls of Campbell's chicken noodle soup. He'd remembered that had been my favorite when I was a child.

"Junie and I wanted to adopt you," he said, "but the g-d state wouldn't let us. Said we were too old. Instead, they put you in a foster place. Do you remember any of that?"

Too well. Old anger seared my insides. I nodded.

"I checked up on where you were. When I saw how bad it was, I got you outta there, pronto." His tone was grim. "As sheriff, I knew where a couple of bodies were buried . . . Not the right bodies to make 'em let us keep you, but I had enough dirt on a certain judge to close down the foster house, put that foul woman in jail, and get you into St. Claire's."

I told Bobby, "That's the Catholic boarding school where I lived from first grade until I went to college,"

Walter Maysfield asked me, "Do you remember Sister Ellen Elizabeth?"

"Oh, yes, I do. She was wonderful!" I explained to Bobby, "Sister Ellen Elizabeth was the head of St. Claire's. From the moment I got there she took an interest in me. She encouraged me to study, and to think of making an exciting future. When she died in my senior year, it was devastating."

"Was for me, too," the sheriff said softly. "Ellie was my sister."

"Sister? Do you mean she counseled you, or something?"

"No, she was my *real* sister." His face split into a smile that was full of love. "My sister—*the* sister. We heard that joke on the old *M.A.S.H.* TV show—got a big kick outta that one."

"You were her brother . . . Was that how you arranged my scholarship to St. Claire's?"

When Walter Maysfield hesitated, Bobby spoke. "You didn't go on a scholarship. The sheriff paid your tuition, all twelve years of it." He turned to Maysfield. "While I was tracking you down, I managed to get into Morgan's school records. You couldn't adopt her, but you gave her your last name, and her education."

I was stunned. "I don't know what to say . . . I'd like to repay you—"

"Don't even think about that!" His tone was so stern it shocked me. Then it softened. "I wanted to do it. An' you made me proud." He beckoned with one big, rough hand. "Come on into the living room."

Walter Maysfield's apartment was a clean and comfortable four-room arrangement at the rear of the building on the ground floor. No view of the lake, but through sliding glass doors his living room opened onto a private patio, complete with a covered barbecue grill and an old-fashioned porch swing.

He gestured toward several scrapbooks spread out on a wooden coffee table in front of a big, deep sofa. "Take a look," he said gruffly. "Both of you."

Bobby and I sat down on the floor in front of the coffee table, our backs against the sofa. I picked up the first scrapbook, and opened it so that Bobby could see, too.

Walter Maysfield (or, more likely, his wife) had carefully saved copies of the papers I wrote in English classes, all of my report cards and class pictures, articles and pictures in the school newspaper, including the list of college scholarships awarded in my senior year at St. Claire's.

Our host answered my unspoken question. "Ellie—Sister Ellen Elizabeth—gave us all that."

The biggest surprise was a small article from the Newark *Star-Ledger*, dated eleven years earlier, now turning yellow behind the plastic page protector. It was a very brief review of a play I wrote at Columbia—the play that was produced for four nights in a fifty-seat theater upstairs over a bowling alley in New Jersey. The reviewer wasn't wild about the work, but he called the young student playwright "promising."

"We came up to New Jersey to see your play," Walter Maysfield said. "The last night it was on. We thought it was damn good."

I stared at him. "Why didn't you tell me you were there? I'd have been so happy to see you."

He shook his head. "Junie was sick then, with the cancer. She didn't want you to see her looking so poorly. Was the last trip she made." He was silent for a moment. I recognized the look of mourning; I'd been in that place.

He cleared his throat and went on. "When Junie passed away, I decided to get in touch with you, see if you needed anything. Went up to the college. Woman in the office wasn't gonna tell me anything, so I flashed the badge. Amazing how that works. She opened right up an' told me you'd just married that photographer fella and gone off to Africa."

"I wish you'd come a few days earlier."

He smiled, a little shyly, but with unmistakable pride. "I was a pretty good investigator in my day, so I managed to keep track of you a little bit, even though you were half way 'round the globe."

I opened another of the scrapbooks, and saw that I'd been right when I guessed that Mrs. Maysfield had put the first ones together. Every item in those books had been artistically arranged. In contrast, these clippings had been put onto the scrapbook pages with an eye toward preservation instead of art.

Between the heavy, padded covers were copies of some of Ian's most famous photographs, and articles about him. A few of them mentioned me as his young wife and protégé. Little ink stars had been drawn next to those references. One story included a picture of Ian and me at one of our campsites in Kenya.

The last scrapbook was filled with articles about *Love of My Life*, and about me. The most recent ones focused on my involvement in murder cases. I shook my head in wonder at the amount of work represented by these books.

"Every day since you went off to college, an' then when I read your husband got killed and you came back to America, I bought the New York City papers," Maysfield said. "When I turned in the old badge an' moved down here, first thing I did was find where the out-of-town newspaper place was. The Main Street News—across the bridge in Palm Beach. Every morning, rain or shine, I walk the mile over for my papers, have breakfast at Cucina's—a nice place couple doors down, an' walk the mile back. The exercise keeps me in good shape."

"Why didn't you get in touch with me?"

"You had your own life. I didn't want to intrude."

WALTER—HE INSISTED I call him Walter—grilled hamburgers for us on his patio barbecue. Bobby and I sliced onions and tomatoes, and set the table in the dining alcove at one end of the living room.

The burgers were delicious. So was the bottle of red wine Walter opened. "To celebrate seeing the little girl again," he said. "So pretty—an' famous."

"Not famous," I said. "I just *work* with people who are famous."

Raising his glass, Bobby said, "To friendship." The three of us clinked glasses.

During dinner, Walter regaled us with some tales of his days as a West Virginia sheriff.

"I yanked cable TV out of the jail, until I found out there's a g-d federal court order that *requires* cable TV for jails! Can you believe that? Well, bein' a law-abidin'man, I hooked the cable TV right up again—but made sure it only let in the Disney Channel, and the Weather Channel."

"Why the Weather Channel?" I asked.

He smiled mischievously. "So they'd know how hot it was gonna be if I had to put 'em to work on a chain gang, clearin' brush out of the drainage canals. When somebody complained, I'd tell 'em, 'This ain't the Waldorf Ass-toria—you don' like it here, don' come back!'"

Later, when I was having a third cup of Walter's excellent coffee, Bobby brought up the proverbial elephant in the room. The reason we were there.

"Sheriff, you said you had something—something you'd only show to Morgan."

Walter sighed and got up. He crossed the room to a cherrywood cabinet and unlocked it with a small key he took from a chain in his pocket.

"I kept this, in case we got together—if you ever wanted to look."

Even though I was sure I knew the answer, I managed to ask, "What is it?"

"My police report—about finding you, and . . . the rest. Before I retired, I made a copy of it."

The file was about half an inch thick, tucked inside an

old envelope folder that was closed with a frayed brown string.

"Everything I know is in there. Downsville, West Virginia, wasn't exactly New York City. We didn't have computers, or much in the way of technology." His voice was hard with suppressed anger. "In those days, there was a national registry for missing autos, but not for missing kids. I got some fingerprints in the van, but I wasn't able to match them then."

I heard the word, "then." Bobby did, too. He leaned forward, alert and eager. "So you *did* get a match."

"Finally. A few years later, I got a name to go with the prints: Ray Wilson."

I was gripping the file at both sides. Afraid to know what was in it—and yet desperate to know what was in it.

Walter said, "Keep the file. I made it for you."

I sat there, frozen, holding on to the file as though in a trance. When it was clear that I wasn't going to open it, Bobby said, "Let me see." I didn't resist when he gently took it out of my hands.

Bobby didn't open it immediately. Instead, he said, "It's getting late. Why don't we go back to the Marriott and get together again tomorrow?"

I looked at my watch, frowning, reluctant to leave this pleasant room, and the man to whom I was sure I owed my life. At least my life as I knew it.

Walter seemed to read my mind. "You could stay here tonight," he said. "Take the bedroom. Many a night I spend out here on the couch anyway—I sleep real good to the TV."

"I'd like to do that," I said.

Bobby stood up, tucked the file under one arm, and pulled the cell phone out of his jacket. "I'll have Emilio bring your bag back here, then take me to the Marriott."

Before he could dial, the cell phone in my skirt pocket

rang. "Damn!" I muttered. This was one evening I didn't want to be interrupted.

It was Penny. She was distraught. "Morgan, it's terrible!"

Fear gripped my insides. "What's happened?"

"Matt just arrested Nancy—for *murder*!"

Chapter 13

THE RED-EYE TO New York landed in Newark at 5:40 Saturday morning. With no baggage to claim, by 6:35 A.M. I was inserting the key into the lock on the front door of my apartment. I pushed it open—and saw something that made me gasp: Detective Matt Phoenix standing in the hallway outside the kitchen, Magic draped over his shoulder, facing backward, the way he likes to ride. His long black tail swished slightly as it trailed down the front of Matt's green sports jacket.

"Matt—why did you arrest Nancy?"

"For murder."

"That's ridiculous!"

Magic scrambled down from Matt's shoulder and galloped toward me. As soon as I knelt down and scooped him up in my arms, he rubbed the top of his silky head along the line of my jaw and started to purr.

Matt took a key from his jacket pocket and handed it to

me. "Here. Nancy gave me your key so I could come over and feed the cat."

"Where is she?"

"In custody."

"Locked up?"

"Of course she is! This isn't a shoplifting case," Matt said. But he wasn't looking at me. His attention was fixed on the broad figure of the man who had come through the door behind me carrying my duffel and his own suitcase. Matt arched his eyebrows quizzically and said, "Hello?" His tone turned the word into a question.

Walter set the bags down, stepped around me, and offered his hand to Matt. "Walter Maysfield. I'm an old friend of Miss Morgan's."

Matt shook Walter's hand, but his manner was stiff. "Matt Phoenix."

I snapped, "This is the *brilliant* homicide detective who arrested my best friend."

Matt snapped right back. "She was caught leaning over the victim, whose body was still warm!"

Reacting to our angry tones, Magic struggled out of my arms, jumped down, and loped off down the hallway. I wanted to reassure him, but first I had to find out about Nancy.

"What victim? Who?"

"Veronica Rose. Her boyfriend's wife."

"*Divorced* wife! Nancy couldn't kill anyone. You've got to let her out."

"There's nothing I can do. She'll have a bail hearing on Monday, then the judge decides . . ." His voice trailed off, and the fact that he didn't finish the sentence sent a jolt of alarm through me.

"Decides? You mean decides how much the bail will be?" He didn't answer, increasing my alarm. "She *will* get bail, won't she? They wouldn't keep her in jail!"

"Why don' we all just take a breath," Walter said quietly.

"You're right," Matt agreed. He looked at me, and I nodded. Peace was declared, at least temporarily.

"Where have you been? Nancy said she didn't know, only that you'd be back Sunday night."

"I was in Florida. Thank you for coming over to take care of Magic." I turned to Walter. "Let me show you where to put your bag."

I saw the surprise on Matt's face when he realized that this stranger was going to be staying with me.

Walter, too, noted Matt's expression. With an amused twinkle in his eyes, he answered the question Matt hadn't asked. "I'm jus' visiting for a spell."

After I showed Walter the den, where I intended to make up the couch into a bed for him, the three of us sat down at the kitchen table. As we drank coffee and ate from the box of apple turnovers Penny had baked and sent over with Matt, Magic came out of hiding to join us. He jumped onto Matt's lap, coiled himself into a circle, and went to sleep. I frowned at Magic's closed eyes and twitching whiskers, and thought: *little traitor*.

I refilled the coffee mugs and we each took another apple turnover. It must be true that carbohydrates are a natural tranquilizer; as I ate the pastry, I felt calmer.

"What happened?" I asked. "When Penny telephoned, all she knew was that you'd arrested Nancy. No details."

"G. G. and I got a call from a pair of uniforms who'd found a one-twenty-five situation at the Vernon Towers."

I knew that 125 was the New York penal code for a violent death. Vernon Towers was one of Manhattan's newest luxury co-ops, on West Sixty-first Street, within the area of the Twentieth Precinct, Matt's headquarters. According to Nancy, Arnold had been one of the building's first residents.

"Nancy and the dead woman were discovered by Mrs. Rose's twelve-year-old daughter," Matt said.

"Didi . . . Oh, poor Didi. How awful for her!"

Matt nodded. "The girl was hysterical. She finally qui-
eted down enough to tell us that she came into the apartment looking for her mother. They hadn't moved in yet
because it was still being decorated. She'd come downstairs from her father's place, where they were living. Her
mother was lying on the floor, head covered with blood.
Nancy Cummings was there. A neighbor heard Didi
screaming and called 911. When the beat cops saw the situation, they secured the apartment. It was an obvious homicide, so we were called in."

"How . . . how did Veronica Rose die?"

Matt's tone, which had been coolly professional, softened. I saw a look of sympathy in his eyes. "Blunt force
trauma to the back of the head. She was struck with an unopened five-gallon can of paint. Forensics confirmed that
the blood and hair on the can came from the victim."

I was trying to swallow the lump in my throat. Walter
reached over and patted my hand comfortingly.

After a moment, I said, "Nancy can't even kill a
spider—she puts them outside on her balcony. She
couldn't murder anyone! She must have told you that."

"She said she didn't do it." Matt shrugged with an attitude that implied, "That's what they all say."

"Where was Arnold?"

"Not home. Didi gave me his cell phone number. I
reached him in his car. He said he was on his way back
from seeing a client."

I tried to keep the horror of the situation from clogging
my mind. I needed to think. *Lawyer!* "Nancy needs a
lawyer," I said. "Who's protecting her rights?"

"She called someone from the firm where she works."

"Better be somebody damn good," Walter said.

I shook my head in frustration. "The best criminal
lawyer I know is Arnold Rose, but he's the ex-husband of
the victim."

"*Not* so ex, according to the daughter," Matt said. "She

told me her parents had gotten back together. That must have made Nancy angry. Jealousy is a classic motive."

My fear for Nancy spiraled up into the red zone.

"You should prepare yourself for bad news," Matt said. "According to the daughter, Nancy and her mother had had some nasty fights. With a history of animosity between those two women, I think the D.A. will feel he's got a strong enough case to charge Nancy with murder. A smart attorney might be able to deal it down to man two. Depending on the charge, Nancy's probably going to spend anywhere from seven years to the rest of her life in prison."

"Stop it!" Even though it was still half full, I removed Matt's coffee mug from in front of him. He got the hint, said goodbye, and left.

As soon as I heard the front door close, I crossed to the kitchen wall phone and dialed the Flynn home, hoping that G. G. was there. I was in luck.

"Hi, G. G.," I said. "No, this time I don't need to talk to Brandi—you're the one. Settle a bet for us. Of all of them that you've dealt with, who's the defense attorney you and Matt absolutely hate the most?"

He growled a name. I thanked him and hung up before he could ask about the "bet."

I felt guilty about tricking G. G., but I pushed the feeling away. Nancy's life was at stake, and I had to do everything possible to help her.

Chapter 14

AFTER SITTING CRAMPED during two plane trips in twenty-three hours, I needed exercise. There was enough time before my appointment to walk from the Dakota down to Fifth Avenue and Twenty-third Street. I'd given Walter the spare key to the apartment, and he said he'd probably go out to explore the neighborhood while I was gone.

My destination was an office on the fourteenth floor of the twenty-one-story Flatiron Building. The Flatiron is a majestic limestone wedge, shaped like the hull of a schooner and adorned with Gothic faces and terra cotta flowers. At its narrowest point, it's only six feet wide. Because it was used in the movies *Spider Man* and *Spider Man 2* as the office of the *Daily Bugle* newspaper, it's one of New York City's most famous landmarks.

As I approached the entrance, I remembered a bit of its history that I'd learned in an architecture class at Columbia. When it was built in 1902, the prowlike shape was supposed to have created bizarre eddies in the wind, causing women's skirts to fly up as they walked on Twenty-third Street. The police had to post uniformed officers to chase away the throngs of men who gathered there to watch.

I took the elevator up to the fourteenth floor. At the far end of the corridor, I found what I was looking for. Fastened to an aged oak door was a brass plate that identified this as the office of B. KENT WAYNE, ATTORNEY-AT-LAW. No partners listed.

Opening the door, I found myself in a small reception room, sparsely furnished with three club chairs, a coffee table covered with magazines, and a secretary's desk and chair. The room was empty, but the door beyond the secretary's desk was open; I heard someone moving around, and papers rustling.

At the door to the inner office, I paused. A man in shirt-sleeves with his back to me was bending over a two-drawer metal filing cabinet, pulling out manila folders, flipping through them, and tossing them onto a chair already overflowing with papers.

"Mr. Wayne?"

At the sound of my voice, the man straightened and turned around. His features were sharp—pointed nose, pointed chin, a mouth that just missed being thin. Blue eyes beneath heavy brows, a head of thick brown hair badly in need of a trim. He was of medium height, with the wiry build of a long-distance runner. The lines etched into his forehead and the twin fissures that ran from his nose to his mouth made me put his age at midforties. He was looking at me—no, he was studying me. I repeated the question. "Mr. Wayne?"

"Yes. Hello. Sorry." He yanked a jacket that matched his pants from the back of a chair and struggled into it. "Are you Morgan Tyler? I didn't expect you until two."

Glancing at my watch, I saw that I was five minutes early. "I'm sorry. Shall I wait in the reception room?"

"No, of course not," he said. "Come in and sit down."

I glanced around his office. Every sitable surface was covered with law books, telephone books, file folders, or stacks of newspapers. In that one respect it resembled Bobby Novello's office. I couldn't suppress a smile as I asked, "*Where* should I sit?"

Without any trace of embarrassment, he cleared off a chair on the client's side of his desk. "I have my own special system of organization," he said. "Drives my secretary crazy, but I pay her well enough to get therapy."

As we took our respective seats, he said, "You did something that very few people have managed."

"What was that?"

"Persuade my answering service to find me on a weekend. Tell me, Morgan—may I call you Morgan?" I nodded. "Just how much trouble are you in?"

"Not me—it's my closest friend. She's been arrested for murder."

His eyes narrowed and his brow furrowed. He looked as though he was searching through a file in his brain. Apparently, he found what he wanted, because he said, "Only two non–drug deal murders occurred in the city during the last forty-eight hours. You don't look as though you'd know the Pakistani cab driver somebody shot and threw off the George Washington Bridge, so I'm presuming it must be the other one. Has your friend been accused of killing Arnold Rose's wife?"

"Yes. Do you know Arnold?"

A slight grimace crossed his face. "We've met." It seemed clear that he didn't like his fellow criminal lawyer. B. Kent Wayne said, "Tell me why you're here."

"My friend is Nancy Cummings. She practices corporate law in Arnold's firm, Newton, Donovan, Lipton, and Klein. She and Arnold are . . . going together. Nancy's been accused of killing his ex-wife, but she's innocent."

Wayne waved one hand in a gesture of dismissal. "That's immaterial."

"It isn't immaterial to me!"

"Let's not quibble over semantics," he said. "The details haven't been made public yet. Why was she arrested?"

I related everything that Matt had told me. When I finished, he said, "She doesn't have an attorney?"

"Nancy called someone from her firm, but I don't know anything about that person. Arnold was the top criminal lawyer at Newton, but he can't represent Nancy in this. I phoned you because I heard you were one of the best in the country."

"Only *one* of?" He smiled wryly. "Who recommended me?"

I opted for honesty. "A homicide detective who despises you."

He laughed. "A defense attorney can't get a better endorsement than that." Picking up a pen from the narrow tray on his cluttered desk, he twirled it in his hands for a few seconds. Finally he put the pen down and said, "Two items before we take this discussion any further. One: I'm expensive. Can Ms. Cummings afford a first-rate defense?"

"She's well-off," I said. "I mean, I think she is. I don't know if she has investments, or savings accounts, but she owns her apartment at the Bradbury, on West Eighty-first Street. Even if she doesn't have enough money available right away—or at all—*I* do. I'll write you a check this afternoon."

"Okay, so, one way or another, she can afford my services. Now part two: Did Ms. Cummings ask you to hire me?"

"Actually, no . . . She doesn't know I'm here because she's in jail and I haven't seen her yet."

"That's a problem. You said she called the Newton office—that means she already has a lawyer. I can't just walk in and take over somebody else's case."

"She *will* want to hire you, as soon as I talk to her."

"Assuming she does, she'll have to say so. Then I'll

contact the other attorney and make arrangements to take over."

"Thank you, Mr. Wayne."

"Call me Kent."

For the first time since Penny phoned me in Florida to tell me that Nancy had been arrested, I began to relax a little. As B. Kent Wayne, attorney-at-law, made notes on a white legal pad—the same kind of pad, I noticed, that I use to plot out the storylines for *Love of My Life*—I began to take in details of his office decor. On the wall directly behind him was a large glass case that held a fascinating display of armaments. Gesturing toward the daggers, several varieties of pistols, an ancient Japanese ceremonial sword, and a medieval spiked mace, I asked, "Is collecting weapons your hobby?"

"I think of them as merit badges. Those pieces were used in some of the cases I've tried—and won."

I couldn't suppress my shock. "One of your clients used a spiked mace?"

In a firm tone, he corrected me. "Was *alleged* to have used it. There were so many inconsistencies and missteps in the prosecution's case that I was able to establish enough reasonable doubt for an acquittal. Situations are seldom black and white. My battlefield is gray."

I was only interested in one thing. "When can you get Nancy out of jail?"

"She was arrested late Friday. That means Ms. Cummings will probably have a bail hearing on Monday. It's likely the D.A.'s office will ask for remand—"

"Remand—that's incarceration without bail." He looked surprised that I knew the term. "Every time I write a mystery plot for *Love of My Life* I have a character arrested," I said. "I had to learn the language."

He smiled. "I must start watching your show. Now, assuming Ms. Cummings wants me as her attorney, I'll ask for release on her own recognizance—citing her ties to the community, and so on. How much family does she have here?"

"None. Her parents are both dead. No siblings. No children."

"Too bad. O.R. is a lot tougher when the accused has no family ties to New York, and can afford to leave the country. I'll fight for bail, but it'll be high."

I waved my hand, signaling that I didn't care. "A bail bondsman will charge ten percent of whatever it is. I'll write a check on the spot. You have to get her released."

"I'll do everything possible," he said.

That wasn't a satisfying answer, but I had to keep pushing for action. "All right," I said. "What do you need first?"

"Find out the name of the lawyer Ms. Cummings called."

I fished around in my handbag for my small personal phone book. Months ago, Nancy gave me a cell number to use in case I had an emergency and couldn't reach her on her own phones. Quickly flipping through it, I found what I was looking for and dialed. As I waited for the call to be answered, I glanced again at Wayne's collection of weapons, and wondered how he was going to fit a five-gallon can of paint into that display case.

Chapter 15

ARNOLD ROSE ANSWERED quickly. "Yes?" His tone was brusque.

"Arnold? It's Morgan. I'm so sorry about—"

"Thank you. I appreciate your sympathy." He certainly didn't *sound* as though he appreciated it.

"How is Didi?" I asked.

"Devastated."

"She's a lovely girl—"

"Yes," he said coldly. Then silence.

"I'm sorry to bother you at this—"

"There is a great deal to do." His manner was impatient. I pictured him on the other end of the line: tapping his foot, or drumming his fingers on a handy surface.

I decided it was useless to make polite conversation, so I skipped right to the point of the call. "What lawyer is representing Nancy?"

"Cynthia Ruddy."

"Cynthia Ruddy?" I repeated her name for Kent

Wayne's benefit. Immediately, he swiveled halfway around in his chair to an extension on his desk and tapped keys on his laptop computer.

"Cynthia's first-rate," Arnold said. "She's the person I'd call, if I were in trouble."

"You've worked with her?"

"I *trained* her. She's excellent. The best."

It seemed to me that Arnold was doing a sales job. I didn't want to hear any more of it, so I said, "Will you let me know if there's anything I can do for Didi?"

"Certainly." With that, he hung up.

I must have been staring at the suddenly dead phone in my hand, because Wayne leaned toward me on his elbows. "I'll bet he behaved like a prick."

In a flash of anger that should have been directed at Arnold Rose, I snapped at Wayne. "It astonishes me when a man uses *that word* to insult another man!"

He jerked up straight and blinked at me in surprise. Then, with a hint of embarrassment, he said, "Frankly, I never thought of it that way." He cleared his throat—to put a vocal period on that subject, I guessed—and indicated the screen on his laptop.

"Cynthia Ruddy: Harvard Law, top grades, graduated five years ago, passed the New York bar on the first try, spent eighteen months as a public defender in Suffolk County. Invited to join the Newton firm three years ago when Lipton, the senior partner, decided to expand their criminal division. She's second-chaired four successful felony trials. Two of them with Arnold Rose."

"But she's never been the lead defense attorney in a case?"

"Not yet. Apparently she's a comer, though."

That assessment wasn't satisfying. "I don't want a lawyer representing Nancy who'll be getting experience in something that involves my best friend's life."

"Has she been Nancy's attorney before—represented her in any matter prior to this situation?"

"Nancy's never been arrested—or been in any kind of trouble at all. Why?"

"Substitution of attorney is much simpler if there's been no ongoing professional relationship. Is Nancy's connection to Arnold Rose strictly . . . social?"

I nodded, not wanting to say anything more specific. Nancy's feelings were hers to disclose. "What's our next step?" I asked.

He shot me a hard, quizzical look. "*Our* next step?"

If the expression on his face was meant to intimidate me, it didn't work. "I'm going to help Nancy. Just tell me what to do."

"All right. Call Cynthia Ruddy and get her to arrange for you to visit Nancy Cummings in jail."

"NO." CYNTHIA RUDDY was adamant. "I can't let you see her. If Nancy tells you anything self-incriminating, it won't be covered by attorney-client privilege."

I felt my heart lurch against my ribs. "You think Nancy's guilty, don't you?"

She hesitated, then answered evasively. "Her situation is serious."

While Kent Wayne had said Nancy's guilt or innocence was immaterial to him, at least he hadn't made up his mind in the negative about her. Now I was even more convinced that Cynthia Ruddy was not the best lawyer to defend Nancy.

"We won't discuss any details of the case," I said. "She's my best friend. I want her to know that I'm here for her."

"If I can get her out on bail, you can see her then."

The word "if" was like a stab in my chest. I hardened my tone in order to persuade Cynthia Ruddy that I wasn't going to take no for an answer. It still took a few more minutes of insisting, but at last she gave in.

"All right." I heard annoyance in her voice. "Be at the Twentieth Precinct at three-thirty. You'll have five minutes with her," Cynthia Ruddy said. "Interview rooms are bugged. There's no expectation of privacy, so the cops will probably be listening in. The microphone's only turned off when a lawyer and client are conferring."

NEW YORK CITY'S Twentieth Precinct is a stubby gray building at 120 West Eighty-second Street, between Columbus and Amsterdam Avenues. When I was here last, it had been a cold day in March, and the trees that edged the street were almost bare of leaves. Today they were bursting with vivid shades of summer green.

During the past year I'd come to this fortress of temporary incarceration several times. All but the first visit had been of my own volition. Quite a few of the officers stationed there had become familiar faces. One of them, Officer Kirk—a young former marine with a shaved head— smiled pleasantly. As he escorted me up a flight of stairs, he asked, "How's it goin'?"

"Fine," I lied, but I smiled, too.

To reach the interview (a.k.a. interrogation) rooms, we had to pass through the detectives' squad room on the second floor. I half expected to see Matt and G. G. at their pair of facing desks, but their chairs were unoccupied. Not seeing Matt was partly a disappointment, and partly a relief.

Interview Room One, a discordant symphony in gray and olive green, looked as though it had last been painted several years before I was born. It was neat in that there was no trash littering the floor, but it smelled strongly of disinfectant. I wondered briefly what substance had been spilled that required such a powerful sanitizer, but I realized it was a question I shouldn't pursue.

Seconds after Officer Kirk closed the door behind me, a policewoman escorted Nancy into the room. She was wearing a gray jail jumpsuit, but at least she wasn't in handcuffs. The policewoman told her to sit on the opposite side of the table from me.

With the stern admonition, "No touching!" she left us alone. Or as *alone* as we could be in a room where I knew the mirror on the wall was two-way glass, behind which other people were probably watching us, and listening.

Suddenly all I could think of was to ask the idiotic question, "Are you okay?"

Nancy's responding smile was wan, but there was no defeat in her eyes. "I'm all right—considering that this wasn't how I'd planned to spend the weekend. Incidentally, you're too loyal to ask, but I didn't kill Veronica."

"You don't have to tell me that," I said. I wanted to grasp her hands in solidarity and support, but I remembered the rule against touching. "I knew you couldn't have done it." Nodding toward the two-way glass, I added, "Maybe we shouldn't discuss the case."

Nancy waved defiantly at whoever was behind the mirror. "I don't care who hears us—my story's not going to change because it's the truth." She grimaced, shaking her head in frustration. "I was such an *idiot*. For Arnold's sake, and Didi's, I decided to try to make peace with Veronica. I phoned her and asked if we could talk privately. She told me she was going down to her apartment to check on what the workmen had been doing, and said I could meet her there. When I arrived, she was dead. I can't believe how stupidly I behaved then, but I'm not the person who killed her!" Suddenly, she looked near to exhaustion. I realized how much effort it must be taking for her to act strong. "Oh, Lord," she sighed, "I'm so glad to see you!" Her eyes filled with tears.

Hoping to lift her spirits, I gestured at her jumpsuit. "It's disgusting, how you manage to look so good—even in that thing. If I gave you a designer scarf to twist and tie in one of those mysterious ways you have, you'd be ready for lunch at the Four Seasons."

She used her index fingers to wipe the tears from her eyes. In a wry tone, she said, "Not quite. They confiscated my makeup. Do you suppose they think I'm going to stab somebody with a mascara wand?"

"Where are the clothes you were wearing when they brought you here?"

"I hope they're hanging up somewhere. Cynthia said they'd give them back to me just before my bail hearing."

Lowering my voice, I said, "They've only given me a few minutes, and there's something important we have to talk about."

"What?"

"Cynthia Ruddy doesn't have enough experience for this situation. I want you to hire Kent Wayne."

"*B.* Kent Wayne?" Nancy was aghast. "Did you know his first name is Bruce? Can you believe it—his parents named him after Batman! Arnold had some tussles with him. He calls Wayne 'The Prince of Darkness.' "

"Of course Arnold would be hostile—they're competitors. If you don't want Wayne, I'll find you somebody else with a great track record, but please don't put your future in the hands of someone at the beginning of her career." I didn't add: *and someone who believes you're guilty*.

Nancy frowned. "But Arnold thinks very highly—"

I interrupted with a joke. "Let's hire her a few years from now—*next* time you're arrested for murder."

Nancy did her best to smile, but I knew it was hard for her to find anything about the situation amusing. "Do you really feel strongly that I should have a different lawyer?"

"With all of my heart! Let me tell Wayne that you've hired him."

The door to the visiting room opened. The policewoman was back, and Matt Phoenix was with her.

"Time's up," the policewoman said.

Nancy stood and looked at Matt. In her most imperious

tone, she said, "We meet again, Detective. I'm sorry I can't offer you coffee."

Matt's face reddened, but he didn't reply. Instead, he glared at *me.*

Nancy leaned down and whispered, "Get Kent Wayne. I'll tell Cynthia that to spare the firm embarrassment I'm going to use outside counsel." Then, with perfect posture and head held high, she swept out of the room. The policewoman trailed behind her, liked the lady-in-waiting to a princess.

As soon as they were gone, Matt growled, "Out, before I think of a reason to lock you up, too!"

Chapter 16

ONE LARGE HAND gripping my upper arm, Matt escorted me out into the street. Rushed me out, was more like it. He didn't stop this forced march until we were nearly a block away, in front of a seedy old brownstone that had been converted into apartments. Below a sign in the window that said VACANCY, the ledge was encrusted with pigeon droppings.

His mouth set in grim determination, Matt steered me down several steps below the street until we were almost at the building's closed basement door, and far enough away from the stream of pedestrian traffic above us to have some privacy. Positioning me with my back against the steps' wrought iron guardrail, he released me, but immediately clasped his left hand around the railing on my "escape route" side. His grip was so hard his knuckles turned white. To get away from him, I would have had to pry that big hand loose, or push through his firmly planted body. Neither option seemed promising.

"This is unlawful detainment," I said.

"It's protective custody!"

"I don't need protection."

"You've needed protection since the day I met you," he snapped. "A couple of months ago you were almost killed—for the third time!"

Actually, that was the fourth time, but I didn't think it would be wise to correct him. "Since I'm still alive, you've just proved that I can take care of myself," I said. "Let me go."

"I will—as soon as you promise to stay out of the Veronica Rose case."

"Then you better use your cell phone to send out for meals, sleeping bags, and a port-a-potty because I'm not making that promise."

He expelled a gut-deep sigh in surrender and stepped back. "It was worth a try," he muttered. "You take so many chances with your life you make me crazy."

I moved away from where he'd imprisoned me against the railing, but didn't go up the steps. Instead, I reached out and took his hand. Reflexively, his hand closed around mine. "Let's go someplace where we can talk," I said.

OVER SURPRISINGLY GOOD diner coffee, Matt and I took off our twin masks of hostility. As angry as I could get at Matt when we were on the opposite sides of a difficult situation, I hadn't been able to rid myself of the physical attraction I felt for him. And that I suspected he still harbored for me.

We had come very close to making love a few months ago, and I'd never stopped wishing that we hadn't been interrupted before we got up to my apartment. An attempt on my life intervened. I really thought that we'd eventually make it up to my bed—or across Central Park to his bed, or to *some* bed, somewhere. Hadn't happened, and wasn't likely to. Matt stopped dating me when I accepted an inheritance that put me into a higher financial bracket than he was in. (On hearing about this, Nancy had referred to him as "an idiot.")

Now we were looking at each other across a scarred old table, its vinyl top discolored from years of scrubbing and beginning to peel off at the corners. Not exactly a romantic setting, but suddenly I felt a stirring of physical longing. Resolutely, I pushed it away. That horse had left the barn, so to speak. *Concentrate on Nancy's situation*, I told myself.

"I'm a lot less likely to annoy you if you'll just give me some information," I said.

He smiled ruefully. " 'Less likely' isn't much of a concession."

"It's something. Come on, please tell me what you know about Nancy's problem."

"Okay, I'll give you as much as I can, because I want to convince you that there's absolutely nothing you can do to help her. What do you want to know?"

I'd been thinking about scenarios other than Nancy as the killer, so I was ready with questions. "Couldn't Veronica Rose have surprised a burglar and been killed because she saw him?"

"The apartment was empty; they hadn't moved in yet. Nothing to steal—and no forced entry."

"Her rings. She wore a diamond engagement and wedding ring set. The engagement ring had a huge stone—I'm guessing ten carats. It had to cost at least fifty thousand dollars, maybe a lot more."

He shook his head. "The rings were on her fingers. And there was a platinum and diamond pendant watch around her neck, and a diamond bracelet on her wrist."

"It could still have been a burglar—somebody who went to the wrong—"

"No mistake. This was personal. Mrs. Rose was hit

more than once, even though the medical examiner says she probably died from the first blow."

I shuddered; I knew that multiple blows were indications of rage. The killer had wanted to utterly destroy the victim, not just kill her.

"Since I saw you this morning, another report came back from the lab. There were no fingerprints on that paint can. It had been wiped clean. That doesn't exonerate Nancy." He reached across the vinyl and took my hand in a gesture of comfort.

"It's hard to think that someone we like could commit a murder," he said.

"Nancy isn't capable of murder. For God's sake, Matt, she's not some stranger suspect—you *know* her!"

"One of the first things I learned as a cop was that you can never tell about people, or guess for sure what's going to push them over the edge into a place you never thought they could go. Nancy had some ugly encounters with the victim in front of other people. One witness said the two women nearly came to blows in the law office."

Alarmed at how damning such a statement was, I jerked my hand away from Matt's and demanded, "What witness? Who said that?"

"Sorry, I can't tell you. Her attorney will get names during the discovery process."

"But if he's going to find out anyway, why can't you tell me now?"

Matt straightened up in his seat and frowned at me. "*He?* Her attorney's a woman named Cynthia Ruddy."

"Not anymore."

"Then who?"

"B. Kent Wayne," I said.

Red spots of anger burned on Matt's face; I half expected steam to start coming out of his ears. "Is this one of your jokes?"

"No joke," I said. "Nancy needs the strongest possible defense."

An astonishing string of expletives spewed from his lips! The vehemence of that reaction shocked me. "What's the matter?" I asked.

"That lawyer you went to doesn't just defend people, he gets his kicks humiliating cops on the stand. A few months ago, he got G. G. so tangled up he made him sound like a damn fool. Our arrest was righteous, but he painted us as a pair of rabid fascists so the perp walked. Whatever that scum of a client of his does next is on Kent Wayne's miserable head!"

Matt stood up so fast he knocked over his glass of water. Angrily gesturing at the mess of soaked paper napkins, he tossed a ten-dollar bill at me. "This is for the waitress. You can pay for the coffee."

He stomped out of the diner. Our pleasant coffee date was over.

I signaled to the waitress. When she came over with the bill, I apologized for the spilled water, gave her Matt's ten-dollar bill, and a five of my own for our coffees.

The diner was almost empty, which gave me quiet and privacy. I telephoned Kent Wayne and told him that Nancy had agreed to hire him, and filled him in on what I'd learned about the murder.

"Thanks," he said. "I'll get to work."

Me, too, I thought. *Just as soon as I figure out where to start.*

Chapter 17

TWENTY MINUTES LATER, when I opened the door to my apartment, I caught the aroma of food coming from the direction of the kitchen. Whatever it was smelled delicious, and made me realize how hungry I was. My salivary glands sprang into action. That had to be the work of the best cook I've ever known.

"Penny?" As I called her name, I wondered how she'd gotten into the apartment, but realized Walter must have let her in.

At the sound of my voice, Magic came loping down the hallway and shocked me by making a graceful leap up onto my shoulder. "Wow," I said, stroking his head. "When did you learn to fly?"

I was in for another surprise when I entered the kitchen. It wasn't Penny at the stove, it was Walter, and he was stirring something in a wok. I'd never owned a wok.

"Hi," I said. Magic stayed on my shoulder, but he was fascinated by what was going on at the stove.

"How'd it go with the lawyer?" Walter asked.

"He's smart, and energetic." I put my handbag on one of the four chairs at the kitchen table and sat down carefully, so as not to jolt Magic. "I just hope I've done the right thing for Nancy."

As Walter continued his activity at the stove, I told him about my meeting with Wayne, seeing Nancy for a few minutes, and about the subsequent fight in the diner with Matt.

"That boy's sweet on you," Walter said. His back was to me, but I heard a smile in his voice.

"Maybe he was once, but not now." Eager to change the subject, I asked, "What did you do while I was gone?"

"Went shopping. Bought some groceries, an' this pot. You didn't have anything in the house except cat food, an' a few cans of tuna. Looks like you take better care of the cat than you do of yourself."

"The neighborhood's full of restaurants and takeout places," I said, a little defensively. "I don't have time to cook."

Walter took a big wooden spoon—also new—out of the wok. He opened the door to the oven and checked whatever was happening inside.

"When Junie found out she wasn't going to be around," he said, "she made me promise to eat healthy, an' she taught me some things. You never know what they put in restaurant food." Walter closed the oven door, took a step toward me, and reached into his shirt pocket. With a grin, he pulled out a shiny new cell phone and held it in one large hand. "I joined the twenty-first century today." Nodding toward a pad on the table, he said, "I wrote the number down for you."

WALTER AND I were sitting at the kitchen table, eating stir-fried chicken and vegetable teriyaki, and the corn muffins he'd baked. Magic was curled up on a pile of newspapers by the back door that led out to the service elevator. He was awake and watching us, but I suspected that the sound of our voices wasn't as interesting to him as the scent of chicken.

"You've never met her, but I want you to know that Nancy's not guilty."

"Tell me why Matt thinks she is."

"Circumstantial evidence." Even as I said the words, I realized how weak that sounded.

Walter lifted one shaggy eyebrow and cocked his head. "What 'circumstances'?"

"Nancy went to see Veronica. They'd arranged to meet in the empty apartment, the one Veronica was supposedly decorating for herself and her daughter. The door was standing open a couple of inches. Nancy went in. She saw Veronica lying on the floor, her head bloody. She knelt down to see if she had a pulse, but there wasn't one. That's when Veronica's daughter came in and started screaming."

"That can was the murder weapon . . . Fingerprints?"

"No prints at all."

Walter shook his head in dismay. "The prosecutor's gonna say she wiped the can clean, but that she didn't have time to get away before she was discovered there."

"Nancy has never had even so much as a speeding ticket. She votes in every election, pays her taxes. There's nothing about her that would suggest to any thinking person that she could commit a murder. She was just in the wrong place, wrong time."

"Any cop worth the tin in his badge would figure she's the most likely suspect. Be fair now. You can't really blame Matt for thinking she's guilty, can you?"

I sighed. "Okay, I suppose you're right. But I know as surely as I'm sitting here that Nancy didn't kill Veronica Rose. She found her after she was already dead."

Walter pursed his lips in thought. "What about motive?"

"Veronica was trying to break up Arnold and Nancy, but that's not enough reason to *kill* someone!"

"In one of my cases, a man beat a stranger to death with a tire iron over a fender bender. Now that's pretty unusual, but history's full of people who killed out of jealousy."

"Not Nancy," I insisted.

Walter swallowed a mouthful of stir-fry. "Taking your word for it that your friend isn't the killer, let's look at the victim. What do you know about her?"

"She comes from Boston, from a rich family. She married Arnold Rose about fifteen years ago. They had one child, Didi. She's twelve. Three years ago, Arnold and Veronica Rose divorced. She took Didi and moved back to Boston. Then suddenly, a couple of months ago, she decided to move back to New York. I think she did it because Didi told her that Arnold was in love with Nancy and it was Veronica who was jealous."

"What you *think* isn't evidence," Walter said gently. "We need to find out exactly why she came back."

I was as surprised as Kent Wayne had been earlier, when I'd said something similar in his office. *"We?"*

"Used to be a pretty damn good investigator in my day," Walter said. "Fact is, when I was out shopping this afternoon I bought me a computer—one of those notebook things that fold up an' fit in a briefcase. Your friend Bobby asked me to do some employee background checks, for a business client he's got."

"It's great, that you're helping Bobby. I'm glad you two hit it off. But you need the Internet—"

"Got that covered," he said proudly. "Old Walter didn't just fall off the turnip truck. I found a coffee shop down the block has Internet access. You just plug the little bugger in one of their outlets. Only drawback is you gotta spend three dollars for a cup of coffee."

"You can work here," I said. "Use my Internet access. I do most of my computer work at the office."

"That's right nice of you—but you're not stuck with me. I'm havin' the cell phone bill sent to Florida. I'll be back there 'fore it comes due."

An unexpected—and unfamiliar—emotion suddenly washed over me: a pang of loneliness. "I didn't realize you would be going back so soon," I said. "Don't rush away. There's plenty of room here."

He looked dubious. "You know what they say: after a week or two guests and fish begin to stink."

Before I could think of a response, Walter picked up the discussion of Veronica Rose. "Most murder victims aren't killed by strangers. Who are her friends?"

"I don't know," I said.

"There are a couple ways to go: find out what kind of life she was leading up in Boston—if she had any enemies. An' find out if there's anybody there or here she could have made mad enough to kill her."

I remembered something Betty Kraft had said, and it gave me an idea.

"What you thinkin'?" Walter asked.

"My assistant, Betty Kraft, is very observant. After Veronica and Didi visited the studio, Betty told me that Veronica was *greedy*. She described her as the kind of woman who had to have men wanting her."

As I told him about Betty, and her pre–Global Broadcasting background as a psychiatric nurse, Walter was scraping teriyaki sauce off of a couple of little pieces of chicken. He put them on a paper napkin and took it over to Magic, who immediately began to munch on the unexpected snack.

"You got a loose-leaf notebook somewhere?" Walter asked. "An' one of those three-hole punchers?"

"Yes, both. With some other office supplies in the bedroom closet."

"Good. We'll need them to start our own murder book," he said.

"A book?"

"Over the years, we had our share of murders in Downsville County. Always made me a book. Most investigators do. We put in notes on everything we learn 'bout the case. After a while, we start to see what the story is."

Remembering my days as a photographer, I said, "Just like seeing a blank sheet of paper turn into a photograph in the developing solution."

Chapter 18

AFTER DINNER, I found that Walter had put his shaving kit on the sink counter in the three-quarter bathroom off the kitchen. It had a toilet, a sink, and a shower, all clean and in good working order, but it was the size of a closet.

"This bathroom is pretty small," I said, concerned.

"It's jus' fine. Growing up, we had an outhouse. No indoor plumbing 'til I was old enough to work an' help pay for it. Junie was born poor, too, but I made sure she always had a nice place to live."

Even though his wife had been dead for more than ten years, I'd noticed that he still wore his wedding ring. "You must have loved her very much."

All he said was, "Yep," but the tenderness in his voice as he spoke was eloquent.

I took a set of clean sheets and a comforter out of the linen closet, and handed Walter a pillow and fresh pillowcase. Together, we transformed the couch in the den into a comfortable bed.

"When I came back to New York from Africa and didn't have anyplace to stay, Nancy turned her den into a bedroom for me," I said. "This is like completing a circle." I took the TV remote from the lamp table between the club chairs and handed it to him, and with it the card listing the channel numbers and what they were.

"We have satellite. The company claims we've got a hundred and twenty channels, but I've never bothered to check out more than a few of them."

Walter settled himself in one of the club chairs, and I plopped down in the other. "I don't want to be in the way now," he said.

I smiled ruefully. "If you're talking about my so-called social life, there's nothing to get in the way of. Frankly, I wish there were."

"What's wrong with the men in New York?"

Joking, but with a grain of truth, I said, "Maybe there's something wrong with me."

The telephone connecting my apartment to the Dakota's reception desk rang. That was a surprise.

"I'm not expecting anybody," I said. Picking it up, I got a bigger surprise when I heard Arnold Rose's voice.

"Morgan, I hope I'm not interrupting you."

"Not at all."

"Please forgive me for just showing up at your building without calling first, but could you give me a few minutes?"

"Yes, of course, Arnold. Come up. I'm on the third floor. Whoever's on the desk will show you which elevator to take."

I stood in my doorway as Arnold got off the elevator. He saw me and hurried forward, grasped my hands, and said, "I feel terrible about how I acted when you phoned this afternoon. I wanted to apologize to you in person."

"There's no need. I understand." I led Arnold into the living room, where Walter was sitting on one of the two sofas flanking the big picture window that faced Central Park.

I introduced Arnold to Walter. Walter stood up, and while they were shaking hands and doing the "how-do-you-do" routine, I took a good look at Arnold under the strong living room light. As always, his clothes were an elegant study in black and gray. During the week he wore black suits and pale gray shirts, or pale gray suits and dark gray shirts, always with silk neckties that matched the shirts. On weekends he wore gray slacks, gray cashmere jackets, and black cashmere sweaters. Usually, Arnold's complexion was ruddy, but tonight it was sallow. Deep worry lines etched his face, but he also looked generally better than when I'd seen him several weeks ago. He'd lost a few pounds, and his abdomen was decidedly trimmer.

A last detail I noticed was that Arnold's thinning black hair seemed darker than previously. I wondered if he was dying it. I probably wouldn't have noted the change, except for the bright overhead light from the crystal chandelier that had come with the apartment—one of the fixtures I hated. I'd joked to Nancy and Penny that I'd replace them as soon as I had time to figure out what my own taste was. I'd gone from living in a boarding school, to a college dorm, to camping in jungles, and finally to this fully furnished apartment. I told my friends, and myself, that since I'd moved into the Dakota, I'd been too busy to pick out my own things. But I'd begun to realize that wasn't the entire truth. I'd gone to Bobby Novello because I suspected that the missing pieces of my past might be keeping me from moving forward.

I said, "Sit down, Arnold, please." I gestured to the couch opposite Walter. "Can I get you something to drink? Scotch? Or wine?"

"No, thank you, Morgan." He sat down, and I sat next to him. "I can only stay a few minutes. My housekeeper is with Didi, but I don't want to be away for long."

"Of course not."

Walter was smiling pleasantly, but behind his round,

owlish glasses he was studying Arnold as though his glasses were a microscope.

"I really just came to tell you how sorry I am that I was abrupt today." Suddenly, he asked, "How is Nancy?"

"Strong," I said. "She's hanging on."

"I want to help her, but I don't know what to do."

"She didn't kill Veronica. You believe her, don't you?"

Just as Cynthia Ruddy had, Arnold hesitated, then: "If she says that she didn't do it, of course I believe her. I understand that she's dismissed Cynthia as her attorney. Do you know why?"

I replied with the excuse Nancy had invented. "To save your firm embarrassment." I added, "She was thinking of *you*."

Arnold nodded. "Hmmm. I see. Then I'll get her another attorney—the best in the country. I'll pay all the fees. Whatever happened in that room, I'm sure it wasn't *murder*. No matter how things look, Veronica's death couldn't have been intentional. I don't want Nancy's life destroyed, too."

"She has a new lawyer. Kent Wayne."

"Wayne?" A sudden flush colored Arnold's cheeks. "That unscrupulous—" With a sharp intake of breath, he managed to rein in his burst of emotion. "Whatever I think of the man is unimportant. He's an excellent defense counsel. As much as I hate to admit it, he's one of the most capable on the eastern seaboard. In these dire circumstances, he's probably the best chance Nancy—he's a good choice." Arnold stood up. In response, Walter and I got to our feet, too.

"I've got to get back to Didi," Arnold said. He took my hands. "Will you accept my apology about this afternoon?"

"Of course. I know what you're going through."

"Thank you." He released my hands, said good night to Walter, and started to go.

"Oh, Arnold. You know I'm very fond of Didi."

"She likes you, too," he said, smiling.

"I'd like to see her. I could invite her to come to the studio—"

His smile vanished. Suddenly his voice was sharp as the crack of a whip. "No!"

"No?"

"I meant not right away. It's too soon for Didi to see anyone." As quickly as he'd flared to anger, he softened his tone. "Now, I really have to go. Call me, Morgan—let me know what I can do to help Nancy."

I followed Arnold to the front door and locked it behind him. Returning to the living room, I told Walter, "When I first met Didi, Arnold was delighted to have me get to know her. Now he's acting like a dragon guarding a cave from me."

Frowning, Walter shook his head. "It's not about you. I was watching that fella. He appreciated your concern for the girl. It was when you mentioned having her up to your studio that he got real upset."

I closed my mind and replayed the conversation in my head, as though it was an exchange in a scene from one of our shows.

"You're right," I said. "I wonder why he's so against her visiting again."

"That goes on the list of questions that need answers."

"Matt's convinced he's arrested Veronica Rose's killer. As far as he's concerned, his job is done, but I know he's wrong. I can't leave Nancy's fate solely in the hands of a defense attorney, no matter how good he's supposed to be."

"Finding the real killer's the one sure way to clear your friend." Walter stood up, stretched, and rotated a kink out of his neck. "I wanna do some research on the dead woman. Show me where to plug in my computer."

"Use mine," I said. "I'll make us fresh coffee."

While Walter rode the Internet through public records and the New York and Boston newspaper archives, I worked at the kitchen table on white legal pads, roughing out future story. I needed to get far enough ahead in my work to take a few days off to go investigating.

COPIES OF THE *New York Times* and the *New York Post* were delivered to my door before dawn every morning. On this Sunday, the *Times* had the usual headlines about the Middle East, but when I picked up the *Post* I was shocked to see Nancy's photograph staring at me from the front page, under the headline "Lawyer Accused of Murder." My stomach muscles clenched in distress as I realized that in Nancy's awful situation, it was probable that every aspect of her private life would be turned into entertainment reading for millions of strangers.

Fur brushed against my ankle. I looked down to see Magic peering outside, poised to go exploring. "No, no. Not out there." I steered him gently back into the apartment and closed the door.

Returning to the paper, I followed the headlines to the story on page three. There was a photograph of Veronica Rose, looking stunning in gown and jewels, taken at an art museum gala she had chaired in Boston earlier this year. At the bottom right-hand corner of the page was a smaller photo of Arnold, with the somewhat snide caption: "Object of their affections." The *Times* had the story, too, with pictures of Nancy and Veronica, but the text was written less sensationally and appeared at the back of Section A, in their New York Report section under the headline: "Wife of Prominent Attorney Found Dead."

SUNDAY EVENING, WALTER got up from the computer. A scowl of disgust creased his broad face, and his drooping gray mustache seemed to bristle. "The late Mrs. Rose was a husband stealer," he announced.

That piqued my interest. "What husband did she steal?"

Walter corrected me. "Husbands, plural. An investment banker named George Reynolds and Ralph Hartley. Hartley's CEO of a Massachusetts utilities company. There might be more, but these happened during the last fourteen months."

He handed me printouts of several newspaper articles and social columns. Reading the material, I saw that the *Boston Chronicle*'s gossip columnist, Cathy Chatsworth, had managed to get the most vivid details of the moral frailties of the socially elite.

"Cathy Chatsworth—that has to be a made-up name," I said, "but she's probably got a phone."

Boston Information gave me a number for her, but it turned out to be for her voice mail number at the *Boston Chronicle.* I left a message, but then called the newspaper's switchboard operator, and asked her to try to call the columnist at home and deliver a message.

Half an hour later, Cathy Chatsworth called me back. Judging from her accent, she was either British or pretentious. After identifying herself, the Boston columnist said, "So, you want to do a TV movie about dear Veronica's murder?"

That had *not* been the message. I'd told the operator to give her my name and tell her that I produced a television show. The columnist had jumped to the wrong conclusion. I didn't want to lie to her, but Nancy's life was at stake, and this woman might be able to help her. Before I could frame an ambiguous answer, she got to what was clearly *her* point of interest. "You pay consultants, don't you?"

"Absolutely. Consultants are well compensated. You'll be paid for background information, and again if the movie is produced. If our company produces it, of course you'll get an on-screen credit."

On her end of the line I heard a gasp. "Oh, no! You

can't use my name! My involvement must be strictly confidential—but I will expect to be paid."

"However you want to work it, that's fine," I said. "But I wonder if you actually have any information about Veronica Rose's personal life that might shed some light on her murder."

"I thought they caught the killer."

"The investigation is ongoing," I said. That was the truth, in that *I* was continuing to investigate, even if the police were not.

"Hmmmmm. This is *delicious*. If your movie needs suspects, there certainly were people who wanted her dead. Four in particular. Interested?"

I certainly was! We made a date to meet for lunch the next day in Boston.

Replacing the receiver, I turned to Walter. "Now we have a place to start."

Chapter 19

AT A QUARTER to nine on Monday morning, Penny Cavanaugh, Brandi Flynn, and I got out of a cab in front of 100 Centre Street, the Manhattan Criminal Courts Building.

The seventeen-story art deco courthouse has a steel frame and a granite and limestone facade. Four towers in front, with a jail behind, the taller tower looks like an ancient Babylonian temple. The building is stepped, and the windows are set in vertical bands, alternating with stone supports. Tall brass and glass entrance doors, both stationary and revolving, are bookended by a pair of huge, free-standing granite columns. A thick, rounded brass railing going up the steps from the street separated those entering the building from those exiting.

Brandi started to go up on the downside, but I caught the strap on her shoulder bag and steered her back to the right-hand section of the divide.

"Remember what we learned in school: 'Keep to the right when passing.'"

"I never did get that one right," she said. "But I aced sex ed."

This morning, Brandi had dressed down from her usual flamboyant style, and wore a simple black dress with long sleeves. She called it her going-to-court outfit, but the plunging V neckline and the wide gold belt around her waist were classic Brandi. Penny was quietly elegant in a beige suit and a chocolate brown silk blouse the same color as her hair. In their separate ways, they were stylish, but in my navy blazer, red skirt, and white blouse, I just looked patriotic. Maybe because I'd been poor for most of my life, fashion wasn't my thing.

The marble lobby was two stories high, with a hanging clock marking the center. There were handsome art deco lighting fixtures, metal doors, and two grand staircases with ornamental railings.

After we passed through the security check, an armed guard pointed us toward the staircase up to the courtroom. So many people swarmed through the lobby and elbowed their way up the stairs that I had a mental image of us as three salmon fighting our way upstream.

We made it, and found the door we sought. A removable sign announced that the Honorable George Dayton would be presiding inside. Still five minutes early, we pushed the door open and went in.

The air in the courtroom was filled with the hum of many low conversations, but none of the people here were smiling. In contrast to the grandeur below, this room where Nancy's immediate fate would be decided was almost stark, with unembellished paneling.

Penny, Brandi, and I found places in the second row behind the railing that separated friends, relatives, and observers from prosecutors, defense attorneys, and clients.

Two rectangular wooden tables, with chairs behind them, faced the judge's bench. One table was reserved for defense attorneys and their clients, and the other for the prosecutors. About four feet of space separated the two sides. Above the judge's bench, in large brass letters affixed to the wall, were the words, IN GOD WE TRUST. I trusted in God, too, but I still wanted Nancy to have the best lawyer money could rent.

Just as we sat down, the court officer stood up.

"All rise," he said.

Everyone in the courtroom obeyed, and a man with a thick pelt of pewter gray hair covering his bulbous head entered from a door behind the raised judicial bench. He was so corpulent that his black robe clung to his body instead of swirling around it. As he took his place, the court officer signaled that all of us could resume our seats, handed the judge a sheaf of papers, and announced Docket number 13759, the People versus Nancy Susan Cummings.

A door—not the one from which the judge had entered—opened behind the bench. Nancy emerged, accompanied by Kent Wayne. She was pale, and her hair looked like it could use a shampoo, but it was combed, and I could tell she'd been allowed to apply some makeup. She looked around the courtroom, saw us, and managed a brave smile.

Nancy and Wayne made their way to the table on the left while an angular woman with short dark hair cut in a shag style moved up to stand behind the table on the right.

Judge Dayton peered over the papers in his hand and said, "Mr. Wayne, always a pleasure to see you." His tone was unmistakably sarcastic. "How does your client plead?"

In the rich baritone of an experienced orator, Wayne replied, "Not guilty, your honor."

"What a surprise." Judge Dayton turned to the prosecution table. "Ms. Robbins, I don't suppose I need to ask, but just for the record, how do the People feel about bail?"

"We ask for remand, your honor. Ms. Cummings viciously murdered her romantic rival."

That set off a heated exchange between the two attorneys, but the judge quickly cut it off. "Enough! If Ms. Cummings did the deed, then the deed is done. Presumably the State isn't claiming she's a danger to others."

"Your honor—"

"Save it for the trial, Ms. Robbins. Bail is set at one million dollars, cash or bond."

With a sharp bang of the judge's gavel Nancy's bail hearing was over. I checked my watch. It had taken all of three minutes. The court officer called out the next docket number, another set of lawyer-and-client emerged from the door to the holding cells, and a young man with a bald spot the size of a yarmulke replaced the woman at the prosecutor's table.

Brandi was shocked. "It happened so fast!"

"This is what it's usually like," I said. "Last year, when the storyline had Link Ramsey on trial, I studied the routine so I'd get it right for the show."

Awestruck, Brandi said, "Boy, writers sure have to learn a lot of stuff."

Penny gently poked me on the arm. "That lawyer is waving at you."

I looked up and saw that Nancy and Wayne had moved over to the far side of the courtroom. He was gesturing for me to join them.

Penny and Brandi came with me. I introduced Wayne to Penny and Brandi, and Nancy hugged us all.

"Thank you for being here," she said.

I asked Wayne, "Can Nancy leave now?"

"My favorite bail bondsman is waiting outside in the hall. If someone can give him a hundred thousand dollars—"

I was about to volunteer, but Nancy stopped me. "I have it. Will your man take a check?"

Wayne nodded. "Certified."

Nancy squeezed my hand. "Kent told me that you offered—"

"Forget it," I said. I didn't want Nancy to thank me for

being willing to pay her bail. It was money I never expected to have, and hadn't earned. Gratitude wasn't merited. "You're getting out of here soon. I hope you don't mind my taking off, but there's someone I need to see right away. I can't tell you anything yet, but this person may have information that'll help you."

"I need all the help I can get," Nancy said ruefully. She gave me a quick kiss on the cheek. "Go!"

"We'll stay with Nancy," Penny said. Brandi nodded in agreement.

FROM THE BACK of the taxi taking me to the airport, I used my cell phone. The first call was to Walter, to let him know that Nancy would be released today. Next, I dialed the office.

"You've got a dozen messages," Betty said, "but only four need immediate attention. In order of time stamp arrival: first, Eva wants to cut her hair."

I thought for a moment. Eva played the role of Sylvia, Evan Duran's sister, a very attractive and vital older woman. With her stepchildren grown, Sylvia had just left full-time homemaking and started a fashion design business. A shorter style would fit her character in that storyline. "Tell her yes, and remind me to add some dialogue about Sylvia's new look. What's next?"

"Jay Garwood wants a change of wardrobe."

"To what?"

"Armani suits. He says he thinks his character should be dressing better than Link's."

"That's ridiculous," I said.

"So what else is new?"

"Tell Jay we'll talk about wardrobe on Friday. We'll have lunch together in my office then."

"He'll like that," Betty said. "He's becoming a bit of a diva."

"Thanks for the tip. I'll have to stop that before it gets out of hand. What else?"

"Clarice just found out she's pregnant."

"Oops!"

"Oops is right," Betty said. "She told me she and her husband weren't planning to start a family for another year. Now she's worried because she knows you can't write a baby into the Jillian-Gareth storyline, at least not in the next several months. She's afraid you're going to fire her."

"Of course not! Tell her we'll hide her pregnancy with props and camera angles when she starts to show, and by the time she's ready to take maternity leave, I'll have worked out a story to explain her temporary absence. I'm glad she told us right away, so we have time to plan. Remind me to talk to costuming about getting ready to dress her to disguise it."

"Will do."

"And stick a note on my computer to go through her future episodes," I said. "I'll take out any physical actions that could hurt her—no climbing, falling, or running. If I can't revise a scene, we'll hire a stunt double. Tell her she has nothing to worry about."

Betty chuckled. "Actually, I already did. I was sure that's how you'd react. She left the office happy, and went to Craft Services to see if they had any lemon meringue pie."

I smiled at the image of delicate Clarice, queen of dressing-on-the-side salads, stalking the caterer for pie. "What's the fourth message?"

"Link wants to see you. He says it's personal."

"All right." I closed my eyes and visualized this week's taping schedule. "He's working Thursday afternoon. Ask him if he'd like to have breakfast with me Thursday morning. Pick some place away from the studio. I don't want anyone on the show to see us together and get the wrong idea."

"How about I get you a wig and a false nose from costume?"

I laughed. "We don't need to go quite that far. I expect to be back in the office tomorrow afternoon. If there's an emergency, you can get me on my cell."

Chapter 20

I MANAGED TO catch the Jet Blue Airbus out of JFK that would get me to Boston an hour before my one o'clock lunch date with the *Boston Chronicle*'s gossip columnist, Cathy Chatsworth. Last night, I'd searched the Internet for a hotel within a few blocks of where I was due to meet her, and chose Adams House—partly because I liked the idea that it was more than 150 years old. Knowing nothing about my own origins, I always seemed to be attracted to buildings full of history.

What I knew about the importance of Boston to the founding of this country came from my American studies classes. Everything I knew about modern Boston came from reading Robert B. Parker's Spenser crime novels. I wished I had the leisure to walk along Boylston Street and try to guess from which window Spenser in his P.I. office could look down on Berkley Street. Another time. Not today.

The cab from the airport dropped me at Adams House,

a Federalist-style white structure, eight stories high, with tall, narrow windows arranged symmetrically on either side of the entrance, and a semicircular fanlight over the front door. The overall effect was stately.

Inside, the decor was Early American, with tables and chairs that were either authentic pieces of the period, or excellent replicas. The wide planks of the dark-stained hardwood floors were polished to a high gloss. Woven scatter rugs added touches of color. A brass chandelier with electric candles and milk-glass sconces provided soft lighting. Murals depicting scenes from the Revolutionary War covered two walls.

I signed in at the front desk, where a short young man in a too large jacket ran the credit card I'd used to secure the reservation, handed me the room's key card, and asked if I needed help with my luggage. I declined his offer, explaining that I had only the tote bag I was carrying.

Within ten minutes, I had dropped the tote off in my room on the fifth floor, quickly transferred cash and credit cards from my wallet into a small "ladies-lunch" clutch bag, exchanged my comfortable shoes for designer pumps, and was on my way.

My destination was the Winthrop Plaza, on St. James Avenue. On my walk, I discovered that it was near Boston's elegant Beacon Hill, and to the Freedom Trail, a narrow, red brick path, two horizontal bricks wide, set into the street. I'd heard that the Freedom Trail meanders past fifteen or sixteen historic sites. I would like to have seen them all, but right now, I was on urgent business. I promised myself I'd come back to Boston when there was time to explore this fascinating city.

The Winthrop Plaza is as grand as an embassy. I entered under an emerald green canopy, and found myself in an impressive lobby that looked to be half the size of a football field. Crossing beneath a crystal chandelier big enough to have costarred in *The Phantom of the Opera*, I found the

KISS OF DEATH   119

concierge desk. Behind it stood a patrician with silver hair and military posture, impeccably dressed in a dark suit. If he had auditioned for us, to play an ambassador, I would have hired him instantly. I told him I was meeting someone in the Santa Maria dining room.

He directed me to an elevator at the rear of the lobby. "The Santa Maria Room is on the third floor," he said. "It's the private restaurant for our Colony guests."

"Colony?"

"It's our charming little hotel-within-the-hotel. For guests who desire the intimate feeling of a traditional inn."

I thanked him and headed for a pair of elevators, one of which opened before I could press the Up button.

Getting off on three, I found myself facing a small, jewel box of a reception room, complete with another concierge desk and a few comfortable-looking chairs upholstered in dark green velvet, a shade deeper than the emerald greens below.

A slender man with slick black hair and the straight posture of a guard on duty approached, introduced himself as the Colony's concierge, and inquired, "Ms. Tyler?"

"Yes."

"Ms. Chatsworth telephoned. She asked me to—ah, here she is."

I turned to see a woman in her late forties, more than six feet tall, emerge from the second elevator. In her cream and navy Chanel suit, she looked almost as thin as a biology lab skeleton, and her skin was pale as one percent milk. What kept her from looking deathly ill was the shimmering auburn hair that reached her shoulders in shampoo-commercial waves, and the bright predator's gleam in her brown black eyes.

I introduced myself to Cathy Chatsworth and extended my hand. She either didn't notice, or simply ignored it, and swept through carved wooden doors into the Santa Maria Room. Like a one-woman entourage, I followed in her wake.

The Santa Maria Room was a small restaurant with perhaps a dozen tables, enclosed in dark wood paneling. All but one of the tables were occupied, with couples or foursomes speaking in soft tones.

A fireplace (unlighted on this day in June) rose tall against the outside wall. Soft lighting came from a brass chandelier with glass hurricane shades over electric candles. Paintings on the walls depicted the voyage of the *Pinta*, the *Nina*, and the *Santa Maria*, a theme which was completed by a portrait of Christopher Columbus. I recognized it as the one reproduced in my middle school history books.

The Boston social columnist headed directly for the unoccupied table. In the center of the room, facing the entrance, it was set for four and had a "reserved" sign on it.

"Sit there," she told me, indicating a particular chair. She claimed the one next to it. Immediately, a waiter approached with menus, and asked what we would like to drink.

"An apple martini." Cathy Chatsworth turned to me. "They have an excellent wine list, unless you'd like something more bracing?"

"Just iced tea," I told the waiter. "With extra lemon and extra ice."

The waiter deposited menus, and was about to leave when she waved one thin hand at the fourth place setting. "Take that away. There'll be three."

The waiter did as instructed.

When we were alone, I asked, "Who's joining us?"

"I invited Laura Reynolds—one of our suspects. Her husband, George, was a plaything of dear little Veronica's."

"Did Mrs. Reynolds know about that?"

"Of course. Laura threatened to divorce him. He gave her a diamond necklace and promised to never, ever, *ever* do such a terrible thing again. When she thought he'd groveled enough, and after she'd had the diamonds appraised, she forgave him. They've lived happily for the last several months."

I had come to Boston for Nancy's sake, to try to find out about other people who might have killed Veronica, but now I faced a moral dilemma. Would evoking George Reynolds's infidelity help Nancy, or just damage his repaired marriage?

Cathy Chatsworth must have sensed my concern, because she said, "Oh, don't worry about upsetting poor Laura. We won't even discuss naughty George's past transgressions." Her lips curved into a wide grin that made her look like an evil happy face.

The waiter returned with our drinks. Before I could put Sweet'N Low into my iced tea, she'd downed half of her apple martini.

When she lowered her glass, I asked, "Did you know Veronica Rose very well?"

"As well as you can know a woman who was, essentially, an empty Prada suit. I'd have said an empty hat, but she never wore a hat. Little Veronica could be moderately amusing, and she photographed well. She was always soo nice to me at the big events because she wanted me to write about what she was wearing, and use her picture in my column. To be frank, I didn't like Veronica, but it was quite a spectator sport to watch her go after men. George Reynolds never had a chance. Neither did Ralph Hartley—and Gloria Hartley was supposed to be Veronica's best friend. There you are: more suspects, just as I promised."

The waiter returned, bringing a basket of rolls and a little ceramic tub of butter, and asked if we'd like to order. Without consulting me by even so much as a glance, she said, "We'll wait. Another martini."

Considering how thin my companion was, and her passion for apple martinis, I wasn't sure how long it would be before we would order lunch. I took a pumpernickel roll from the basket and buttered it.

Cathy Chatsworth looked at me biting into the roll with an expression on her face that was somewhere between disdain and disgust. "Bread has killed more people than guns," she announced.

Before I could swallow and reply, she continued telling me her theories about the Veronica Rose murder. "George and Ralph were Veronica's two most recent conquests. Then she suddenly tossed them both on her personal trash heap and flew off to New York to recapture her ex-husband. Either of them could have killed her out of jealousy." She lowered her voice. "I met Arnold Rose. Speaking woman to woman, I didn't get any *sexual* vibes and never could understand what Veronica saw in him. He doesn't come from a distinguished family, and it wasn't money. Arnold's very well-off—I've heard his income's in seven figures—but Veronica's late father was a billionaire, and she inherited everything."

"How did George Reynolds and Ralph Hartley feel about her dropping them?"

"Miserable and desolate!" Cathy Chatsworth flashed a wicked smile. "The dolts didn't know about each other—not until they read some tiny little hints in my columns. After that, right outside the Harvard Club, Ralph and George duked it out."

"Were either of them hurt?"

"Lord, no. They were both too drunk. But it was a delicious blind item for my column the next day. Laura figured it out because George came home with a black eye and a ridiculous tale about running into a door. Honestly, wouldn't you think an investment banker could come up with a better lie than that?"

"Did the other wife—Gloria Hartley—know that her husband was cheating on her?"

She chortled, and said in a childlike, singsong voice, "Not until she received an anonymous note . . ."

Cathy Chatsworth was one of the nastiest people I'd

ever met. If I'd been on any less important mission than clearing Nancy's name I would have left the table. But I stuck it out, pretending not to be revolted by how she played with people's lives. "What did Gloria Hartley do when she found out about her husband cheating?" I asked.

The columnist shrugged. "She had a nervous break-down. In the paper, I referred to her sudden disappearance from the social scene as an 'around the world cruise,' but the truth is she went to a hospital for the rich and upset in Geneva."

"Is she seriously ill?"

"Oh, no, no, no. Not Gloria. After a few weeks she went to France to have her face and most of her visible body parts lifted. Now she's living in Paris, spending Ralph's money on a West Bank artist with a big . . . shall we say *potential*?"

Okay, at least this unpleasant meeting had produced four possible suspects: Laura Reynolds, George Reynolds, Ralph Hartley, and Gloria Hartley. Each of them had been hurt badly by Veronica Rose. Even if Gloria Hartley was in Europe, that didn't necessarily eliminate her. She could have flown to New York and returned to Paris the same day. Or she could have hired a hit man.

My companion suddenly raised a gaunt arm and waved at the entrance to the dining room. A middle-aged woman with a blond pixie cut framing her broad face waved back and came toward us. She had a deep tan, and in a short-sleeved summer dress that revealed muscular arms, she looked healthy and athletic.

As the new arrival reached our table, Cathy raised her voice to a cheerful trill. "Laura, darling, I'm so glad you could meet us. This is my new friend, Morgan Tyler. She's a television writer and producer from New York. Morgan, this is one of my oldest, closest friends, Laura Reynolds."

"Hi," she said. Her smile seemed genuine, but I had to wonder. If Laura Reynolds was really such a close friend to this woman, she might simply be putting up a pleasant front.

Cathy scooted her chair closer to me and patted the cushion of the chair on her other side. "Sit here, Laura." That put the columnist between us, with Laura Reynolds facing the restaurant's entrance. Cathy's voice took on a sympathetic tone as she asked, "How are you, Laura, dear?"

Laura Reynolds seemed a bit startled. "I'm fine, but from that solicitous note in your voice, I must look a wreck." She turned to me. "I played four sets of singles with the pro at the tennis club this morning. Cathy says I should confine myself to doubles now, and I suppose she's right—" she flashed a friendly smile at the columnist— "but I can still run the legs off other women my age. I'm not ready to settle for doubles just yet."

Cathy signaled the waiter, ordered another apple martini and more iced tea for me. Laura Reynolds asked for white wine. Reaching for a menu, she said, "I'm ravenous. I hope they have the cracked crab today."

"We'll order later." Cathy took the menu out of her hands, and shooed the waiter away.

I saw a flash of irritation in Laura Reynolds's eyes, but she politely let Cathy Chatsworth's rudeness pass and turned to me. "Is this your first visit to Boston?"

"Yes, but it won't be my last. It's a beautiful city."

"I wouldn't want to live anywhere else," Laura said. "Where are you staying?

"Adams House."

"That's a lovely place. They have a desk in the lobby that's been authenticated as having been owned by Abigail Adams. It's supposed to be the desk where she wrote her wonderful letters to John. Did you ever read them?"

"Yes, I did. She was an amazing—"

"She's dead," Cathy Chatsworth said, taking a verbal ax to that conversational thread. Toying with her martini, she leaned closer to Laura. "Morgan's up here investigating our Veronica's murder."

I saw Laura Reynolds flinch slightly, but she kept her voice even as she said to me, "How terrible it must be for Veronica's daughter, and for Arnold."

"They're both pretty devastated, as you can imagine."

Beside me, I heard Cathy Chatsworth gasp. Both Laura and I turned to look at the columnist. She was staring at the entrance to the restaurant.

"What is it?" Laura asked.

"I thought . . . No, I *did*! I just saw George go past."

"*My* George?"

"Yes, George Reynolds."

Laura shook her head emphatically. "It couldn't have been. He's in Cambridge today."

Cathy gave her a pitying look. "Oh, you poor dear."

"What are you implying?"

The columnist patted her hand. "I heard a rumor—and *prayed* it wasn't true. I came here today to prove to myself it absolutely wasn't true." She reached into her handbag and removed a room key card. "But I found out that George keeps a suite here at the Colony. Room 317."

"No! Not after . . . he wouldn't dare!"

Cathy moved the key card across the tablecloth until it rested against one of Laura Reynolds's clenched hands. "Room 317."

Laura stared down at the card. Her lower lip trembled, but then the line of her mouth hardened. Slowly, she uncurled her fingers and picked up the card. Without a word she stood up and moved toward the restaurant's entrance and out into the reception area. I glimpsed her turning left.

"Cathy, what are you—"

The columnist shushed me. "I got a tip that George is being naughty again. Laura needed to know." She picked up a menu. "Shall we order now?"

"I've lost my appetite."

As though I hadn't spoken, she said, "I'm going to have the tripe. I hate tripe, but that's how I keep slim—by only ordering something I hate and then not eating it. Occasionally, if I'm feeling playful, and to give the waiter some exercise, I'll send the dish back to the kitchen." She glanced over at me. "You should talk to Ralph Hartley about Veronica. You can find him at his AA meeting. I've heard he goes to the same one every afternoon at four o'clock. In the basement of saint somebody's Episcopal church on the corner of Sutter and Concourse. Find a taxi driver who speaks English. You can't miss the building."

I wondered how Cathy Chatsworth could drink those martinis on an empty stomach and not be drunk. She wasn't even slurring her words.

Suddenly, a woman's shriek split the genteel air of the Santa Maria Room, followed by sustained screaming of a volume that could have reached from the stage to the top balcony at the Metropolitan Opera House.

All conversation stopped. A hush enveloped the room like a shroud.

The *Boston Chronicle*'s gossip queen broke the silence. "It's better to know the truth than to live in blissful ignorance."

Another yell from the hallway—this time it was a male voice, followed by pounding footsteps and the sight of a half-naked man wearing only pants and trying to struggle into a shirt. Just as he raced in front of the restaurant's doorway, a water glass sailed through the air after him. It missed its target and shattered against the door frame as the man sprinted out of sight.

Cathy Chatsworth gave a little wave toward the hallway. "Goodbye, George," she cooed. "Have a nice day."

I gripped my purse and stood up. "That was cruel!"

"It's foolish to waste your sympathy on Laura." She smiled like a thirsty vampire who'd just discovered an unguarded neck. "Why do you think she takes so many tennis lessons? I can assure you it's *not* because that pro is famous for his backhand."

Cold, bony fingers fastened around my left wrist. "Don't forget my consultant's fee." She shoved a card into my hand. "This is my home address. Send it there, not to the paper. And make the check out in the name of Olive Flitt—with a double *t*."

"I'll remember the spelling," I said. "With one *t* you'd be an insecticide."

Chapter 21

AFTER LEAVING THE Winthrop Plaza I started walking to rid my nostrils of the stench of spending time with Cathy Chatsworth–Olive Flitt. It took twenty blocks before I managed it.

I had no intention of invading Ralph Hartley's AA meeting, but I telephoned his office.

"I'm sorry, but Mr. Hartley's out of town," his secretary told me.

I gave her my name, said that I was an old personal friend of "Ralph's," and asked where I could reach him.

"He left for Tokyo last night," she said. "But if you'll leave your number, I'll give it to him when he calls in."

"I would appreciate that," I said. "It's very important that I speak to him." I gave her both my cell phone and my home numbers.

"What can I say this is in reference to?"

"It's personal," I said. "Please tell him it's about a mutual friend of ours."

She agreed to give him the message, but cautioned me that unless he knew what my business was, he might not return the call. "He's a very busy man," she said.

Telling her that I would take my chances, I hung up.

I spotted a convenience store, bought a small bottle of orange juice, and drank it on the street outside. With that shot of temporary sustenance, I had the clerk point me toward a telephone directory where I found the location of the Boston Public Library. A call to their main number let me know that they had newspapers from all over the country on Microtext, and that the room was on the first floor of the library's McKim Building at 700 Boylston Street.

Out on the street, I saw a UPS man delivering packages. I asked him how far it was to 700 Boylston and learned that it was less than half a mile. An easy walk.

The McKim Building's Copley Square facade has magnificent arched windows, and a triple-arched main entrance. Among the inscribed tablets beneath the window arches and the medallions in the spandrels, I recognized the head of Minerva, goddess of wisdom, carved in the central keystone.

Inside, the entrance hall ceiling is vaulted, with domes in the side bays. The turn of the main staircase is guarded by a handsome pair of lions, carved from unpolished marble and crouched on pedestals. I wished I could examine all of the visual wonders of the building, but there wasn't time. Instead, I crossed the white marble floor to the information desk and told the woman there what I wanted.

"Go to the left," she said. "When you pass the pay phones turn right, and you'll see the Microtext Room."

The librarian in charge of the library's vast collection of newspapers on microfilm directed me to a viewer, supplied me with a year's worth of copies of the *Boston Chronicle*, and showed me how to use the machine.

Threading the films into the viewer, I located Cathy Chatsworth's columns. Her reports from the social front alternated between fawning and sarcastic, but I had to admit that the woman could be entertaining. Although what I read left a bad taste in my mouth, I kept at it until my eyes ached.

Returning the rolls of microfilm, I thanked the librarian for her help. Outside in the evening air I had to admit to myself that this library visit had been a wasted effort. Of the people Veronica knew in Boston, the Reynolds and the Hartleys still seemed to be the most likely murder suspects.

Because I felt so grubby after my session with Cathy Chatsworth and after reading nearly one hundred of her gleefully nasty columns, I stopped at the nearest drugstore for a bottle of body wash. As soon as I got up to my room at Adams House, I filled the tub with hot water, stripped, and pinned up my hair. Adding several generous squirts of lilac liquid, I sank to my chin in fragrant foam and tried to scrub away images of the apathetic, overprivileged, ethics-challenged class of people who cheat on their spouses as routinely as they add to their wardrobes.

Judging from what I'd learned today, Cathy Chatsworth and her "dear friends" thought sexual betrayal was some sort of game. To read their quotes in the columns, it seemed they gave more consideration to their designer wardrobes than to those they'd once sworn to cleave only unto. In front of family and friends they'd promised to let no man—or woman—put them asunder, but in Veronica Rose's lofty circle, a lot of "asunder" had been "put." Tonight I knew more about her, and liked her even less.

When the bathwater finally lost its heat, I got out of the tub. Shrugging into the hotel's terry cloth robe hanging on the back of the bathroom door, I took the pins out of my hair and went to the desk next to the king-size bed to see what the room service menu had to offer this hungry traveler.

I was trying to decide between Boston clam chowder or a hamburger, when I heard a knock on the door.

It was a little after eight o'clock, about time for a maid

to turn down the bed. I crossed the room to the door. Automatically cautious, before I touched the knob, I looked through the peephole. It wasn't a maid. What I saw produced a gasp of surprise.

My unexpected visitor knocked again, louder this time. I opened the door.

"Matt!"

He stared at my robe and his jaw tightened. "Are you alone?"

"Of course I am." I stepped aside to let him in and closed the door. "What are you doing in Boston?"

"Apparently, the same thing you are—except *you're* not supposed to be doing it."

"What are you talking about?" I asked.

He wasn't smiling, but for once he didn't look angry. "You're so convinced Nancy couldn't have killed the woman that I dumped all Veronica Rose's phones and found she made close to a dozen late-night calls to Boston. I came up—on my time off—to nose around. Most of the calls were to the home of George and Laura Reynolds. I couldn't find him, but I met his wife. She was upset, but she told me she'd been talking about Veronica Rose earlier. To you. She told me where you were staying."

I could hardly believe what I was hearing. "You're here because you're trying to help Nancy?"

"I'm trying to find the truth," he said.

"Thank you!" Without thinking, I threw my arms around Matt in a hug of gratitude.

It was either the wrong move, or the right one. Before my brain processed what was happening, his arms went around me, his mouth was on mine, and we were kissing. My lips opened, our tongues met, and suddenly all restraint vanished. Matt slipped his hands through the opening of my robe and began to caress my breasts. All I wanted was *more*—more of his mouth, more of his hands. I wanted to feel his skin against mine.

Wriggling out of the robe, I let it fall to the floor. He stripped off his jacket and shirt, and in moments we were naked, kissing . . . On the bed, at the point when I wanted nothing else in life except to feel him inside me, he drew back slightly. "I didn't expect—I don't have anything with me."

"It's all right," I whispered. "I can't get pregnant."

Before he could ask anything else, I lifted my lips to his. He kissed my mouth, my neck, my nipples, until at last . . . Only a few deep thrusts, and then we exploded together in that ecstasy I had no words to describe. We made love again, and this time it lasted much longer.

In that magical afterglow, relaxing in each other's arms, I thought about the fact that I was lying to Matt by misdirection. I'd told him "I can't get pregnant," wanting him to assume I meant I was on birth control. He trusted me, and we made love, but if we were going to have a real relationship—if this was more than just a powerful attraction to each other—then I'd have to tell him that I couldn't have children. He deserved the chance to back away from me . . .

"What are you thinking about?" he asked softly.

"How happy I am." That was true; it just wasn't the whole truth.

"I'm happy, too," he whispered.

Later, we ordered Boston clam chowder from room service. Both ravenous—Matt had skipped dinner, too—we consumed the bowls of thick soup and the crackers, and then the cheese and fruit that came with them. While we were eating, I asked Matt if he'd learned anything from Laura Reynolds that might help Nancy.

"She and her husband are worth taking a look at, but I've got to work that angle on my own time. G. G. will help, but as far as our captain is concerned, we cleared the case when we arrested Nancy."

I said, "I found out about two other possible suspects:

Ralph and Gloria Hartley," and shared what I'd heard about that couple.

Matt nodded thoughtfully, and said he'd see what they could find out, but he cautioned me that he'd have to work outside the department.

Walter and I don't have to worry about a department, I thought, and had one more reason to be grateful that Walter Maysfield was back in my life.

Matt pushed the rolling cart out into the hallway for the waiter to collect, and came back to bed. Wordlessly, we reached for each other again. When we finally fell asleep in each other's arms, we slept for eight hours.

The touch of Matt's fingertips lightly caressing my breast woke me. I opened my eyes and smiled at him. "Good morning . . ."

Showering together, our naked bodies slick with soap, we kissed. What began as a sweet, playful brush of our lips became passionate. We began to make love as the water streamed over us. After months of frustration and self-denial at last we were free to savor each other, and we did . . .

As we were drying ourselves with thick towels, Matt's cell phone rang. He muttered, "Damn it," hurried into the bedroom, and picked up his jacket from where he'd dropped it last night. Finding the phone, he answered, "Phoenix."

Following him into the bedroom, I heard Matt say, "I'm in Boston, Captain," and knew the call was from his boss at the Twentieth Precinct. As he listened, Matt's expression—relaxed and smiling just seconds ago—became sober. "I'll get right back."

Matt disconnected and grabbed his clothes. Dressing at warp speed, he said, "Half an hour ago, one of our young cops was murdered, shot down a block from the precinct house. Everybody's on deck for this one."

"Oh, that's terrible! I'll go back with—"

"Sorry, I can't wait for you to get your things together." He pulled me into his arms for a quick kiss. "See you in the city." Hair still wet and uncombed, jacket in his hand, Matt rushed out the door.

An hour later, after I'd dried my hair, brushed my teeth, dressed, and was ready to check out, I discovered that Matt had stopped long enough to pay the hotel bill.

Outside on the street, waiting for a cab, I thought about him. Leaving, he'd said, "See you in the city." Remembering his words brought back to me a scene I'd written for the show a couple of years ago. Our Sylvia character explained to her unhappy stepdaughter that there were really *two* English languages. "There's the one we use every day, and then there's *man-speak*." Sylvia comforted the tearful girl by saying that, in man-speak, " 'I'll call you tomorrow' can mean he'll call you in two or three days, or even in a week. Men are wonderful, sweetheart, but they don't figure time the same way we do."

Every woman I knew told me she related to that scene. We'd received more positive mail about it than for any other bit—until my "pool scene" a few months ago. In that scene, still being discussed in the *Love* chat rooms, the character Jillian, naked, pulls Gareth into her swimming pool where they make passionate love.

I couldn't help wondering what Matt's "see you in the city" was going to mean . . .

Chapter 22

AS SOON AS the Jet Blue Airbus landed in New York, I turned my cell phone on and called Walter. I told him I was on my way back to the Dakota.

"Did you get some useful information in Boston?"

"We have four new suspects to check out."

I heard Walter's deep chuckle. "That was a good trip."

The trip was even better than he knew. I smiled, remembering how wonderful it felt to be in Matt's arms.

Walter met me at the door with Magic riding on his shoulder. "Come into the kitchen. I made us sandwiches for lunch."

While Magic munched on his Natural Balance dry food, Walter set out thick turkey sandwiches and a plate of sliced fruit.

"A very nice woman named Penny called about an hour ago. She's having a little shindig for your friend Nancy tomorrow night." He scrunched his face, summoning Penny's exact words. "She said it's a getting-out-on-bail party." He grinned. "She invited me, too. That okay?"

"Of course it is! I want you to meet Penny. Matt's partner, G. G. Flynn and G. G.'s wife, Brandi, will probably be there, too. The Flynns are my favorite couple."

"I'd like to meet your friends," he said.

Meaning Matt, I asked, "Did anyone else call this morning?"

"Nope."

That was a pretty dumb question. Matt was on a case, trying to find out who murdered one of their police officers. I couldn't expect to hear from him so soon.

I handed Walter the list I'd made on the plane: Laura and George Reynolds, and Ralph and Gloria Hartley. With Boston addresses and phone numbers. "The two men had affairs with Veronica Rose in the last year or so. Both the wives found out. To say the least, they didn't take the news well."

"That's about as sure a thing as skunks showing up in the spring."

I filled Walter in on my nonlunch with Cathy Chatsworth, recounting the scene in the Santa Maria Room.

Walter shook his head. "Anybody who thinks that Chatsworth woman is their friend is a fool."

"Gloria Hartley had a nervous breakdown over her husband's affair, and is now supposedly in Paris, getting even, but I don't know if any of that is true. Yesterday, I saw for myself that Laura Reynolds has a very bad temper. George and Laura Reynolds are in Boston. Ralph Hartley's secretary *said* he went to Tokyo, but I don't know if that's true. According to Cathy Chatsworth, he goes to AA meetings in Boston every day."

As an afterthought, I took back the list and added two more names: Cathy Chatsworth, a.k.a. Olive Flitt. "This woman is vicious. I don't know what she'd be capable of if she thought she was in danger of losing something she wanted. Suppose Veronica stole a man from her—or maybe Veronica was in a position to threaten her job at the *Chronicle*. I don't think we should overlook her. Maybe that's why she tossed us the other suspects."

"All six of these folks—we gotta count Chatsworth with her two names as two people—will have to be checked out: police records, court records, financial records, where they go, who they know, what their bad habits are, what they're hiding—all kinds of stuff. Deep-sea fishing, so to speak. It'll take a while."

Trying to sound casual, I said, "I heard from Matt. He's going to try to help us, unofficially. I'm going to tell Kent Wayne about our list. Nancy needs all the resources we can gather."

"Don't tell the lawyer 'bout Detective Phoenix being on our side," Walter said. "The NYPD isn't going to take kindly to one of their own working to free somebody they already arrested. Professionally, he's on dangerous ground."

I realized Walter was right. "Any help Matt gives us will be our secret," I said.

MY CELL PHONE rang just before midnight. It was Matt.

"Hi, honey. Did I wake you?"

"Yes, but I don't mind." Remembering our delicious night together, a happy little shiver went through me. "What's happening with your case?"

"We caught the guy who shot Officer Drew. A miserable crack addict, so out of his head he said he didn't know Drew was a cop—he thought the uniform meant Drew was in the Navy!" He took a deep breath and let it out. That seemed to relax him a little. "Killing a cop is murder one. New York hasn't put anybody to death since the nineteen sixties. He'll die of old age in prison." Matt's voice took on an edge. "Unless he gets a lawyer like Kent Wayne. Then he'll probably get off with a fifty-dollar fine."

"That isn't very likely." Quickly changing the subject, I said, "Penny's having a little party for Nancy tomorrow night."

"Yeah. Because we arrested her, I wasn't sure G. G. and I should be at her getting-out-on-bail party, but we talked it over and decided that since technically the case is closed, it's okay. We just won't advertise it."

"Thank you for keeping an open mind about Nancy."

"I'm glad I did." I heard a teasing smile in his voice. "Are you bringing a date tomorrow night?"

"Walter Maysfield. Did you tell Penny about him?"

"What little I know, which isn't much."

That was another subject I was eager to avoid. "I'm looking forward to the party." *To seeing you,* is what I meant.

"Me, too," he said. "Go back to sleep."

WEDNESDAY EVENING, WALTER and I met Nancy at her building, the Bradbury on West Eighty-first Street. I'd called her just as we were leaving the Dakota, so she was downstairs, waiting for us.

Walter and I climbed out of the back of the cab, but left the door open. I introduced Nancy to Walter.

Walter acknowledged her with a "Pleased to meet you," and a gallant little incline of his head, but Nancy reached out and drew him into a hug.

"You're Morgan's friend, so you're part of our little family," she said warmly.

We reached Matt's red brick townhouse on East Sixty-eighth Street a few minutes past seven. The big terra cotta pots on either side of the black lacquer front door were full of gloriously blooming scarlet geraniums. And, at the beginning of summer, Penny had edged the house with an eighteen-inch-wide bed of pink and red begonias.

Matt greeted us at the door, smiled at me, and said to Nancy, "No hard feelings, I hope."

"I was in the wrong place at the wrong time. You were just doing your job," she said graciously.

Matt shook hands with Walter. "Nice to see you again, Mr. Maysfield."

"You, too, but call me Walter."

"Brandi and G. G. are here already," Matt said, leading us into the living room.

G. G. was sunk into the soft cushions on one of the two sofas that flanked the fireplace, and Brandi came from the wet bar against the wall, bringing him a drink.

"Hi, there," Brandi said with a cheerful little wave. She handed G. G. his Scotch over ice, then gave Nancy a hug. "I'm so glad you're here with us!"

G. G. heaved himself up from the downy depths of the sofa's cushions. He greeted me with the gruff warmth I'd become used to, and offered a big, rough hand to Nancy. "No hard feelings."

"None at all," Nancy said.

G. G. Flynn was two inches shorter, ten years older, about twenty pounds heavier, and had only a fraction of Matt's hair. He looked like a TV stereotype of the overweight cop a few years short of retirement, but Matt had said G. G. was one of the sharpest investigators he'd ever known, and there was no one with whom he'd rather risk his life on the job.

After Matt introduced Walter to the Flynns, Brandi and I went into the kitchen to see if we could help.

"Out, both of you," Penny said, shooing us back in the direction of the living room. "Everything is under control. I'll be with you all in a minute."

When Brandi and I rejoined the others in the living room, we found Walter and G. G. chatting like old friends.

"You have more murders in New York—you got a lot more people—but we got the corner on weirdness," Walter said. "Did you ever find a body that'd been hit on the back of the head with an ax handle, then drowned in a tub of moonshine?"

G. G. snorted. "Kid stuff. Did you ever find one vic in two separate parts of a building?"

Yuck, I thought.

Brandi shuddered with revulsion. "Oh, Georgie, stop that. Can't you two boys talk about something besides dead people?"

Walter was immediately contrite. He stood up from the club chair next to G. G.'s end of the couch. "My apologies, ma'am."

Brandi beamed a delighted smile at him. "How nice." She maneuvered around the other end of the couch to sit next to her husband.

Nancy said, "I'm going into the kitchen to say hi to Penny."

"She'll throw you out," Brandi warned.

G. G.'s mouth curved into what I called his "Brandi smile," that loving expression his big face took on whenever he looked at his wife. She settled onto the couch and he squeezed her hand. "I'll be good," he said.

Conversation turned to sports, with Walter and G. G. arguing the relative merits of the Miami Dolphins versus the New York Jets.

Returning from the kitchen, Nancy took the club chair opposite Walter, and charmed the men with her knowledge of both teams, and of her personal favorite, the Pittsburgh Steelers. She'd been a football enthusiast going back to our college days, but I'd never learned to tell a scrimmage from a down. I'm a baseball fan.

Behind the bar, Matt was pouring glasses of wine, and watching me. Being in the same room with him after our night together was a little awkward. I was as nervous as a teenager, but it was a good kind of nervousness, ripe with anticipation. Matt brought me a glass of red wine, we exchanged smiles, and I began to relax.

Penny came out of the kitchen, carrying a tray of

deviled eggs, baked mushrooms, and eggplant caponata with tiny little triangles of Italian bread for dipping.

"Something for everybody," she said.

Matt took the tray from her and set it in the middle of the coffee table between the sofas, within easy reaching distance of all of us, while Penny passed out cocktail napkins and little hors d'oeuvre plates.

G. G. surveyed the tray. "Before I decide on this stuff, what's for dinner? I gotta pace myself."

"Chicken Parmesan, roasted red and yellow peppers, and steamed green beans. For dessert we're having pineapple sherbet and miniature brownies."

"Penny's using us to test out things she's going to make on her TV show," Matt joked.

"Ma'am, I'll be your guinea pig anytime," Walter said.

Without my asking, Matt put two deviled eggs and a scoop of the eggplant mix on a plate and handed it to me. Nancy saw that gesture of intimacy—his knowing what I liked without asking—raised her eyebrows, and flashed me a smile of approval.

Matt picked up another plate and asked, "What can I give you, Nancy?"

Echoing the famous punch line from *When Harry Met Sally*, she said teasingly, "I'll have what *she's* having."

Brandi got the joke and giggled, causing Penny to look up in curiosity.

"What's funny?" G. G. asked.

Brandi nudged him and said, "Tell you later, sweetie."

Before I could steer the conversation onto less embarrassing ground, the doorbell rang. Penny went to answer it.

Matt told a story about his first week out of the police academy. "I got a tip from a numbers runner on my beat that there was a big-time drug trafficker in the Wildwood projects—he gave me the apartment number. Imagining winning citations and a gold shield, I went to the captain.

Based on my information he got a warrant and arranged a full-on raid with the drug guys. I got to come along, but I had to stay in the back. I was still trying to Velcro my vest when they broke down the door and found a little old lady rolling joints for her husband who was going through chemo."

"Oh, how embarrassing," Brandi said. She was sympathetic, but G. G. and Matt were laughing.

Penny returned to the living room. "Now we're all here," she said.

Matt's and G. G.'s laughter died when they looked up to see the man standing beside Penny.

Jaunty in a navy cashmere blazer and gray slacks, and carrying a gorgeous bouquet of tulips, daffodils, and tea roses, was B. Kent Wayne.

Chapter 23

PENNY WAS SMILING. "Matt and G. G., this is Kent Wayne, the defense attorney who got Nancy out on bail."

Wayne nodded at Nancy, Brandi, and me, said, "Hello, again," and handed Penny the flowers. "Thank you for inviting me to dinner."

G. G., red faced and nearly apoplectic, exploded. "You son of a bitch!"

Shocked, Brandi squealed, "Georgie!" and grabbed his balled-up fist.

Wayne retained his cheerful demeanor as he asked G. G., "Have we met, sir?"

"Don't you 'sir' me, you barnacle on a butt."

"That's colorful," Kent Wayne said amiably.

Nancy was aghast. "G. G., what's the matter?"

G. G. pulled out of Brandi's grip and was struggling to his feet from the depth of the soft sofa cushions. Matt stepped over behind him. Placing both hands on his partner's shoulders, he gently kept the older man seated.

Astonished, Penny looked back and forth between G. G. and Wayne. "What is going on?"

"We've met Mr. Wayne," Matt said, his tone cold. "Professionally."

Penny got it. "Oh, Matt, if he defended someone you arrested, you can't hold that against him. That's his business. Kent is our guest."

"You call him Kent?" Matt's teeth were clenched so hard I was amazed that he could speak clearly.

Wayne touched Penny lightly on the arm. "Perhaps I should leave."

"Absolutely not!" she said. "We're having dinner to celebrate Nancy's release, and you belong here with us."

I stood up and faced Matt. "This is my fault. When I persuaded Nancy to hire Kent Wayne, I didn't know you and G. G. had a history—"

G. G. turned his burning gaze toward me. "He was *your* idea? Was that why you called me?"

"You called G. G.?" Matt asked.

Walter stood up, made the classic T sign with his hands, and said, "Why don't we all jus' take a time-out?"

Matt ignored him and kept his focus on me. "Why did you call G. G.?"

"I tricked him into telling me what criminal lawyer you two disliked the most because I wanted Nancy to have the strongest person to fight for her."

Nancy was on her feet, moving to my defense. "Whatever Morgan did, she would have done the same for you, Matt, or Penny, or anyone who needed help. You know that."

"It's all right, Nancy," I said. "Matt has every right to be angry with me." I turned to G. G. "I'm sorry I lied to you—saying I wanted you to settle a bet about defense attorneys when I was really looking for the name of a legal top gun. I should have been honest with you."

G. G. grunted and finally settled back against the sofa

cushions, close to Brandi. "Forget it," he said. "When a friend's in trouble, we do what we have to do."

"I won't lie to you again, G. G.," I said.

"So," Penny said brightly to Kent Wayne, "now that everything's all right—what can I get you to drink?"

If Penny thought that the evening's rough spot had been smoothed over, she was wrong. From the stiffness of Matt's shoulders, and the fact that he was not looking at me, I knew that everything was far from all right between the two of us.

IF ONE DEFINES "a pleasant evening" as being one during which blood is not spilled, then Penny's celebration dinner party was a success. The food was certainly a hit. Matt didn't eat much, but G. G. had his usual three helpings. Kent Wayne said he'd never had a better meal, and sounded as though he meant it. Several times I caught Wayne watching Penny with more than casual interest. She was particularly attractive tonight, with her gleaming brown hair falling loose around her heart-shaped face. Again, I thought that her warm smile and her easy laugh made her look like an earthy Madonna. What surprised me was when I realized how often that smile of Penny's was aimed at Kent Wayne.

The small-town sheriff and the big-city lawyer turned out to be an entertaining team of storytellers. They kept most of us at the table laughing as they related some of their stranger experiences on opposite sides of the crime-and-punishment equation.

When the last drop of pineapple sherbet and bite of miniature brownie had been consumed, we all got up to help Penny clear the table.

"I don't need help, really," she said. "Besides, there's only room for one other person in the kitchen."

"Then I'll help," Kent Wayne announced. "Please let

me—it's a way to say thank you for including me this evening."

Penny started to protest, but Wayne took a stack of plates out of my hands and maneuvered himself around behind her. "Lead the way."

Penny said, "Well, if you insist . . ."

Matt glowered at Wayne's back, but he followed Walter and G. G. back into the living room.

Nancy, Brandi, and I watched Wayne and Penny disappear into the kitchen.

"Wow," Brandi said. "That guy's some operator."

"He won't get anywhere with Penny," Nancy said. "She's still convinced her dead husband is alive."

The skeptical expression on Brandi's face made it clear that she wasn't so sure this was true. "In my opinion, if Patrick Cavanaugh wasn't dead he'd have come back to Penny by now. She's been alone for seven years—that's a long time without somebody to snuggle with."

From Matt's coldness toward me after he found out that I'd tricked G. G. into telling me about Kent Wayne, it didn't look as though I was going to be snuggling with him again anytime soon.

IT WAS NEARLY eleven when Walter and I took Nancy back to her building at Eighty-first Street and Central Park West. On the sidewalk, we said good night, and promised to call each other tomorrow.

"I enjoyed your stories," Nancy told Walter. She kissed him on the cheek and hurried toward the entrance. We watched through the glass doors until she was safely inside and at the elevator.

"Do you mind if we walk home?" I asked Walter. "It's only nine blocks."

"Fine idea. I'd like to stretch my legs." Walter paid the

cab driver, and we started walking down Central Park West.

Even though it was June it wasn't hot yet. Vehicle traffic was light at this hour. We saw a young couple holding hands as they waited for a bus, but the only other pedestrians were on the other side of the street, strolling along the stone wall that bordered Central Park.

After a couple of blocks of companionable silence, Walter said, "I like that G. G. You know where you stand with him. No big-city bull hockey pucks."

"I shouldn't have tricked him."

"You'll prob'ly do worse in your life. Most people do. We ain't perfect creatures."

We were nearly home when Walter said, "You got nice friends. I even like the lawyer."

"Matt doesn't. He told me Kent Wayne gave G. G. a terrible time on the witness stand a couple of years ago. That's why he's so angry with me. G. G.'s like a father to Matt."

"Your young fella has a stiff neck that goes all the way down to the soles of his feet. If he doesn't loosen up some, he's gonna lose the best thing that could ever happen to him."

"What's that?"

"You," Walter said.

"Matt and I have other problems," I said, remembering that a few months ago he'd said we couldn't see each other because I had more money than he had. Maybe he forgot about that in Boston, but maybe it was still a barrier between us, and he was using what I did with G. G. to keep us apart. "I don't have time to figure Matt out. We've got to help Nancy beat a murder charge."

"Best way to do that is to find out who killed the woman. Then maybe everybody kin relax a little, have some fun."

I replied with a quote: " 'Tis a consummation devoutly to be wished.' "

"Shakespeare?"

"Yes."

"Thought so," Walter said. "Junie an' I used to watch *Jeopardy* every night."

Chapter 24

IT WAS THE morning after Penny's awkward dinner party, and Matt hadn't phoned. I wondered if I was living under some kind of a curse. Romantically speaking, I'd been alone for five years after the death of my husband, Ian. Six months ago I'd finally worked up the courage to start living like a grown-up woman again, and what happened? Twice in those six months I'd made love with a man—and both of them promptly vanished from my life, either literally, like mysterious Nico Andreades, or figuratively, like Matt.

Magic was still curled where he'd slept on the pillow next to mine. I reached down to give him a few loving strokes. "I guess it's still just you and me, fella."

Magic's response was a wide, pink yawn.

A few minutes later, as I was about to leave the apartment to meet Link for our Thursday morning breakfast, the phone rang. My pulse quickened with anticipation. I snatched up the receiver—but it wasn't Matt on the other end of the line.

"Morgan, it's Arnold."

That was a surprise. "Hello. How are you, and how is Didi?"

"Didi is still in great distress, as you can imagine. I'm calling because I understand you went to Boston."

"Who told you?"

"Cathy Chatsworth." I heard the distaste in his voice as he pronounced the name of the Boston gossip columnist. "Vile woman."

"I'm not too fond of her myself."

"She said you were investigating Veronica. I wish you hadn't done that."

"Nancy's been accused of murder," I said sharply. "I thought if I knew something about Veronica I might be able to develop a theory as to who really killed her."

"And did you?"

"I learned about some people who didn't like Veronica. One of them might have killed her. If Nancy's actually put on trial, other possible names will at least let her lawyer plant reasonable doubt in the minds of the jury. I'm sorry if you're upset, Arnold."

On Arnold's end of the line, I heard a heavy sigh. "All Cathy Chatsworth knows are a few . . . about certain activities Veronica wasn't proud of. She never knew who my wife really was. I did."

"Then tell me about her, please. I would have gone to you in the first place, but I know how hard this must be for you, and Didi."

"It's terrible," he said softly, "but I'd like to talk about Veronica. After spending time with that bitch in Boston, your opinion of Ronnie is probably negative. I want you to know about the woman I fell in love with, who gave me Didi."

I looked at my watch and decided that I had to see Arnold while he was willing to talk. Later, he might change his mind. "What are you doing right now? I could come over to your place—"

"No! Didi's resting. I have an appointment on the West Side this morning. I could come to your apartment first. Say, in twenty minutes?"

"Perfect."

As soon as we said goodbye, I dialed Link's number. He picked up on the second ring. "Hi, it's Morgan. Something's come up. I'm sorry, but I can't meet you for breakfast. How about an early lunch in my office? Tommy will be away at an Affiliates meeting."

"Yeah, okay," he said. "What I want to talk about can wait a few hours. If I can't see you this morning, I'll go to the gym."

"Thanks, Link. I'll tell Betty not to interrupt us."

"Oh, I like the sound of that," he joked, adopting an exaggerated version of the tone he uses when his character is about to make love to a woman in our story.

With affection, I said, "You're a nut," and hung up.

Walter was in the kitchen, getting ready to make scrambled eggs. Magic sat on the stool next to the counter, watching him intently.

"Use a bigger bowl," I said. "I'm staying for breakfast, and we're going to have company."

WALTER SET OUT a great spread: eggs, toast, muffins, fresh orange juice, and a Variety Pack of dry cereals, but all Arnold wanted was juice and coffee. The three of us sat at the kitchen table; Walter and I ate quietly while Arnold talked.

"When I met Ronnie I was in my senior year at Harvard Law. On scholarship. She'd just made her debut." He glanced at Walter. "That means she was presented to society at a grand ball."

"I know," Walter said. "I'm from West Virginia, not Borneo."

Arnold had the grace to look embarrassed. "Sorry. I'm used to explaining things to juries."

"No offense taken," Walter said.

I refilled Arnold's coffee mug. "Go on."

"I saw her picture in the paper, and must have said something about how beautiful she was. One of my classmates knew her, and introduced us. Much to my amazement, she agreed to go out with me. She didn't care that I had very little money. She was happy eating pizza and renting videos. We fell in love . . ."

Arnold paused for a moment, as though trying to keep his emotions in check. I sat still and silent, letting him take the time he needed. When he continued, his voice was stronger. "I made top grades, Law Review, all that, so after graduation, I had my choice of several major firms. I wanted to do criminal defense, and the best offer for that was in New York. Ronnie urged me to take the opportunity. We got married and she moved here, leaving all her friends and everything familiar and comfortable. She was fascinated by my work—wanted to know everything about the cases I took . . ."

There was a dreamy expression on Arnold's face—a look I would never have associated with that lion of the courtroom. It was as though he was reliving the past in his mind. I saw that he really had loved her. Perhaps, as Nancy feared, he had fallen in love with her again.

To keep him talking, I said, "I'm not surprised she was interested. Criminal law is an enthralling profession."

Arnold snapped back into the present. "It was more than just interested. We'd been married for a year when she confided to me that she had always wanted to become a lawyer. Her father told her that she'd been brainwashed by television shows, and that law wasn't at all the right career for her."

"What did he want her to do?"

"Nothing." Arnold's mouth hardened and his tone turned bitter. "Her father was a king of the leveraged buyout, and did a lot of lavish entertaining while making big deals.

He told Ronnie that she'd just waste time in college, because she'd only get married one day and have a husband
to take care of. In the meantime, because her mother was
dead, he insisted it was Ronnie's duty to be his hostess."

"That's pretty medieval," I said.

"She wasn't strong enough to go against his wishes—at
least not until she married me." Arnold laughed, but it was
a sound without a trace of mirth. "That was her first rebel-
lion. The old man didn't approve of me—I was poor then,
I wasn't well connected, 'not of their social set.' He
wouldn't come to our wedding, and he didn't come to the
hospital when Didi was born. I think marrying me was
Ronnie's revenge on her father for not letting her have the
life she wanted. In a way, she tried to have a law career
through me, by helping me. She was a wonderful hostess—
charmed the partners in the firm where I worked. As I got
more important cases, my income grew, and finally I could
give her all the material things that she'd turned her back
on. I insisted we have live-in help, and that she hire cater-
ers when we gave parties. When I took a high-profile criminal case out of state, I'd have to be gone weeks at a time,
and I couldn't fill her in on the day-to-day business of
preparation and trial. Worst of all—and I'll never forgive
myself for this—when Didi started kindergarten, Ronnie
told me she wanted to go to law school. I thought she was
joking, and treated it that way. I didn't know how badly I'd
hurt her until she got her revenge on me by having an affair. I wouldn't have known about it, but she told me. I was
furious, of course. Told her she broke my heart, that I'd
never be able to forgive her. She left me; took Didi and
moved back to Boston. At the time, I didn't put her affair
together with her frustrated ambition."

"When you divorced, did she try to go to law school?"

Arnold shook his head. "I'd made her feel ridiculous for
wanting to. She plunged back into the social whirl, entertaining again for her father. Joined the charity committees

he asked her to. When the old man died, she inherited a fortune."

Before I could frame a tactful version of the question, Walter asked boldly, "Who inherits her money?"

"Didi. Everything is in an unbreakable trust, to be administered by Ronnie's personal attorney, in Boston." Arnold stiffened and glared at Walter. "I'm a wealthy man. Are you implying that I might have killed my wife for her *money*?"

"Just asking," Walter said calmly. "The police think they got the killer, but the question about you is prob'ly gonna occur to Miss Cummings's lawyer."

Arnold's voice was close to a snarl. "I'll be happy to show him my bank statements." He tamped his anger down and added, "When Ronnie and I divorced, she took nothing from me, and I took nothing from her. However, I insisted it be put in writing that I was to pay all of Didi's expenses— personal and educational—through graduate school, if she wants to go. In a week or so, Ronnie's will is going to be a matter of public record. You can read it for yourself. And I'll make our divorce papers available to anyone. I will gain nothing from Ronnie's death, nor from Didi's trust."

To get things back on a cordial footing, I said, "From what I've seen, you're a wonderful father."

That seemed to mollify Arnold. "I love my daughter more than anything in the world," he said. "Naturally, I was very happy when she and her mother moved back to New York. Ronnie and I had long ago gotten over our hard feelings and become friends again. I bought an apartment for them in my building." Arnold's face flushed with embarrassment. "Morgan, I'm ashamed to say this, but with Didi and Ronnie back in my life, I was unkind to Nancy. I loved Nancy . . ."

I caught the past tense. "*Loved?* You don't love Nancy anymore?"

"It's complicated." He shifted in his seat and looked

uncomfortable. "I didn't stop loving Nancy, but—I'm not proud of this—I found myself falling in love with Ronnie again, too."

"That's crap!" Walter said. To me, he added, "Excuse my language."

Arnold stood up. "I behaved atrociously to Nancy before . . . before Ronnie was killed. But please believe that I never meant to hurt her. Right now, I have to focus on getting Didi through this, but if there's anything that I can do for Nancy, all you have to do is let me know."

"I will," I said.

Politely, Walter stood up. Arnold gave him a curt good-bye nod, and squeezed my hand lightly.

When I returned from showing Arnold to the front door, Walter was clearing the kitchen table. "What do you think?" I asked.

"After the personal things he told us about her, Veronica Rose isn't just a victim anymore. I feel kinda sorry for her."

"Me, too. Maybe she behaved the way she did because she never got to live her own life."

"Or she wasn't strong enough to tell her father and husband to go to hell," Walter said. "You know Arnold Rose. Did you believe that—how he felt about his wife?"

"I'm furious at him for hurting Nancy, but I think he's sincere about his feelings."

"Yeah, I believed him, too. But just for the record, I don't buy it that a man can be in love with two women at the same time. Your friend Nancy's well rid of that guy."

Chapter 25

I STILL HADN'T heard from Matt when Link Ramsey arrived in my office. As always, his unruly nut brown hair looked as though it would need a trim in another day. That was the impression it always gave; I wondered how he managed to keep it in precisely that state.

There was a devilish gleam in Link's dark chocolate eyes. "I told Betty if she gave us a half hour of privacy, I'd let her tie me up and discipline me."

I laughed at that ridiculous image. "You're safe with Betty, but be careful. One day somebody might take you up on one of your crazy proposals."

"I like living on the edge." Link held up the takeout bag he was carrying. "Betty told me about your favorite deli. She said you like egg salad on whole wheat with mustard, mayo, and lettuce. Hold the pickles and chips. I brought cole slaw and potato salad."

As Link unpacked our picnic lunch, I cleared space on the desk. "I got us a couple of cold sodas from the machine."

"This is great," I said, dividing the paper napkins and plastic forks.

Link pulled one of the visitor's chairs up to the edge of the desk, opened our sodas, and unwrapped the corned beef on rye he'd brought for himself.

After we'd each taken a bite of our sandwiches, I asked, "What did you want to talk to me about? Betty said it was personal."

He took a swallow of soda and set the can down on the napkin I'd folded to use as a coaster. "Nancy Cummings. How's it going with her?"

"She's still the number one suspect, but some other people are being looked at."

Link grinned at me. "Looked at by *you*, I bet." He took another swallow of soda. "I like Nance," he said, "but even if I didn't, I'd care about this mess because she's your best friend. According to the papers, the cops think Nancy killed Veronica Rose out of jealousy. Maybe they got the theory right, but the killer wrong."

My pulse rate jumped. I put down my sandwich and looked at Link with hope. "What do you know?"

"When Veronica Rose came up to the studio that day, I pegged her right away as a scalp collector—the kind of dame who wants men to fall for her just to feed her ego."

"Betty got that impression, too."

"I wouldn't tell you what I'm about to if the woman hadn't been killed, but in the couple of weeks before she died, I saw her with somebody who wasn't Arnold Rose. They were way out of her high-rent neighborhood, and she and the guy had that 'we just had sex' look."

I was getting excited at the prospect of having another suspect. "Describe him."

Link shook his head. "No need. We know him. It was your resurrected actor, Jay Garwood."

"Jay! I remember Betty telling me that when Veronica was up here, turning on the charm, he'd reacted to her—how did Betty put it?—like a hungry dog looking at a steak, I think she said."

"Yeah, I was there. That's a pretty good description. I didn't think anything about it, until I saw the two of them together, and I still wouldn't have given it a thought except that she was killed." Link added, "Not that just seeing them together proves anything."

"No, but this is information I didn't have before. Jay didn't say anything about their having become friends. Or whatever they were. Just between us, what do you think of him?"

"He's okay—knows his lines, and doesn't get in my key light." Link flashed his alpha-male grin. "At least, he didn't do it more than once."

"Have you spent any time with him out of the studio?"

"No. He didn't socialize with the cast, and I realized why when I saw him out with Veronica Rose. They were sucking face as if they thought they'd be dead the next day. A week later, he shows up for blocking wearing a gold Rolex watch. He sure didn't buy it with his tax refund."

"You think Veronica gave it to him?"

"I'm as sure as I am about the sun rising in the east."

After lunch, Link went back to his dressing room.

"Where can I find Jay Garwood?" I asked Betty.

She consulted her Master List, which tracked each of the actors during any days they were at the studio. It made it possible to know where everyone was at all times.

"He's in Makeup," Betty said, "getting covered in fake blood for that new flashback scene—the one where he's in the guerrilla prison camp. They're taping the scene at two."

It was 1:15; allowing time for him to go through the final blocking before tape rolled, I'd have about twenty minutes alone with him.

Makeup was located next to Costume, on the far side of the twenty-sixth floor from my office. I made my way past our two stages, 35 and 37, and saw set people putting the finishing touches on the jungle prison on Stage 35. Stage 37, dressed as Sylvia's design showroom, was being lighted. Link and Eva, who played Sylvia, were running lines for the comedy scene we'd tape after the jungle flashback.

I hadn't written the scene in which Link goes to Sylvia's dress salon to buy a formal gown for the new woman in his character's life—a new associate writer had—but it was one of my favorite scenes this week. All I'd had to do with this script was revise a few of Link's lines to make them more specific to his quirky character.

Jay Garwood was alone in the Makeup room, standing up in front of the long, brightly lighted mirror, looking into it and mouthing his lines.

If I hadn't known he'd been made up to look like the only survivor of a plane crash, on seeing him I'd have immediately called for an ambulance.

"You look appropriately awful," I said with a smile.

"Thanks. You want me?"

"Where are the makeup twins?" I asked, referring to the identical sisters in their fifties, former models, who were in charge of makeup for the show.

"When they finished with me, they went to lunch," he said.

It seemed odd that he hadn't turned around to face me since I'd come into the room. I was having my conversation with his reflection.

"I wanted to talk to you, Jay."

"Yeah?" I heard a note of strain in his voice and saw him transfer his script to his left hand while he wiped his right hand down the side of his slacks. It was a nervous gesture, denoting sweaty palms. He'd turned slightly away from me, but I could observe what he was doing in the mirror.

I perched on the chair next to where he was standing. "Sit down a minute, okay?"

With all the enthusiasm of a teenage boy called into the principal's office, Jay Garwood turned away from the mirror and sat down in the canvas-back chair, where he started to fidget.

"So, what can I do for you?" He'd made his tone casual, but I saw the look of worry in his eyes.

"It's what I want to do for *you*, Jay," I said.

He brightened. "I'm getting the Armani suits?"

"No—at least, not immediately. I'll have to see what I can do about the costume budget. No, I came to offer you my sympathy. This must be a painful time for you."

In his chair, Jay Garwood suddenly became very still. "Sympathy?"

"About the death of Veronica Rose. This must be a difficult time—because I heard you two had been seeing each other."

"That's not true—where'd you hear that?" he demanded.

"Just around . . . I mean, I thought someone said you two were dating—"

"No! I didn't know her. The only time I was ever with her was that day she came up to the studio with her kid."

"Oh, then whoever thought they saw you together must have been mistaken. I guess I was worried about you for nothing."

"That's okay. Are we still having lunch tomorrow, to discuss my wardrobe?"

I got up. "It turns out that I won't have time tomorrow, Jay. We'll discuss this next week." *But we'll talk about more than your suits.*

I said good-bye, wished him luck with the scene he was about to tape, and left the Makeup room.

Outside in the corridor I reviewed what had just happened. I believed Link, which meant that Jay Garwood had just looked straight into my eyes and lied.

Back in my office, I was about to dial Walter to tell him

to put Jay Garwood at the top of our list of suspects when Betty buzzed me.

"Your private detective friend is on line one," she said.

I picked up the receiver to hear Bobby Novello say, "I just found the man in the van."

Chapter 26

HEARING BOBBY SAY that he'd found the monster from my childhood made my insides lurch in shock.

"Can you talk?" he asked.

Two more lights on my phone console flashed. Outside at her desk, Betty was being kept busy. "Yes," I said. Short of a catastrophe, Betty never interrupted me when I was on a personal call. "Tell me."

"I'll give you the detailed report in writing, but the shorthand version is that I tracked him halfway around the world. After Sheriff Maysfield got you away from Ray Wilson, the creep disappeared completely for two years."

Like a snake vanishes down its hole.

"There wasn't any trace of him until he surfaced in San Pedro, California, at the Port of Los Angeles," Bobby said. "He was calling himself Raymond Woods then, and worked on cargo ships sailing the Far East routes. Did that for thirteen years, and most of the time he was out of the country. Back in San Pedro, he suddenly disappeared, and surfaced a year later, in Oklahoma, using the name Ray Wyatt. Tended bar for a while—that's when his finger-prints entered the system again. Three weeks after he started, he was fired for drinking on the job and left Oklahoma. He probably wandered around the country, doing odd jobs in the underground economy, never lighting in one place long enough to show up on the official radar. Finally, a little more than a year ago, he stopped moving around. That's when his Social Security number popped up."

I had the sensation that my stomach was filled with ice water. Cold perspiration dampened my hairline; I felt it beading on the top of my skull. My hands—one holding the receiver and one on my desk—were clenched so hard the knuckles were white. I forced my voice to sound calm as I asked the most important question in this conversation: "Where is he now?"

"That's the crazy thing," Bobby said. "Maybe this guy is nuts, or he just thinks that after all these years he's safe, but he's living in a town called Belle Valley, Ohio. It's only two hundred miles from Downsville, West Virginia—where he's still on the wanted list—and he's calling him-self Ray Wilson again."

"Does he . . . does he have a child with him?"

"I was afraid of that, too. No. He lives alone. I found him because he's collecting SSI disability. In other words, our tax dollars are supporting this crud."

The word *disability* sent a new jolt of fear through me. I didn't want Ray Wilson to die before I confronted him. "What kind of disability?" I asked.

"It's nothing visible. I got a look at him from a distance. He's got both his legs and both his arms. I'm guessing it's alcoholism or drugs or a mental disorder. It'll take a little more digging to find out the specifics."

"No!"

"*No?* What do you mean?"

"I'm sorry, Bobby. I didn't mean to snap at you. Where are you right now?"

"In Belle Valley, Ohio, room twelve at the Dew Drop In Motel. It's down the block from the house where the subject is living, at four-oh-four Webster Street."

"Forget about him for now. I need you to come back to New York right away and help Nancy. We've uncovered five suspects—people who might have murdered Veronica Rose." Quickly, I told him about the two couples from Boston who had reason to hate her, and about my conversations today with Link Ramsey and Jay Garwood.

"We've got to find out who the real killer is before Nancy has to go on trial," I said. "Or at least we have to come up with someone else who looks so guilty that the prosecutor will have to drop the charges against Nancy. Right now, she's the only person they're even considering."

"Okay. I'll be back at my place tonight."

"Tomorrow's Friday. Let's get together in the evening for a meeting with Walter and Nancy, and Nancy's lawyer, if he's available. We'll make plans for the investigation over dinner. How's seven o'clock at my apartment? And Chinese food?"

"That's all good," Bobby said. "Be sure to get chopsticks. Chinese food doesn't taste as good with a fork."

"Agreed. Oh, Bobby, about what you've been doing? Don't bother to write a report. We need to concentrate on saving Nancy. Just give me your bill for time and expenses tomorrow night, when we have a moment alone. I'll send you a check the next morning."

"Great."

After we said good-bye, I replaced the receiver and thought about what Bobby had told me: Ray Wilson was in Belle Valley, Ohio. Now that I knew he was alive, and where he could be found, it was time to make some plans.

Taking a clean white legal pad from my desk, I began a list of the things I had to do in the next couple of weeks.

First, I'd go to a library tomorrow and use a computer there to look up information about Belle Valley, Ohio, and get driving directions. I had to do it at a library so as not leave any trace of my interest on either my office or home computers.

Next, I'd start taking money out of my savings account, three or four thousand dollars at a time, well below an amount that would attract attention. I'd make the first withdrawal this evening, just before six, when the bank closed. Already, at home, I had ten thousand dollars of emergency cash in the bedroom closet safe. Keeping hidden emergency money was a habit my late husband, Ian, had taught me when we were traveling in dangerous parts of the world.

"You never know when cash for a bribe could mean the difference between life and death," he had said. Twice, before Ian was killed in the crash of our Land Rover, we were captured by separate sets of poachers who discovered us photographing evidence that they'd slaughtered elephants for the ivory and a rhino for its horn. Rhino horns, ground to powder, were thought to be aphrodisiacs—primitive Viagra. The money we had hidden in boxes of film had saved our lives.

AT FIVE O'CLOCK, I insisted that Betty go home. "Tommy's getting back from the Affiliates meeting tonight," I said, "and I'm meeting with the breakdown writers tomorrow morning, so we might have a long day."

"I haven't copied the script revisions you made yet," she said.

"Do that tomorrow. We're not taping those scenes for another week."

She reached into the bottom drawer of her desk for her handbag and said with a smile, "Then I'm taking off." She came out from behind her desk, but paused. "Oh—do you want me to order lunch in for the breakdown meeting?"

"Good idea. Find out what each of them want when they arrive, then have the order delivered at one o'clock. Thanks for reminding me. Now go home."

"Yes, ma'am," she said, giving me a comic salute.

I waited until the elevator doors had closed behind Betty, and then went back into my office and took a key from the collection hanging from a hook beneath my desk. Quickly finding the key marked "Small Props," I crossed the floor to a door behind Stage 35. The stage was dark; the last scene of the day using that set had wrapped an hour ago.

The room where small props such as hospital I.D. tags, police and fire department badges, passports, and such were kept in filing cabinets was not much bigger than a storage closet.

My first act was to open the drawer marked "Misc. Devices" and remove a lock pick. I knew we had one because a few months ago I'd written a scene in which Link Ramsey's character used it to get into a bad guy's office. I slipped it into my pocket.

Next, I went to the drawer marked "Driver's Licenses" and rummaged through them until I came to a Chicago license with a picture on it of a woman about my age. The name on the license was "Charlotte Brown." She'd been a minor character in the story three years ago. The actress who'd played Charlotte had short dark hair, bangs that brushed the top of her eyebrows, and she wore glasses.

For my purpose, the only thing that was wrong with the license was the expiration date, but I could have that changed by one of our studio prop artists. Tommy called them "our forgers" because they were so skillful at making fake documents that looked real. He joked that we paid them well so they wouldn't use their talents for crime. All I had to do was tell one of them that I needed the expiration date changed on the license to use as a prop in a future storyline.

I stared at the picture on the laminated rectangle in my hands. Unlike Charlotte's short dark hair, mine is shoulder length, and a kind of blondish reddish shade Matt says is the color of marmalade.

With a pair of clear, nonprescription glasses, and a short black wig that I could buy at any one of a thousand shops in the city and customize, I would look enough like Charlotte Brown to pass for her.

Chapter 27

FRIDAY NIGHT, BOBBY arrived first, shortly followed by Kent Wayne and Nancy. Wayne, who lives on East Eighty-first Street, directly across the park from Nancy, had picked her up on his way to the Dakota.

From the brightness of her voice, to her quick smile, it would seem to a stranger that Nancy was holding up well under the stress of being accused of murder, but I saw the stiffness of her shoulders, and the hollows in her cheeks. Movements that used to be smooth were now abrupt, and when she wasn't holding something, her fingers tended to twist around each other when they used to lie gracefully at rest. Nancy had been the best and kindest friend in the world to me when I first came to New York City on scholarship to Columbia, and again, after Ian's death. Whatever it took, I had vowed to help her now.

By the time Bobby, Walter, Wayne, Nancy, and I were seated at my dining room table eating Chinese takeout, it had been forty-four hours since my argument with Matt at

Penny's dinner party, and he still hadn't contacted me. I was fuming. I might not have been so angry if we hadn't spent Monday night and Tuesday morning making love with such enthusiasm. Apparently, those hours hadn't meant enough to Matt for him to get over his snit about my tricking his partner. G. G. got over it. Why couldn't Matt?

Well, to hell with him. Who needs a man with—as Walter put it—a stiff neck that goes all the way down to the soles of his feet? Not this woman!

"Who'd like some more cashew chicken?" I asked.

Bobby and Wayne signaled with raised chopsticks. I got up to put more of that dish onto their plates as Nancy refilled glasses: bottled water for Bobby and me, beer for Walter, red wine for herself and her lawyer.

"I've never been in this building," Kent Wayne said. "Always been curious about it, but I never knew anybody who lived here."

"First time I took Morgan home," Bobby said, "we were on my motorcycle. I thought the Dakota looked like the set of a mad scientist movie."

"You're close," I said. "The first actor who lived in this building was Boris Karloff."

Glancing around, Wayne said, "I find your decor interesting."

Nancy defended me. "The place was furnished when Morgan bought it. She didn't pick out that wallpaper with the tiny rosebuds, or this table with the gilt trim."

"I wasn't making a critical judgment," Wayne said. Using his chopsticks, he gestured toward the most unusual object in the room—or in the entire apartment, for that matter. "Do you mean to say that authentic-looking ancient Egyptian mummy case in the corner came with this apartment?"

"I wondered about that thing. She's not a bad-looking woman," Bobby said, referring to the painted female figure on the front of the case. She had large dark eyes and even features, and wore a headdress fashioned in the form of a hawk's head, with its feathers fanning out on either side. Her straight black hair reached to the middle of her breasts. Narrow arms, crossed at the level of her rib cage, displayed long, slim fingers.

Nancy, who had been staying here with me when the mummy case was delivered, and knew from whom it had come, glanced at me, but didn't say anything. Instead, she turned her attention to the last few bits of Mongolian beef and snow peas on her plate.

Noting the sudden silence, Wayne said, "I'll bet there's a story about that thing."

There was, but I wasn't about to tell him that the mummy case had arrived containing the missing piece of a murder mystery that I'd been involved in several months ago.

"Not a very interesting story," I lied. "It was just a gift from someone."

"When I was a young fella, we gave a bunch of *flowers* to a pretty girl. Guess the world has changed more than I knew," Walter said.

"Anyway, I've been promising Nancy and Penny for months that I'll get around to redecorating this apartment with things that *I'm* going to choose."

Nancy asked, "When? I need something fun to look forward to, so I want a firm commitment."

"As soon as we get you out of this mess, I promise to start redecorating. You and Penny can go shopping with me."

"I'm going to hold you to that," Nancy said.

Wayne's attention had remained fixed on the mummy case. Gesturing toward it, he asked, "Mind if I take a closer look?"

"Go ahead. Are you interested in that sort of thing?"

"I wasn't, until a former client paid my fee with an Egyptian sarcophagus." He got up from the table and moved over to the mummy case. "I didn't know anything about antiquities, but I live a couple of blocks east of the Metropolitan Museum, so I did some studying and found out the sarcophagus was from the early years of the Ptolemic dynasty, around three hundred B.C. This case might be several hundred years older, Morgan. You probably know this held a female mummy—the painting on a case was usually a representation of the person they put in it."

"I didn't know that," I said, and felt a little embarrassed that I hadn't tried to find out. *As soon as I have time, I'll do some studying on the subject.*

"An expert could tell you the exact age of the piece and where it came from by the panel of hieroglyphics that run down the center of her gown, and from the colors of the paint and the style of the artist."

"Antiquity detectives—everybody wants to get into my act," Bobby joked.

Wayne leaned over and pointed out a design on the side. "See this drawing of a doorway? Something like it was on my sarcophagus. The man at the Met told me that's supposed to be the portal for the spirit to exit, allowing it to roam between the world of the living and the world of the dead."

"Was it worth as much as you were charging the client?" Bobby asked.

"More. My fee was eighty thousand, and according to an appraiser at a big auction house the sarcophagus was worth over a hundred. From the catalogue prices I saw, this case of yours would probably go for a bigger number."

Walter was peering closely at the mummy case. "From all the work that went into decorating this, the woman must have been somebody important."

With a faint note of wistfulness in her voice, Nancy added, "Or somebody who was loved."

Wayne reached for the latch. Before I could say, "Don't open it" he opened the mummy case—and exposed one of my housekeeping secrets.

Surveying the contents inside, he asked, "What's this?"

Embarrassed, I admitted, "I'm using it for storage. Those are old *Love of My Life* scripts."

Wayne closed the case carefully. "You've got a treasure here."

"What did you do with your sarcophagus?" Bobby asked him.

"Ah, thereby lies a sad tale. In a wild burst of affection, I presented it to the woman I was seeing at the time." He added ruefully, "It turned out she'd wanted a diamond. She stamped her feet and cried—not a pretty picture. The irony is she didn't realize that what she angrily referred to as 'an old coffin' was worth more than any diamond even *she* would have picked out. We broke up, and I kept it. If I ever again think I've found 'the one,' I'll give it to her as a test of our compatibility." He expelled an exaggerated sigh. "For now I'm just a lonely bachelor, overworked and underloved."

LATER, DINNER FINISHED and dishes cleared away, the five of us began to brainstorm Nancy's case.

"The girl, Didi, found her mother dead," Wayne said. "I'll want to talk to her, to find out if she saw someone in the hall before she went into the apartment."

"Arnold won't let you anywhere near her," Nancy said. "And I can't blame him. Didi's traumatized."

"Didi likes me," I said. "Or at least she used to. If I can find a way to get to her, maybe I can persuade her to talk to me."

"I appreciate what you want to do, and I wish you luck," Nancy said, "but I don't think anybody's going to get through the barricades Arnold's stacked up around her."

"Unless she's in a coma, I'll think of some way to see her," I said. An idea had already occurred to me. "Tomorrow's Saturday. Didi is obsessed with horseback riding—she's won ribbons in competitions. To keep up her skills, I'll bet she's going to insist on practicing."

"Yes, she would!" Nancy's voice was full of excitement, and hope. "She's registered in three big shows before the end of the year. Arnold doesn't ride—he's afraid of horses. He won't go near one unless it's to see Didi compete, and then he'll stay outside the ring. I'll bet he *will* let her go to the stable alone, but with his chauffeur to drive her and to make sure nobody tries to talk to her as she leaves or enters the building. The driver's name is Max." She turned to Wayne. "I know Max pretty well, but I don't think he's ever seen Morgan."

"Would he go inside with Didi?"

"I doubt it. When Max took us places, he'd always stay out in the car and read a book."

"A few months ago Didi invited me to see her perform," I said, "so I know where she goes through her ring exercises. The Woodburn Academy on Amsterdam Avenue."

Nancy nodded in agreement. "Because she spends so much time practicing, Didi doesn't go to school—Arnold has private tutors come to the apartment. I think the riding ring is probably the only place you could get to her."

"Then that's my first move," I said.

Talk turned to the list of suspects Walter and I had compiled: Ralph and Gloria Hartley, Laura and George Reynolds, Cathy Chatsworth—a.k.a. Olive Flitt—and Jay Garwood, who lied about being romantically involved with Veronica Rose.

"One of the things I'll ask Didi is what she knew about her mother's relationship with Garwood. When she saw him last, and how he acted."

"Also, if she came down via the stairs, or used the elevator, and if she saw anyone at all between leaving Arnold's apartment and getting to her mother's," Wayne said and turned to Nancy. "Is there a back way out of the apartment?"

"Arnold has a back service entrance for deliveries and trash pickup—an elevator and stairs. It's likely that all of the apartments there do."

Wayne frowned. "Back entrances mean easy escape, if the killer knew anything about the building. Let's hope the girl saw something that she doesn't realize is significant." Proceeding to the next subject, he said, "There's a detective firm in Europe that I've done business with. I'll have them track Gloria Hartley's movements in Paris the last few weeks. Find out who she's seen, what she's done, if she left the city."

"If she knows any hit men," Nancy added.

Walter volunteered to locate Jay Garwood's ex-wife. "I'll go have a talk with her, find out what she has to say about him—like for instance if he was violent, an' why they got a divorce."

"Excellent," Wayne said.

Bobby said, "I'll hire some reliable Boston operatives to help. We'll do a full-court press on Ralph Hartley, George and Laura Reynolds, and Cathy Chatsworth."

"Be careful of the Chatsworth woman," Wayne cautioned. "She's a journalist."

Bobby snorted. "She's a journalist like I'll be playing center for the Boston Celtics."

"Nevertheless, she's employed by a major newspaper," Wayne said. "Stay below her radar."

"Where's she's concerned, I'll be the Invisible Man," Bobby said facetiously.

"When I get what I can out of the Garwood woman, I'll join your team, Bobby," Walter said.

"What can *I* do?" Nancy asked.

"Go over all the bank and investment records we dig up," Wayne said. "With your corporate law and finance expertise, you might spot something significant—a clue, an anomaly—that the rest of us would miss."

We all agreed that we'd share everything we found out with each other, but with no one who wasn't at this table.

I held up an index finger. "Except we'll give what we learn to the police, when we've discovered who the real killer is."

"*When* you find out who it is. I like your optimism," Nancy said. She tried to smile, but the attempt wasn't successful. At that moment, our eyes met, and I saw how terrified she was about what would happen to her if we failed.

Chapter 28

BOBBY, NANCY, AND Wayne hadn't been gone for more than a few minutes when the telephone rang.

"Your guests got into a cab," Matt said.

"Did you just drive up, or are you watching my house?"

"I'm not spying on you. I was on my way home, but then I suddenly found my car turning onto Seventy-second Street."

"All by itself?"

"My subconscious is smarter than I am," Matt said.

In man-speak, this was an apology for how he'd acted Wednesday night. "Would you like to come up for coffee?" I asked.

"No, thanks. I've had a long day and want to hit the sack, but will you come down for a few minutes?"

"Where are you?"

"Across the street. I'll meet you at your entrance."

On my way out, I stopped at the door to Walter's room. I used to think of it as the den; how quickly it had become Walter's room.

"I'm going downstairs to talk to Matt for a little while," I said.

"Glad he came to his senses," Walter said. "I reckon you'll be safe, so I won't wait up."

Matt was standing at the arched entrance to the courtyard.

"Hi," I said.

Without a word, he took my hand and led me a few yards west on Seventy-second. It was a dark night, but in the spill from a streetlight farther down the block, I saw the outline of his Crown Victoria, and recognized the communications aerial rising from the trunk.

To my surprise, it was the rear passenger door he opened instead of the front.

"Get in," he said.

I did, and he followed me inside. No sooner had he closed the door than he took me into his arms and kissed me. My own arms went around his neck, welcoming the feel of his chest pressed against mine. We kissed until we were breathless, then gently pulled a few inches apart.

"I missed you," he whispered. "I haven't had a good night's sleep since . . ." He paused.

I finished the sentence for him. "Since Boston."

"Boston . . ." His voice was soft. "I never thought just hearing the name of a city would make me hot."

I pulled a few inches farther away. "So it's only sex?"

"What we had in that room wasn't just sex, and you know it."

I did, but I wasn't going to admit it. Instead, I asked, "Have you changed your mind about that money I inherited?"

Matt inclined his head an inch or two. It wasn't an acquiescing nod, but it was something nearby. "I still wish there wasn't such a financial disparity between us," he said, "but I've been thinking that maybe the thing to do is to keep it completely separate from *us*. Never talk about it."

"You mean you want to pretend the money doesn't exist? I can do that. It's not as though *I've* ever brought it up."

"No, you haven't. I'm the one who made it a problem."

"We could start over—forget about old issues." I smiled at him mischievously. "I'm sure we can find new subjects to fight about."

"You'd make a joke if somebody was tying you to a post in front of a firing squad."

"I hope I never find out if that's true."

Matt leaned over to kiss me lightly on the tip of my nose, then sat up straight again. "Right now, with your best friend accused of murder, we can't see each other, but when this situation is resolved—"

"When Nancy is cleared!"

"For your sake, I hope that's what's going to happen. What I'm trying to say is that when this situation is over, I want us to see each other."

Man-speak again. "See each other? What kind of *see* each other?"

"Jeez, you're difficult," he said, but there was warmth in his voice. "I want us to see each other . . . seriously. How do you feel about that?"

"I like the idea."

Matt took me in his arms again. Our lips met in the darkness.

After a few minutes, he said, "That's about as much as I can stand without carrying you off to my cave." He opened the door and helped me out of the car.

We held hands as he walked with me back to the Dakota's entrance. "If G. G. and I find out anything that could help Nancy, I'll let you know," Matt said.

"Thank you."

He squeezed my fingers lightly. "Stay out of trouble."

We whispered our good nights, and I passed beneath the archway into the center courtyard. As I crossed the few yards to my section of the building, I ran the tip of my index finger lightly over my lips, recalling how sweet was the feeling of Matt's mouth on mine.

I wondered if Matt would still want to see me "seriously" if he knew that at some point in the near future I was planning to slip away from New York for a couple of days, with a convincing cover story that would explain my absence.

How would he react if he knew what I intended to do when I reached Belle Valley, Ohio?

Chapter 29

AT SEVEN O'CLOCK Saturday morning I put on a pair of jeans, an old pair of desert boots, and a cotton shirt. By stashing keys and cash in the pockets of my jeans and clipping the cell phone to my belt, I wouldn't have to carry a handbag. I was dressed for riding, in case it was necessary for me to get on a horse while I was sleuthing.

I didn't have riding boots, but my anklebone-high desert boots had a heel that was three-quarters of an inch high—just enough for the stirrups. Although I'd ridden horses a couple of dozen times during my almost six years in Kenya, the only talent I can claim is an ability to stay in the saddle. Ian, who was a superb rider, said he admired my grit, but he never praised my horseback-riding form.

Walter and Magic were already active in the kitchen. Walter was heating the grill and mixing pancake batter, and Magic was crunching on a bowl of Natural Balance crunchies.

"Don't make pancakes for me this morning," I said.

"I'm off to the riding stable to see if I can catch Didi alone."

"Did you find out she'll be there?"

I shook my head. "It's a guess. There's no way I can ask when she's scheduled to ride. Arnold's probably told the woman who owns the place to let him know if anybody inquires about Didi, so I'll plant myself in the coffee shop across the street and watch for her. If she does come, I'll wait a few minutes, then go across to the stable to ask about taking riding lessons."

"And you'll be so surprised to see Didi," said Walter with a sly grin.

"You got it."

"Suppose she doesn't come?"

"If I'm not home by six, don't include me in what you make for dinner. To hang on to a table by the window, by the end of the day I'll have ordered practically the whole menu, one thing at a time."

Walter gestured to a tan cloth hat on the table, folded flat. It had a brim and was the kind of hat that fishermen wore. In the green camouflage version, game wardens in East Africa wore them to keep the scorching sun out of their eyes while they scanned the horizon for signs of poachers.

"What about the hat?" I asked.

"Tuck your hair up under it an' you got a handy little disguise. Obscures your face without calling attention."

I smiled with appreciation and tucked the hat into my belt. "Thanks."

"Good hunting," Walter said. "After breakfast, I'm going to start looking for that Garwood fella's ex-wife. The neighborhood library has current telephone books for all the boroughs, and the phone company office has a collection of old books. You said he had a child, so the mom probably kept her married name."

"Unless she married again."

"No plan is perfect," Walter said. "If we can't find her on one road, we'll try another." He gave the pancake batter a final turn in the mixing bowl. Dropping spoonfuls carefully onto the sizzling griddle, he added, "I have a couple more ideas."

I said I'd see him later, gave Magic a gentle head rub, and set off for Didi's favorite New York City stable.

THE WOODBURN ACADEMY, on Amsterdam Avenue near West Eighty-sixth Street, opened its wide pale yellow barn doors to customers at eight A.M. Fifteen minutes earlier, I'd claimed a seat by the front window of the Amsterdam Diner and ordered coffee and scrambled eggs. A dozen people were already having breakfast. Five of them sat at the counter that ran along the back wall separating the open kitchen from the eating area. The other patrons, singly and in pairs, occupied the dark orange fake leather booths.

A few minutes before eight, two giggling preteen blonde girls accompanied by a young Hispanic woman arrived. Apparently unhappy that they had to wait, they stamped around, marching in circles. I could hear the sound of their whining across the street. The girls resembled each other, but there was at least a year's difference in their ages; they were probably sisters. They wore riding pants and boots, topped by T-shirts with writing across their undeveloped chests. I was too far away to read the messages.

The woman with them was present in body, but her attitude was detached; her attention was not focused on the girls. Her body, beneath a dress that belonged on a much older woman, was firm. A sour expression marred her otherwise pretty face.

While eating slowly, I watched this trio, idly wondering about their lives. At the same time, I kept an eye on the vehicles in the street.

Just as the big doors opened, a taxi pulled up to the entrance and a harried-looking man got out, followed by a dark-haired girl of about ten. This girl's riding clothes were so new I doubted they'd yet been worn near a horse. I wondered if the man was a divorced father with weekend visitations, indulging his child with expensive things. The man tried to hold the girl's hand as they headed toward the stable, but she yanked away from him and screwed her face up into an unattractive pout. I'd tried one of those pouts, when I was about that girl's age, but Sister Ellen Elizabeth at the orphanage-like boarding school had asked me, "What will you do if your face freezes in that expression, and you have to go around looking like that for the rest of your life?" I never did it again.

By 9:30 I'd had two more cups of coffee, a glass of orange juice, and half an English muffin. I'd given up watching the foot traffic on Amsterdam and concentrated on the passing cars. In particular, I was interested in a silver Lincoln Park Avenue. Nancy had told me that Arnold's car was a silver Lincoln Park Avenue, but she didn't know the license number.

This particular Lincoln had circled the block three times, slowly. When I saw it making its second pass, I jotted down the plate number. It was DD 617, and that made me sit up straight. Having been in that city so recently, I knew that the telephone area code for Boston was 617, and "DD" could stand for Didi. The thrill of discovery made my pulse quicken.

A man in a chauffeur's cap was at the wheel. Wearing black-rimmed glasses, in his fifties, big shoulders. That was pretty much how Nancy had described Arnold's chauffeur, Max. Because the rear windows were tinted, I couldn't see if Max had a passenger in the back, but I doubted that he was driving around and around the block for his own amusement.

The fourth time the silver Lincoln rounded the corner

onto Amsterdam, it stopped in front of the riding academy. The chauffeur got out, opened the rear door, and extended his hand to his unseen passenger.

Yes! I congratulated myself on a good guess as Didi emerged from the car, but I was startled at what I saw. This was a changed Didi. She was dressed for riding and carried her safety helmet, but her hair—which used to cascade down her back in thick, coffee-colored waves—had been cut to just below her ears. And it didn't seem to have been the work of a stylist. It looked like Didi herself had hacked off her long hair. She said something briefly to Max, and headed toward the stable. The driver stood on the sidewalk, watching until she disappeared inside.

I signaled the waitress for my check, and after leaving a large tip, I paid the bill at the cash register. The cashier gave me change for the twenty I handed her, and I stuffed it into a pocket without looking at it because I was still watching through the diner's front window. Max-the-driver climbed back into the vehicle, eased it forward, and parked in front of a fire hydrant a few yards past the barn door entrance. I waited to see whether he was going to stay in the car or follow Didi into the riding academy.

He stayed in the car.

In the diner's restroom, I took the cloth hat from under my belt, pushed my hair up beneath it, and pulled the brim down to the middle of my forehead, securing it on my head. A glance at my reflection in the restroom mirror proved that Walter had been right. This was a pretty good disguise because it made me look dull. Dull doesn't call attention to itself.

Ten minutes after Didi disappeared through the barn doors, I saw that Max had settled behind the steering wheel and was reading a book that he'd propped up against it.

I left the diner and strolled down the block, away from the barn doors and the Lincoln. At the corner of Eighty-fifth and Amsterdam I crossed over to the Woodburn side of the block and ambled back up toward the stable's entrance.

Every parking place on Amsterdam was filled, but vehicle traffic was light, and there were only a few people walking along the street this morning. Lucky for me, the fire hydrant Max had illegally pulled up beside was a few yards beyond my destination, keeping me behind the Lincoln, with Max's back to me.

Because I had asked more than once to see Didi, Arnold might have described me to Max, and told him to look out for me. But if he had, he'd probably only alerted Max about my coming to their apartment building. If Arnold let Didi go riding, he must think Woodburn was a safe place for her to be alone.

It was only a remote possibility that Max knew what I looked like, but in case he glimpsed me in his rearview mirror, I kept my head angled slightly away from the curb, letting the brim of the hat shade the top half of my face. It was so important that I talk to Didi, in case she knew something or had seen something that could help Nancy, I didn't want to take even the slimmest chance of being thwarted.

Max's attention was still on his book when I reached the academy's yellow barn doors. Standing outside and leaning against the exterior wall was the father I'd seen earlier. He was speaking heatedly into a cell phone and ignored my approach.

As soon as I entered, I was hit with the powerful aroma of horses, but I've never found that smell unpleasant. Horses, like cows and elephants and antelopes, are herbivorous; their natural deposits don't have the stench of a carnivore's leavings.

My eyes adjusted quickly to the difference between the electric lights inside and the brighter June sunshine on the street. In my peripheral vision, I saw Didi mounting a horse, but deliberately kept my gaze aimed away from her.

I took off my hat, letting my hair fall free, and raised one hand to attract the attention of a lean and leathery gray-haired woman who wore a sweatshirt with a picture of a big brown horse on the front. From my visit a few months ago, I recognized her as the owner, Mrs. Woodburn. She was in the farther of the two riding rings that took up most of the space on the building's sawdust-covered ground floor, working with the young girl whose father was outside on his cell. The two blonde sisters and a red-haired child were riding awkwardly, supervised by a pair of young women wearing shirts that said "Woodburn Academy."

As the older woman came toward me, I said, "I don't have an appointment for a riding lesson, but I just took a chance and came in." With my back to Didi, I couldn't tell if she'd spotted me yet.

Mrs. Woodburn said, "My instructors are busy right now, but one of them will be available in a few minutes. How much riding experience have you had?"

"Not much. Consider me a beginner."

Behind me, I heard the slap of hooves on the sawdust floor, and the sound a horse makes when it blows air out the sides of its mouth.

"Morgan? Is that you?" Didi steered her horse around so that I could see her. I played "surprised."

"Didi—hi! I came to see if I could get some lessons." I added with a warm smile, "Actually, you inspired me. When I saw you ride, I got the urge to learn, but this is the first chance I've had."

"Sunny's a good teacher," Didi said, "but she's out sick today." She looked down at Mrs. Woodburn. "Woody, if it's okay with you, I could show Morgan things like getting on and how to sit, and lead her in a walk."

The stable's owner pursed her lips and looked dubious.

"I'll pay for a lesson anyway," I said quickly, "and a riding fee. Whatever."

Mrs. Woodburn glanced at her watch. "I'll have an instructor for you in fifteen more minutes, but since Didi's practically a member of the staff, she can start you off."

In baseball terms, I'd made it to first.

Chapter 30

"THIS IS MOON Glow," Didi said. She leaned forward to give the big brown horse an affectionate stroke on its neck, then she dismounted gracefully. "Hold his reins while I go get you a horse."

I took the long leather straps attached to the bridle and held them the way she had.

"Are you sure you want to go to this trouble, Didi? I don't want to take up your time if you're practicing for a show."

"It's okay. I can be here as long as I want." She hurried toward a hitching rail attached to the south wall, a dozen feet outside the riding ring, where a saddled horse with a reddish coat was tethered.

Returning with the red horse, Didi said, "This is Cinnamon. She's a good one to get started on—kids ride her." She took back Moon Glow's reins and placed Cinnamon's in my right hand. "Now to get on, you have to face the same way as the horse."

I laughed. "That's the one part I'm sure of."

Didi said solemnly, "You think that's funny, but you'd be surprised at some of the things I've seen people try to do on their first lessons." She regarded my desert boots with a critical frown. "That's not the right footwear. I guess it'll be all right this time, but get some good riding boots."

"Will you tell me where to buy them?"

For the first time since we met this morning, Didi smiled. "I know the best places for all the stuff you'll need, and what bootmaker to go to. It's much better to have boots molded to your foot. Those store-bought ones can mess you up."

Standing as close as I was to Didi, I saw that the two inches of hair visible below her helmet were ragged at the ends, strong indication that she had done the cutting herself. The dark shade that had been shining with natural highlights only a few weeks ago was now dull and limp, and the healthy pink tint was gone from her lovely face. She'd lost some weight, too; her custom-tailored riding jacket was a little too big on her. Thinking of the grief she suffered, my heart went out to her.

Didi regarded me with the serious concentration of a brand-new teacher with her first pupil. "Put your left foot in the stirrup, and swing your right leg over the horse and get your foot into the other stirrup," she said.

I did as instructed—a little awkwardly, but I got up on my first try. Once in the saddle, old muscle memories awakened and I automatically gripped the horse with my knees.

Didi vaulted easily into Moon Glow's saddle, and now we were next to each other on our respective mounts.

"Hold the reins the way I am," she said, demonstrating. I did.

"Now copy what I do." Didi inclined her head slightly toward Moon Glow's neck and made a clicking noise with her mouth. Moon Glow started to move forward. I followed

Didi's lead and we walked our horses side by side around the ring. Didi was a patient teacher; before I realized it, I was feeling comfortable on horseback.

At first, from just inside the second ring, Mrs. Woodbury watched us with narrowed eyes and an apprehensive frown. Then, apparently satisfied that Didi was being careful, her face relaxed and she turned away to check on other students.

"This is fun," I told Didi, meaning it. "I don't think I'd have thought of trying to ride if I didn't know you."

She looked pleased. "You mean I inspired you?"

"Absolutely."

We had almost completed our first circuit of the ring when I said gently, "I'm so very sorry about your mother."

Tears started to form in her eyes. "I don't want to talk about it."

"Okay, subject closed," I said quickly. "I had an idea. Remember how impressed I was that night we first met when you told me you'd spotted Cody's previous girlfriend as a phony? So, I wonder if you'd like to come to the studio when you have time. I'll show you some tapes of future episodes, and you can tell me what you think. You'll be my special test-marketer."

Didi turned toward me enough so that I had a three-quarters view of her face..

She asked cautiously, "Will *he* be there?"

" 'He'? You mean Jay Garwood? If you like, I can arrange to have you come up when he's there—"

"No!" Her voice was so sharp it startled both of our horses.

I'd touched a nerve in Didi, and pressed the point. "Jay and your mother were seeing each other, so I thought you must like him."

"I hate him!" Didi pulled back on Moon Glow's reins so hard the horse tossed his head, shorted, and lifted his front hooves off the ground for a moment. From across the stable floor, Mrs. Woodburn yelled an admonishing, "Hey! Don't do that!"

I saw Didi's eyes fill to overflowing with tears—and I saw something else in those eyes: fear.

"I hate him!" she cried, "And I hate *you*!" Then she jumped off Moon Glow and raced toward the big barn doors and out onto the street. The horse started to follow Didi, but I leaned over and grabbed the reins to stop it.

Mrs. Woodburn hurried and over took Moon Glow's reins as I dismounted.

"What happened?" she asked sharply.

Digging into my pocket for cash, I asked, "How much is it for her time and for mine?"

She shook her head in confusion. "I bill Didi's father. And you didn't have a lesson . . ."

I handed her a twenty and a five. "Will this do?"

"Sure. But what—"

I pushed the money into her hand and hurried out of the stable before she could finish the question.

Out on the street, I looked for the silver Lincoln, but it was gone.

Chapter 31

THE CAB I'D hailed on Eighty-fifth Street pulled up to the entrance to the Dakota just as Walter stepped out through the archway.

I waved at him. As I was paying the driver, Walter opened the rear passenger door and greeted me. Climbing out, I asked, "Where are you going?"

"I located Mrs. Garwood." He patted the front of his jacket, indicating the inside pocket where I knew he kept his investigator's notebook. "On my way to see her. She's still Mrs. Garwood and lives down on West Ninth Street."

I took him by the arm and steered him back toward the entrance to the Dakota's courtyard. "I've got to tell you about what just happened with Didi," I said. "Give me a few minutes to change my clothes. I'm going with you to see Jay Garwood's ex-wife."

"You smell a little bit like a horse," Walter said. "I don't mind, but this is the big city. You might want to clean up before we go."

FIFTEEN MINUTES LATER, as I was getting out of the shower, the phone rang. I wrapped myself in a big terry-cloth bath sheet and picked up the receiver. "Hello?"

"Morgan, this is Arnold Rose." It wasn't just announcing his full name that signaled he was furious; I could tell by the snarl in his voice.

"Arnold—"

"Listen to me," he snapped. "I have just drawn up a request for a restraining order to keep you away from Didi. Be assured that this order *will* be granted, and if you violate it, you *will* go to jail."

"Arnold—"

"However, because we both care for Nancy, I am willing to give you one more chance. If you will give me your word that you won't come near Didi again, I will table the R.O. But if you try to contact her in any way, I will slap you with this order so fast your teeth will rattle. Have I made myself clear?"

"I understand perfectly, Arnold." I was seething at his arrogance and his heavy-handed attempt to control me, but I kept my tone carefully neutral.

"Do you promise to have no further contact with Didi?"

"Yes, Arnold," I said. But behind my back, my fingers were crossed. A promise doesn't count when it's extracted under duress. I wasn't going to let the threat of legal action stop me from trying to help my best friend.

"I'm glad you understand the jeopardy you've put yourself in," he said.

"Yes, I do."

"Then goodbye." Arnold Rose hung up.

I dressed quickly and tossed the essentials into a handbag.

In the kitchen, while checking to make sure Magic had plenty of fresh water and food, and giving my ambulatory purr-machine an affectionate head rub, I filled Walter in on the call from Arnold.

Beneath his big gray mustache, Walter pursed his lips. "I'd say that was a significant overreaction," he said. "What did you do that was so terrible?"

"When I told Didi how sorry I was about her mother, her eyes started to tear up but she just said she didn't want to talk about it. She was all right. But then when I mentioned Jay Garwood's name, her reaction was almost violent."

"What do you think caused that?"

Remembering the look of fear in Didi's eyes, I took a deep breath. Walter was watching me so closely I had the uncomfortable feeling that he was reading my mind.

"Something might have happened with Garwood," I said carefully.

Walter grunted. His eyes narrowed. "You mean you think maybe Garwood did something to the girl?"

Nodding in agreement, I took another breath. "If I find out that Garwood behaved inappropriately to Didi I'm going to fire the bastard." Silently, I wished I could do more to him than toss him off the show.

"That sort of thing's hard to prove if the girl won't talk," Walter said. "It's hard even then, unless there's physical evidence." *Like there was physical evidence in your case twenty-four years ago*, he might have said. I was grateful that he didn't.

Pushing past the awkward moment, I told Walter, "That's why I want to go with you to see his ex. The woman who was married to him probably knows Garwood better than anyone. I want to know what broke up their marriage." I didn't want to voice my fear that he might have hurt his own daughter, so I went back to Veronica's murder.

"Walter, how's this for a theory? Say Garwood . . . bothered . . . Didi and she told her mother. Veronica was furious, broke up with Garwood, and told him she was going to have him arrested. That might have panicked him so much he killed her."

"Could be," Walter said. "Whoever killed the woman didn't go to the apartment planning to do it. That heavy can of paint was a weapon of opportunity."

LORETTA GARWOOD LIVED on the second floor of an undistinguished fifteen-story concrete apartment building on West Ninth Street, in between the Avenue of the Americas and Broadway.

"Let's hope she's home," I said.

"It's Saturday, so she probably wouldn't be at work."

There was no doorman, and the front door was locked, but there was a speaker above a list of names on the wall. I pressed the little black button next to "L. Garwood" and heard a distant buzz. Within a few seconds we heard a woman's voice; it was tinny through the electronics.

"Yes? Who is it?"

"Mrs. Garwood?"

"Yes. What do you want?"

"My name is Morgan Tyler. I'm a producer of *Love of My Life*."

"Oh, God! Is Jay in trouble?" There was an unmistakable note of apprehension in her voice.

"No," I said reassuringly. "Not at all." (That was true at this moment.) "This is just a routine background check." (That was a lie.)

"Background check?"

"There's nothing to be concerned about, Mrs. Garwood. May we come up and speak to you for a few minutes?"

Seconds of silence, then: "Well . . . I have to go out in a little while so we can't talk for long."

The advance cop-out, I thought. She's nervous about something. "We just need a few minutes," I said.

"All right. It's apartment two-oh-three, on the second floor. Come up the stairs because the elevator's on the fritz."

As soon as she sent the electric message to unlock the front door, Walter pushed it open.

Across the small, unadorned lobby a hand-lettered OUT-OF-ORDER sign was stuck to the elevator with a ragged piece of duct tape. To the left of the elevator the door to the stairway was propped open with a metal trash can. The stairwell was dimly lighted and painted a color I called "prison movie gray."

By the time we got to the second floor, Walter was breathing heavily. "Guess I let myself get out of shape," he said. "I have gained ten pounds since I retired."

An attractive, dark-haired woman in her early forties was waiting for us in the doorway of apartment 203. On the thin side of slender, she was dressed casually in beige cotton slacks, a pink T-shirt, and running shoes. "I'm Loretta Garwood," she said. She didn't extend her hand, so I simply said hello, and introduced Walter and myself.

"Come in." She stepped aside to let us enter the apartment. We walked directly into a living room that was painted in yellow and white, and furnished in an eclectic style that mixed periods comfortably. The nine-foot sofa, the deep upholstered chairs, and the highboy were all too large for the proportions of the room. I guessed they had come from the house on Long Island that Garwood told me they'd owned before he lost his job ten years ago.

Loretta Garwood gestured for us to sit down. "I'd offer you coffee, or iced tea, but I really am on my way out and don't have anything prepared." The worry lines creasing her face and the concern in her voice indicated a high degree of nervousness.

"Please don't think about it," I said, taking one of the chairs. Walter sat down on the end of the sofa near my chair, which meant that both of us would be facing our hostess. On the lamp table between us was a framed picture of a very pretty teenage girl.

Loretta Garwood sat down tentatively, perching on the edge of the chair opposite us. "What do you want to know?"

I picked up the photo. "Is this your daughter?"

She smiled. An easy smile, nothing forced about it. "Yes. That's Annie."

"She's lovely," I said.

"We named her after the singer, Annie Lennox. When we were dating, we played her songs all the time."

"I like Rosemary Clooney," Walter said. "Guess that's the generation gap."

Loretta Garwood faced me directly; all traces of social pretense were gone. "Just tell me why you're here. Is Jay drinking? Is he going to be fired?"

"I haven't heard anything about drinking," I told her. "He's been thoroughly professional on the show."

She sighed with relief and settled an inch farther back on her chair. "Thank God. I was afraid he was going to lose his job again."

"I wasn't with the show when Jay was on it before. Do you know why they let him go?"

She grimaced with distaste. "Jay mouthed off—said something insulting about a woman the head writer was hot for. So the guy just forgot about Jay, left him out of the story until his contract ran out. I told Jay he'd been a jerk, and blamed him for what happened to us financially. We'd overspent on the house because we naively thought the good days would last forever. We were sure Jay was going to be a star." She shrugged. "Didn't happen, and the life I thought was solid just disappeared."

"That was a bad break," Walter said.

She shook off the old sadness and brightened. "At least we kept our health. Good thing, too, because for a few years there we couldn't afford medical insurance. Now that Jay's earning good money again, we're beginning to climb out of the hole we've been in since we lost the house."

I nodded sympathetically. "I'm glad things are turning around. Most of us have been through rough times." I paused a moment, then took the plunge and went after what we had come to find out. "Mrs. Garwood, I wouldn't ask this if it weren't absolutely necessary, but what kind of a father is Jay?"

"He's a wonderful father," she said warmly, sounding sincere. "Even when he was so broke he had to crash on a friend's couch, he managed to give me money to take care of Annie. I moved to this apartment to be near the place Jay worked as a bartender, so Annie and Jay could see each other often."

I studied the photo of Annie Garwood. Her smile was wide and infectious. There was nothing in her large eyes that hinted at secret pain. "She looks happy," I said.

"Jay and I weren't a good match, but he gets high marks as a father. Annie couldn't have a better dad. Why are you so interested?"

"I have absolutely nothing to base this question on," I said, "but how would you react if someone alleged that Jay took . . . too much of an interest in a twelve-year-old girl?"

"I'd say they were crazy!" Her eyes blazed with shock, and outrage. "Jay and I couldn't go the distance, but there is absolutely nothing *sick* about him! Who in the world said something like that?"

"No one," I said quickly, and added a lie about doing "background" on everyone new to the show because we were casting parts of preteen girls, and had to be sure there wouldn't be any inappropriate behavior.

"Well, you can trust them with Jay," she said firmly. "Believe me, if I'd ever had even the *tiniest* suspicion, or if Annie had acted in any way that made me think he'd done something to her, you couldn't have taken him back on your show because he would have been a dead man. I wouldn't have divorced him, I'd have killed him!"

OUT ON NINTH Street again, Walter said, "I believed that woman. What did you think?"

"I believed her, too." I shook my head, now doubting my interpretation of Didi's behavior. "Maybe I was wrong."

We were walking toward the Avenue of the Americas, weaving our way through the Saturday pedestrian traffic. Walter didn't say anything, but I saw him nod thoughtfully.

"Didi's reaction was so extreme that I leapt to a conclusion."

"You mentioning Jay Garwood did set her off," Walter said. "If it wasn't what we thought, what do you s'pose it could have been?"

I put my arm through his. "Thank you for that 'we.' *I'm* the one who assumed that a reaction like hers could only have one meaning. My tunnel vision, not yours."

Walter asked, "Do you think Didi was faking her little drama?"

"No. I'm absolutely sure I stepped on some kind of emotional land mine—I just don't know why it exploded."

As we walked, I thought about Didi, and what I knew of her, trying to figure her out as I would a character I was creating for the show. Sometimes it helped to talk the questions out.

"Didi wanted her mother and father back together," I said. "She was so determined about it that a few months ago she staged a horseback riding accident. She got Nancy to help her saddle a horse, but then she made it impossible for Nancy to get the girth tight enough for safety. When the saddle slipped and Didi fell off, it made Nancy look guilty of carelessness. Arnold was furious at Nancy. They made up later, but then Didi's mother moved them back to New York. Nancy's and Arnold's relationship never really got back to being as strong as it had been, because Nancy wouldn't tell Arnold that Didi's accident was just a stunt she pulled to get Nancy out of her father's life. She said it would break Arnold's heart to know the truth."

"Maybe the kid talked her mother into breaking up with the actor," Walter said, "an' now she feels guilty about it because her mother's dead."

"Possible, but that seems a little weak, considering the powerful reaction she had to the mention of Jay Garwood's name."

"I'm gonna comb through the registries of sex offenders an' see if I can turn up something on your actor."

Walter searched thoroughly, but he didn't find anything on Jay Garwood supporting my suspicion that he'd molested Didi. I had to admit my guess was wrong.

"If conclusion-jumping was an Olympic sport," I told Walter, "I'd have taken home the gold."

Chapter 32

TUESDAY MORNING, AS I reached the Global Broadcasting building, I was surprised to see Nancy standing outside, waiting for me. That was so uncharacteristic I asked immediately, "What's happened?"

"They've set the date for my trial. September twenty-fifth."

A jolt of apprehension shot through me. "So soon? That's less than three months away!"

She gestured toward the building's ground-floor coffee shop, the Central Park Café. "Do you have time for coffee, so we can talk about things?"

"Absolutely. The show's crisis du jour can wait."

The cafe was only half full this morning. Summer vacations had temporarily thinned the ranks of the regulars. Nancy and I took a booth in the back.

I asked her if she'd had breakfast.

She shook her head. "I'm not hungry."

In an attempt to lighten the dark atmosphere caused by an approaching trial, I told her, "At times like these, best friends say, 'you've got to keep up your strength.' At least have some toast, or a muffin."

Without waiting for her to agree, I ordered coffee for both of us and a blueberry muffin for Nancy. As soon as we were alone again, I asked, "Can't Kent get the trial date moved back, maybe to after the New Year?"

"He doesn't want to. We refused to waive my right to a speedy trial. Kent says that the quicker we get to court the better it is for me, because the State will have to rush in preparing their case."

"And when people rush, they make mistakes. The prosecutors have a lot of cases to handle," I said. While Kent Wayne's strategy made sense, still the thought of Nancy going to trial so soon, or at all, made my stomach muscles clench with tension.

"Don't look so worried," she said brightly. "I've got an invincible team around me."

I matched her bravado. "Bobby and Walter and Kent and Matt, and the two of us. Six against the State of New York." I wanted to think the State didn't have a chance, but I knew that in this David and Goliath battle to save Nancy, we were David. Unfortunately, we didn't have a slingshot. At least, we hadn't found one yet.

"There's something else," Nancy said.

"What?"

"Have you heard from Chet?"

"He calls a couple of times a week," I said. "Last I heard, his father was almost ready to leave the hospital."

"He's home now. And Chet's on his way back to New York."

"I didn't know that." *So he told Nancy before he told me. That's interesting.* "Chet's been worried about you," I said. "Every time we talk he asks how the investigation is going."

"He's been very supportive," Nancy said. "Do you mind?"

"Of course not! I'm glad he's such a good friend." But I realized Nancy wasn't really asking if I *minded* that Chet called her. Something else was going on. "We've been best friends for almost thirteen years. Out with it."

Nancy looked down at the blueberry muffin her fingers were taking apart. "I know you and Matt . . . well, what I mean is . . . if things aren't going to work out with you and Chet, how would you feel if Chet and I saw each other once in a while—I mean, just as friends."

"I'd be very happy about it," I said sincerely.

"I don't even know if he would want to. He hasn't said anything about it. I was just asking."

"Don't turn that muffin into crumbs, eat it," I said. "You've got to stay healthy while we find out who really killed Veronica Rose. Chet's going to be a great addition to Team Nancy."

And maybe he'll turn out to be the right man for you, I thought. *Chet's a wonderful person—almost as good a man as my best friend deserves.*

CHET CALLED THAT night to invite me to lunch—*lunch*, not dinner. That told me I was right to sense that our relationship had changed.

"Name the restaurant," Chet said. "How about something Broadway glamorous, like Sardi's? Or French elegant, like Jean Luc's?"

"I've got so much work to do. What if we just have lunch in the Central Park Café on the ground floor of the Global building?"

"You're a cheap date. Here I'm willing to spring for the fresh fish of the day, and order chocolate soufflés for dessert."

"How about we go to the cafe, and I promise to order the most expensive thing on the menu?"

"Whatever you say." Pause. "How are you doing, Morgan?"

Now he's calling me Morgan. He used to call me "gorgeous."

"I'm okay, but I'm worried about Nancy, as you can imagine. Hey, wait a minute," I said, as though the idea had just this moment occurred to me. "Instead of taking *me* to lunch, why don't you take Nancy? Between my workload and following leads in the murder case, I barely have time to sleep. It would cheer Nancy up a lot if you could spend some time with her. Take her to dinner—maybe to a show. It's been months since she's had any fun. When you see her, she can fill you in on the investigation. You might even come up with some brilliant idea nobody else has thought of."

On the other end of the line, Chet was silent for a moment. Then: "You're a good lady," he said softly. His words were a perfect example of an unspoken communication.

"Yeah, yeah. I'm going to run for saint, but if I win I'll demand a recount," I joked. "Go on, call Nancy. Give her something to look forward to."

After we said goodbye, I picked up the Yellow Pages. It was time to buy a black wig.

Chapter 33

AT A QUARTER past twelve the next day, I told Betty that I needed fresh air. "I'm going for a walk and have a hamburger somewhere. Can I bring anything back for you?"

"No, thanks," she said. "Craft Services has Swedish cabbage rolls today. I'm going to fill up a plate and eat lunch with the makeup twins."

I flashed my cell phone at her. "The electronic leash. Call me if there's a crisis." Giving her an affectionate salute, I left the Global Network building and hurried up the street toward the subway entrance at Sixty-sixth and Central Park West.

It was hot and noisy under the city streets. Even in the middle of the day, when the tunnels weren't crammed with people, the odor of sweat was the heaviest perfume in the air, but for traveling long distances around New York City, there's no transportation that's faster or cheaper than the subways. I bought a MetroCard at a vending machine and caught the A train.

There were a few vacant seats in my car as it sped north, but I was too full of nervous energy to sit. I hooked one elbow around a standing pole and watched the stations flash by the subway car's dirty windows.

It took almost half an hour to get to my destination: Dyckman Street, in the Inwood section of the city.

The neighborhood of Inwood, at the northern tip of Manhattan, is one of many small town–type areas in New York City, with schools, a lovely big park, high-rise apartment houses on tree-lined streets, and many local businesses. It was to three of those businesses that I was headed today. I'd chosen to come to Inwood on this shopping trip because no one who worked on the show lived up here, nor did anyone else I knew. The chance of my running into someone who recognized me was about as low as a chance could get.

Using the Yellow Pages, I'd found a wig shop on Dyckman Street. Next, I'd looked up stores that sold the other items I wanted, and found everything within a three-block radius.

Armed with my list of addresses, I made my way through heavy pedestrian traffic on Dyckman until I reached Marilyn's House of Hair. The shop occupied a narrow space between an Italian grocery store and a three-story commercial building with a blue and white sign that advertised the office of a CREDIT DENTIST on the second floor.

Wig stands with painted faces, sporting a variety of hairstyles and colors, filled a shelf in the shop's front window. Propped on a display easel at the end nearest the entrance was a faded eight-by-ten framed publicity photo of Marilyn Monroe.

A little bell jingled over my head as I entered. There were no customers, but a girl with rainbow-streaked hair came through a curtain that screened the front of the store from whatever was in the rear.

Rainbow Hair was about twenty. She stopped within a

few feet of me—close enough to see the pair of little silver rings that pierced her eyebrows, and the silver stud on her chin. In a bored voice, she asked, "Help ya?"

Forcing my eyes away from her face hardware, I said, "I'm looking for a black wig."

"Real hair, or fake?"

"Real."

"We got three styles made with human." She ticked them off on her fingers. "The Snow White model—ya know, like in Disneyland? We got a Diana Ross Afro. An' the Cleopatra. I saw all about Cleopatra on TV. A snake bit her on a boob."

"I'm not superstitious. Let me see the Cleopatra, please."

She removed a wig from a glass case below a display of beaded necklaces, and gestured for me to sit in the chair that faced a tabletop mirror. The Cleopatra looked like it was going to be exactly what I needed: straight black hair, shoulder length, with bangs.

In seconds, the girl had expertly pinned my own hair flat against my scalp and fitted the wig to my head.

The transformation was amazing. When I added the pair of nonprescription eyeglasses I'd bought in a drugstore, I was pretty sure that not even Nancy would recognize me, at least not at first glance. If anyone in Belle Valley, Ohio, ever described me, their details wouldn't match Morgan Tyler.

As I stared at my reflection, the girl asked, "Wha'cha want this for?"

"A costume party."

"Oh, good!" She sounded relieved. "I was afraid you were gonna have chemo an' lose your hair. If that was the problem, then I was gonna recommend a blonde wig, something close to the color of your own hair. That way, nobody would have to know."

Nobody would have to know. In the mirror, I saw genuine concern in the girl's eyes and realized that I'd formed a wrong impression of her. By focusing on the piercings, I hadn't looked for the person beneath the metal. Shame on me.

I paid for the wig in cash. Waiting for a receipt, I asked if she worked on commission. When she said she did, I bought a hundred dollars worth of the beaded necklaces that hung on a Plexiglas stand next to the register.

Back out on Dyckman Street, I went to the end of the block and turned left. My next stop was a store called The Blessed Event, to buy a maternity dress. After I selected one, I'd leave the necklaces in the dressing room, for whoever might like to have them.

Finally, I would go to the hardware store a block farther down for the last two items on my list: a roll of duct tape, and a pair of needle-nose pliers.

Chapter 34

I BEGAN GETTING up at five A.M. instead of six. With a mug of coffee on the right side of my bedroom keyboard and Magic curled up on the left, in easy petting distance, I worked on scripts and new storylines for the show. At six-thirty, I zipped off what I'd written to my office computer and to Betty's, and closed the program.

While I showered, I thought about Walter because I was going to have to lie to him. He'd spent years in law enforcement, seeing through phony stories. I'd have to give a really convincing performance if I was going to succeed in leaving town without sending his "lie meter" flashing.

At seven, dressed and ready for the day—and hiding my nervousness behind a sunny smile—I met Walter in the kitchen for breakfast. Magic, scurrying ahead, jumped up onto the counter and sat next to his can of Natural Balance salmon, swishing his tail. He fixed me with the "open-that-now" stare he'd perfected. I obeyed.

"Good morning," I said—and right away wondered if I was sounded too cheerful.

At the other end of the counter, Walter was whipping eggs with a fork. "Morning."

I removed the top from Magic's salmon, put the food into his dish, and watched as he attacked his breakfast.

"You're getting up pretty early these days," Walter said.

He'd provided an opening for my lie. I yawned, hoping that would disguise any hint of nervousness in my voice. "I've decided to treat myself to a three-day weekend at a spa, so I'm getting ahead on my work. I haven't taken a vacation in three years."

Walter didn't say anything. Because he was facing away from me, I couldn't see his eyes. He slid the beaten eggs into the heated frying pan and reached over to put slices of whole wheat bread into the toaster.

"I'm looking forward to my trip to the spa." Immediately, I regretted saying that. It was one sentence too much. When people lie, they tend to overtalk.

Walter turned and peered at me through the round glasses that, with his spherical face, made him look like an owl. A skeptical owl. "A spa. That one of those places where they make you drink juice made out of grass? You don't need to lose weight."

I busied myself setting the table. "I won't be on the weight-loss program. I just want a weekend of facials, massages, and sleep."

I felt him watching me. A nervous fluttering began in my stomach, and I wondered if he'd had this same effect on the people he'd arrested back in his sheriff days.

"When are you plannin' to go?"

"Friday morning, and I'll be back Sunday night."

The toast popped up. I took the slices out and put them into the silver toast rack on the table. I never thought of myself as a silver toast rack kind of person, but Penny had given it to me last Christmas, and I kept it polished. My one attempt at domestic elegance.

Walter turned off the flame under the eggs and divided them onto our plates.

"You don't mind taking care of Magic while I'm gone, do you?" I asked. "His cupboard is stocked with food, and taped inside the door are the name and number of his veterinarian, Dr. Jeffrey Marks."

"I know where everything is. The little fella and I get along real well."

"I'll keep my cell phone on," I said. "If something breaks in Nancy's case and I'm needed here, I'll come back right away."

"Bobby an' me, and Kent Wayne's people, are still checking out the Boston suspects. It'll probably be awhile before we know anything concrete. You go on your trip."

Eager to change the subject, I said, "At the studio today, I'm going to talk to people who work with Jay Garwood, to see what I can find out."

"Good," Walter said. His tone was pleasant, but his smile was perfunctory: lips only, no eye contact involved. That told me he was somewhere deep in his own thoughts.

WHEN I REACHED the office an hour later, I repeated my lie to Betty.

"You could use a little time to yourself," Betty said. "Sometimes I think you work an eight-day week." She picked up her notebook. "Where will you be?"

I shook my head. "That's my secret. If there's a crisis you or Tommy can't solve, you can get me on my cell. Short of a catastrophe, from Friday morning until Sunday night, I don't want to be bothered."

"I'll be the dragon guarding your cave," Betty said.

Ten scripts for future episodes were waiting for me on

my desk. They'd come in from my staff of associate writers. Going over them, making minor revisions, and rewriting the dialogue where necessary occupied me all morning. It was intense work, and kept me from thinking about where I would really be on this coming Friday night.

At lunchtime, I went looking for Eva Martin. On the days she worked, Eva, who played Sylvia, usually had lunch in her dressing room while she studied her lines.

Her dressing room door was slightly ajar. I knocked.

When Eva called, "Come in," I pushed it all the way open and saw that she was rehearsing with actor Bill Randall, who played Stuart, Sylvia's longtime nemesis on the show. That was a piece of good luck for me. I'd planned to talk to Bill after my chat with Eva. Now I had both of them together. These two actors, who had been on *Love* for twenty years, might be able to tell me something I needed to know.

Eva, "with the movie-star face," to quote an enchanted male magazine writer who rhapsodized about her mature beauty, was in her early fifties. She'd been an actress in Hollywood, doing moderately well playing leads in low-budget films. It wasn't until she moved to New York that she'd found stardom and lasting success in Daytime drama as one of the most beloved characters on *Love of My Life*. As Tommy had remarked one day when we were watching her on-screen, Eva had been wasted in movies; her exquisite face was made for Daytime drama's many lingering close-ups.

Bill, in his late fifties, had dark blond hair that was going silver at the sides. He was attractive in an off-center way; his features would never be described as handsome, but his eyes were so lively and intelligent that the effect made him compelling. Even though Bill played a character with few scruples and a bushel of flaws, he brought such emotional nuances to the role of Stuart that he had acquired many loyal fans.

With his usual courtly manners, Bill Randall stood when I came into the room. As though I were a guest in his home, he began clearing scripts off a chair and said, "Here, please sit down, Morgan."

I thanked him and sat. "I hope I'm not interrupting you two."

"I wish," Eva joked. "Bill and I haven't had a naughty scene with each other since your predecessor turned Sylvia and Stuart into enemies fifteen years ago. *Unfortunately*." She glanced at Bill with a teasing smile. He responded by giving her hand a gentle stroke.

Such strong sexual sparks were flying between them, I was half afraid that if I touched something metal, I'd get an electric shock.

What's going on here?

Two years ago I'd written a story in which she shot him, and it hadn't been an accident. Evil Stuart had hovered between life and death during the February sweeps, and then recovered, much to the delight of the viewers. Those same viewers also felt that Sylvia, who was the show's ultimate "good woman," had been right to put a bullet in him.

Since I'd been with the show, I'd only seen an easy professional comradeship between Eva and Bill, but now their attraction to each other was unmistakable. Watching them gave me an idea for a storyline that would shake up the lives of both their characters. Because Sylvia and Stuart were separately connected to so many of *Love*'s other contract players, this new plot twist could affect, to some degree, nearly everyone in the cast.

I said, "After all these years that Sylvia and Stuart have been enemies, I think I'll create an event that brings you together as lovers."

"Eva's a joy to work with," Bill said enthusiastically.

Eva squealed with delight. Bill folded one of her hands into his and beamed at me. "Is that what you came to talk to us about?" she asked.

"Actually, I just wanted to compliment you on the beautiful work you've been doing with Jay Garwood."

"The brother and sister reunion scenes were great!" Eva said. "As soon as I read them, I knew you were the one who wrote our dialogue."

I thanked her for the compliment, but I needed to get to the point of my visit. "How do you like working with Jay?"

Eva and Bill exchanged a quick glance. Awkward silence.

"What? Please be honest with me. I won't repeat what you say, but I really need to know if there's any reason you're concerned about him."

" 'Concerned' is too strong a word," Eva said.

"It's just that he can be a bit annoying sometimes," Bill told me. "For weeks he was bragging about not needing this 'soap' job much longer because he expected to marry a rich woman."

"Jay's a little full of himself, but he's on time and knows his lines," Eva said. "When he was on the show before he was sometimes . . . difficult."

"How?" I asked.

"He made fun of the dialogue and would improvise during taping," Bill said. "It was hard to play scenes with him. I'm theater-trained—we don't make up our own lines."

"But Jay's behaving better now," Eva said. "More respectful of other actors."

Bill gave a short, mirthless laugh. "Being out of work for ten years certainly improved his conduct. Jay's not a guy I want to have a beer with, but I don't know anybody on the show who has a serious beef with him."

Trying to make the question sound casual, I asked, "How does he behave around the kids in the cast?"

Eva shrugged. "He pretty much ignores them."

Bill asked, "Do you mean does he use vulgar language when they're around?"

"That . . . or behave in any other way that might seem inappropriate."

Both Eva and Bill shook their heads. "No. I can't remember him even talking to the kids," Eva said.

"Has one of those dreadful stage mothers complained about him?"

I assured Bill that nothing like that had happened. "Please don't say anything about this conversation. I wouldn't want false rumors to start."

Bill raised his right hand, as though swearing to tell the truth. "Not a word."

Eva's eyes suddenly widened and she gasped. "Oh, Lord—you don't think he's got a sick thing for kids!"

"Absolutely not," I lied. "Forget I asked anything about Jay." I regretted starting this conversation because if Garwood didn't do what I'd suspected, my questions could destroy his reputation in a way that could never be repaired.

To steer them in another direction, I told Bill, "While Stuart's arguing with Sylvia today, look at her with just a hint of softness in your eyes."

Bill nodded. A good actor, he understood how to communicate with his eyes.

"What should I do?" Eva asked.

"Play it exactly as you are now. Be angry with Stuart. Let what happens in a few weeks come as a complete surprise to Sylvia."

I left two happy actors to go back to their rehearsing.

Outside in the corridor I had to admit to myself that I'd made a serious mistake with my theory that Garwood had killed Veronica Rose. Bill and Eva, who knew him well professionally, and Garwood's ex-wife, who knew him better than anyone, had said essentially the same thing: that he had his faults, but an inappropriate interest in minors was not one of them.

I wanted to kick myself. In flashing red neon lights it was obvious now that I'd misinterpreted Didi's violent reaction to the mention of Garwood's name. By listening to my emotions instead of using my brain, I'd made a dazzling leap to the wrong conclusion.

Apparently, Garwood thought of Veronica Rose as his "golden goose." If he hadn't done anything that would make her threaten to have him arrested, then he had no motive for killing her. Without a motive, I couldn't offer Garwood to the police as an alternative to Nancy.

I was back to square one in the investigation.

Chapter 35

THURSDAY AFTERNOON I phoned Nancy, Penny, and Matt and told them my going-to-a-spa story. Nancy and Penny told me to have fun. Matt wanted me to hurry back.

Thursday night, after Walter went to sleep in his room, I took the emergency sewing kit out of my bureau drawer and did some needlework. It wasn't artistic, but it was creative.

First, I sewed strips of Velcro onto the edges of two sides of the round throw pillow I'd bought to wear beneath the maternity dress.

Next, with the homemade straps attached, I slit the seam at the bottom of the pillow, stuck my hand inside, and with my fingers made a cavity in the stuffing. The hiding place prepared, I took the Glock 19 out of the drawer of my bedside table, removed the magazine, ejected the bullets, and snapped the empty magazine back into the pistol.

I have a premises permit for the 9-mm automatic. It's legal for me to keep it in the apartment for self-protection, but I'm not allowed to carry it concealed. That regulation was only one of several laws I planned to break during the next three days.

My Glock—black, almost eight inches long, and eighty-three percent steel—could be spotted on a security X-ray machine. It wouldn't pass unseen through properly monitored metal detectors, either, but I wasn't worried about it being discovered. I'd worked out a way to cross four state lines without going through any security checkpoints.

I slipped the automatic pistol inside the pillow, repositioned the stuffing so that it cushioned the piece, then restitched the seam.

Placing the pillow against my stomach, I attached the Velcro straps so that they gripped around my back. The Glock, unloaded, but with the magazine in it, weighed about a pound and a half. I spent a couple of minutes bending, stretching, and reaching out to the sides, replicating movements a person would make in the course of normal activities. The pillow stayed in place.

Next, I took the fifteen rounds I'd ejected from the Glock's magazine and opened a thick old copy of *A Tale of Two Cities*. Halfway into the story, I'd hollowed out a well in the pages. Now I dropped the bullets into the created space, stuffed enough cotton balls around to keep them from clicking against each other, closed the book, and shook it. No sound from the ammunition. I wrapped the book in bright gift paper and tied it with a ribbon.

Finally, I wrote a goodbye note to Walter, apologizing for not seeing him before I left, but explaining that I hadn't wanted to wake him. I reminded him that I'd be home Sunday evening.

FRIDAY MORNING I got up at four A.M. That was too early for Magic. As I eased out of bed, the little furry heating pad who slept curled up next to me opened his eyes, blinked, yawned, and went back to sleep.

I took the world's quietest shower, and dressed in black cotton slacks, black running shoes, and a loose, safari-style navy blue cotton jacket that would conceal the money belt I fastened around my waist. It had twenty thousand dollars in cash in it—more than I thought I'd need, but allowing for unexpected problems. I had another six thousand dollars, mostly in hundreds, in my wallet, along with my fake "Charlotte Brown" driver's license displayed in the wallet's plastic window. That done, I folded the piece of paper I'd torn from the *Daily News* classified ads, and shoved it into the pocket of my jacket.

Taking an old tote bag from the closet, I stuffed in the maternity dress, the "baby bump" pillow with the automatic pistol inside, the black wig, glasses, the roll of duct tape, the needle-nose pliers, and a flashlight with fresh batteries. On top of these items, I added underwear, socks, and a toothbrush, paste, the lock pick I'd taken from the studio property room, and the gift-wrapped book that concealed fifteen rounds of 9-mm ammunition.

I left the note to Walter on the kitchen table, and slipped out of the apartment.

TWENTY MINUTES LATER, the woman who emerged from an all-night diner's restroom carrying my tote bag looked nothing like me. *She*—Charlotte Brown—had shoulder-length black hair with bangs, wore glasses, and, in her dowdy green maternity dress, appeared to be about seven months pregnant. The weight of the automatic pistol in the pillow strapped against my stomach reminded me to move with the abdomen-first walk of a genuinely pregnant woman.

At six A.M., my subway car pulled into the 191st Street Station in upper Manhattan and I got off.

In spite of the nagging voice of reason that kept telling me to go home—I had come to buy the last item I needed for my trip into the distant past.

Chapter 36

I'D MADE AN appointment with a woman on West 190th Street for seven o'clock this morning. I couldn't show up an hour early, so I found a diner in the neighborhood and ordered breakfast.

A middle-aged waitress with dyed platinum hair and lipstick that reached beyond the natural shape of her mouth didn't want to serve me coffee.

"You're pregnant," she said.

"I'm allowed two cups a day," I replied. Firmly.

She picked up the pot with the orange plastic lip. "Okay, then decaf."

I clamped my hands over my cup. "No—*caf*."

She moved the decaf pot away, but she was still reluctant. "Do you smoke cigarettes, or drink?"

"Not a puff. Not a drop," I assured her. "Now, please, *I want that coffee.*"

Something in my caffeine-deprived attitude told her not to mess with me this morning. She poured from the "strong-stuff" urn, and I ordered orange juice, scrambled eggs, and crisp bacon.

"Take the fresh fruit instead of the hash browns," she said. "It's better for the baby."

Having triumphed in the caffeine battle, I agreed to have the fruit with my eggs. Smirking like a winner, she headed for the kitchen to place my order.

Because I'd never been pregnant, it hadn't occurred to me before, but now I wondered about something. How did the millions and millions of people whose mothers smoked cigarettes and drank alcohol, whose mothers ate fried potatoes instead of fresh fruit, who drank coffee and water that wasn't bottled—or, heaven help them, drank water that came from a *tap*—how did all of those people grow up to be healthy and productive? And how did generations before our current age of enlightenment survive while breathing in secondhand smoke and eating red meat and white sugar?

The waitress brought my breakfast, and it was very good. She even refilled my coffee cup—after I'd asked her twice.

AT EXACTLY SEVEN A.M., I stood at the entrance to an apartment building on West 190th Street and pressed the bell button next to the name "Harrison."

A woman's voice answered the buzz. "Hello? Who is it?"

"Mrs. Harrison? We spoke on the phone yesterday. I'm here about the car you're selling."

"Oh, yes. It's the second one past the fire hydrant—the gray Buick Skylark. Take a look. I'll be right down."

The ad in the paper had said the car was a 1998. I couldn't tell one year from another, but it didn't matter. The paint on the car was a bit faded, there were a few little nicks and scratches but no distinctive marks that might cause someone to remember it. I examined the tires. The tread on them was worn, but the tires weren't bald. They would serve me well enough for as long as I needed them.

"What do you think?" The woman had come up behind me while I was running my fingers over the surface of the tires.

I stood up. "It looks pretty good."

"Hi, I'm Adele Harrison." She was in her fifties, with a narrow frame and a head that was a little large for her body. Her brown hair was cut short and shot through with gray. Her complexion was pitted with old acne scars, but her eyes were lovely: large and pale blue, with naturally thick lashes.

"I'm Charlotte Brown," I said. Gesturing to the car, I asked, "Why are you selling?"

"It was my husband's. He passed away last year. I wanted to keep it, but I just can't afford the insurance any longer. It's in good condition."

"What's the mileage?"

"Seventy-nine thousand and something. My husband worked in New Jersey and drove it to and from work. He bought it new, and said it was the most reliable car he'd ever had." Her voice full of sarcasm, she added, "When they stopped making Skylarks, he said it was because they were too good, that people kept them longer than the car people wanted."

I nodded as a signal of shared irritation. "It's like lipstick. As soon as I find a shade I like, they stop making it."

"That's the truth! Let's drive around the neighborhood."

Adele Harrison took a key from her pocket and unlocked the driver's side. She flipped the button that unlocked the other doors. "Get in," she said, as she walked around to the passenger side. "You can see how it drives."

I piloted the Skylark up one street and down another without detecting any problems. It was a simple basic car, and operated smoothly.

"Your husband must have taken good care of it," I said.

"Oh, he did. He had the oil changed every three thousand miles."

When we got back to her apartment house, we saw that her old parking spot had been claimed by a new Honda. I eased the Buick into the space in front of the fire hydrant.

"How much do you want?" I asked.

"Well . . . my brother said it was worth six thousand dollars . . ." She stated this so hesitantly, I was sure she didn't believe what she was saying, but instead was trying to trick me into paying an inflated price.

According to the used car ads, other vehicles of this age and type, with lower mileage, were being offered at four thousand, sometimes less. I was willing to let her think she was taking advantage of me, because I didn't want the paperwork trail there would be if I went to a dealer.

Although I was prepared to overpay, I didn't want to raise her suspicions by seeming too eager. "That's a little higher than I'd hoped." I heaved a sigh of regret.

From her sudden frown of concern, I guessed she was afraid of losing the sale. "How much can you spend?"

"Fifty-eight hundred is really as high as I can go," I said. "But I brought cash."

An instant smile lighted her face. "Okay. If that's all you've got, I'll let you have it for fifty-eight hundred, in cash."

Adele Harrison pulled the key out of the ignition and practically leaped out of the passenger seat. "The pink slip is upstairs—I'll go get it." Her greed apparently blinded her to the possibility that I might have an ulterior motive for overpaying.

I took fifty-eight hundred dollars out of my wallet. When she returned, I counted the money into her hand. She gave me the key to the Skylark and turned over the pink slip.

"I signed on the back," she said, showing me that she'd

transferred ownership. "I'm going to cancel the insurance this morning so I don't have to keep paying."

Now that she had the money I'm sure she didn't care what I did. For the sake of the charade, I assured her that I would register the car in my name and buy my own insurance right away.

Just as I put the key in the ignition, she asked, "When are you due?"

I had been ready for that question ever since I decided on this phony pregnancy disguise. "Late August." To be polite, I added, "Do you have children?"

"Two. They're both grown. Enjoy them while they're little—you never know how they'll turn out." Her voice held a note of melancholy.

I thanked her for the advice and drove away.

After filling the Skylark's gas tank, I headed south toward the George Washington Bridge, to begin my 445-mile trip to Belle Valley. Unless the car broke down, I'd be there by late this afternoon.

I wasn't worried that either Adele Harrison or the waitress in the coffee shop would remember me, because by late tonight, "Charlotte Brown" would cease to exist.

And I would be taking the greatest risk of my life.

Chapter 37

THERE IS NOTHING "belle" about Belle Valley, Ohio, and it isn't in a valley. It is a depressed—and depressing—town strewn carelessly across a dusty plain. From the deteriorating cluster of buildings I saw behind a sagging chain-link fence, the town had once been host to a large manufacturing plant, but the factory had been boarded up and abandoned. Belle Valley is nearly as dead.

I thought about what I'd learned when I Googled Belle Valley, Ohio, from the library computer. Land area: 1.9 square miles. Population as of two years ago: 4,759. That was down 17.2 percent from the previous census. Twelve percent were unemployed. Median annual household income: $19,390. Median house value: $41,100.

The crime stats were especially interesting to me. During the past three years, there had been no murders in Belle Valley, but there had been 20 rapes, 198 assaults, 71 burglaries, and 409 auto thefts. My conclusion was that it was relatively safe to walk through this town at night, but that it was dangerous to leave a car unattended.

I drove slowly around Belle Valley's outer limits, and then along streets dotted with fast-food stops, mini-markets, and liquor stores.

Driving in an ever-shrinking square grid, I noticed small houses with yellowing lawns, a few kids on skateboards, tired-looking men and women coming home from work. On the patchy athletic field next to Belle Valley High School, boys were playing baseball while girls, giggling together, watched from one section of the old bleachers.

Block by block, I drew closer to Webster Street, where Ray Wilson lived.

As the afternoon waned and shadows deepened, I slowly passed number 404 Webster Street, and observed that Bobby's use of the word "house" had been an exaggeration. The monster's place was little more than a shack. There was no vehicle parked in front of it or in the oil-stained, cracked concrete driveway on the left side.

On my second turn around the block, I stopped in front of number 404. While pretending to consult a map, I studied as much as I could see of the structure.

Single story. Constructed of concrete blocks visible through a layer of stucco that had flaked off in large chunks. Concrete was a good material for my purposes; it contained sound better than did wood.

A pair of windows bracketed the front door. The one on the right was boarded up with plywood. On the left, the view inside was hidden behind a shade pulled down to an inch above the sill. No light shone through that crack. Between the lack of a vehicle near the place, and no interior lights turned on, it didn't seem that Ray Wilson was at home.

As far as I was concerned, this hovel did have one very attractive feature: a hatchlike door on the left side, just aboveground. I guessed that it led down into a cellar. There was a window just above it. No light was coming from that portal, either.

If I could get into the house through the cellar, it would eliminate the risk of using the lock pick on one of the doors, where I might more easily be spotted.

Not wanting to call attention to myself by sitting in the car any longer, and possibly raising the suspicions of someone who lived in a nearby house, I folded the map and drove away.

It wasn't very far to the edge of town, where earlier I had passed a diner called the Blue Fox. There was a faded painting of a fox—red, not blue—on the sign outside. I hadn't eaten since breakfast and needed nourishment. On the drive from New York I had only stopped for coffee.

The small lot in front of the Blue Fox Diner was half full when I pulled into it at fifteen minutes after six P.M. I pushed open the door and entered a brightly lighted rectangle with a twelve-seat counter and eight booths. Elvis Presley's voice singing "Are You Lonesome Tonight" flowed from a jukebox.

The booths nearest the entrance were occupied, as were three of the counter seats. The booths were upholstered in yellow vinyl, torn over the years in many places. Rips in the fabric had been repaired using black masking tape.

Yellow and black. The diner should have been called the Bumble Bee instead of the Blue Fox.

As soon as I took the first breath inside, I was assailed by the smell of hamburgers grilling. Normally, it's an odor that alerts my salivary glands to be ready for action, but this evening it made me feel a little nauseated. I wondered if it was the power of suggestion, because I was disguised as a pregnant woman.

No. I'm queasy because of what I've come to this town to do.

A teenage waitress with short, curly black hair and a name tag that said "Violet" must have seen some indication of distress because she came over to me with a concerned frown on her face.

"You feel okay?" she asked.

"Oh, yes," I said brightly. "Just the smell of the meat . . ."

Looking at my protruding tummy, she nodded. "I know what that's like. When I was pregnant with my first, the smell of eggs cooking made me puke!"

When *she* was pregnant? Her *first*? Up close, she seemed to be about fifteen, but she had to be older than she looked.

"Come on. I'll put you where you don't smell the burgers."

Violet led me to the farthest table from the kitchen. It was empty, but still had dirty dishes on it from the previous occupant.

"Can you squeeze in?" she asked, as she gathered up the used crockery and utensils.

I maneuvered into the booth, with a couple of inches to spare. Mercifully, I couldn't smell the grill from here.

"Thanks," I said.

She deposited the dishes at the end of the counter, returned, and wiped the surface of the table clean with a damp cloth. "What can you eat, without going upchuck?"

"This is my first pregnancy," I said. "What do you suggest?"

"How 'bout a milk shake? They kept me going. I'll make it real thick."

"That sounds good," I said. "Chocolate, please."

Violet returned a few minutes later with a glass the size of a flower vase; she used both hands to carry it. A straw was sticking up from the middle of her chocolate concoction. It resembled a flagpole anchored in cement.

"This *is* thick!" I said. Too thick, it turned out, to suck through the straw. I ate her delicious ice cream and milk creation with a spoon.

After consuming the world's thickest shake and paying the bill, with a generous tip added, I again drove slowly past 404 Webster Street.

The first thing I saw were the flickering lights from a television set, visible through the inch of space below the window shade. Someone was home.

The next thing I noticed struck me like a blow to the stomach. Parked in the driveway was a van. Old and dirty, like the one the monster had when Walter found me. That van of my nightmares had been light gray; this one was a dark color, had patches of primer paint on the back, and one rear tire was missing its hubcap. Worse than the familiar silhouette was the fact that in this vehicle, too, the windows were blacked out.

Terrible memories of being weak and helpless came flooding back.

For a moment I thought I might heave up everything I'd swallowed for the last six months, but I fought down the urge to retch and drove on.

You're a grown-up now, I told myself. *Tonight you will have a 9-mm automatic—and the element of surprise.*

Breathing deeply to calm my racing pulse, I steered the car around the corner to Franklin and up to Cook Street, which ran parallel to Webster, on the north. In my earlier reconnoitering, I'd noticed a motel on Cook that had a VACANCY sign. It was in the block just beyond 404 Webster.

Two cars were parked in front of the line of ten cabins that comprised the Happy Hours Motel. A rusting marquee advertised cable TV. The T in TV was missing.

In the motel's tiny office, I registered as Charlotte Brown and paid in cash for two nights, even though I had no intention of staying that long.

The motel manager was a thin, elderly man. Nearly toothless. What little hair he had shot upward from his mottled scalp in odd little outcroppings.

I said, "I don't like to park next to other people. They

always seem to bang their doors into mine and chip the paint, so I'd like the cabin at the end of the row."

The manager shrugged, shot a stream of dark liquid from his mouth into a metal basket behind the desk, and wordlessly handed me the key to room number 10.

THE MOTEL HAD been dark for more than an hour, and I didn't hear any sounds coming from the two other occupied cabins. Without turning on the light, I dressed again in my black slacks and navy blue safari jacket and fastened the money belt around my waist. In the deep left side pocket of the jacket I put the lock pick, the roll of duct tape, and the needle-nose pliers. The flashlight was stuck in the waistband of my slacks. In my pants pocket, my cell phone was set on vibrate.

The Glock rested in the right-hand pocket of my jacket, loaded with a full fifteen-round clip. It felt comforting, there against my hip.

Chapter 38

AT FIFTEEN MINUTES before two A.M., I slipped out of my room at the Happy Hours into the humid late June night. Way off on a distant highway, I heard an eighteen-wheeler roar by the dot on the map that is Belle Valley. During the two minutes I waited in the shadows, only three cars sped past the motel.

Leaving the Skylark parked in front of my door, I moved swiftly down Cook Street to the corner, and turned south on Franklin toward Webster.

The sidewalks in this little patch of the town were deserted, and the houses mostly dark. Only about one in three streetlights were working, creating eddies of glimmer and eddies of gloom.

At the corner of Franklin and Webster, shards of glass crunched beneath my running shoes. I saw that the globe above my head had been smashed. The milk-colored spheres on the other streetlights were intact; the bulbs inside the darkened ones must have burned out. I'd observed such a feeling of apathy in Belle Valley that I wondered if anyone who lived on the street had bothered to call the power company to report the dead lights. Maybe someone had phoned, and was put on eternal hold, still waiting to speak to a human being.

While driving around this afternoon, I saw that everywhere I looked there were manifestations of defeat, an attitude of "why bother." It was in the faces of the residents, in the poor maintenance of their homes and streets and public buildings.

There was a working streetlight at the corner of Franklin and Webster, but the rest of the block where the monster slept was dark.

Being careful to walk quietly and stay in the shadows, I reached number 404 Webster. No longer was there a sliver of flickering light from a television set coming through the crack below the front window shade. The decrepit van was still parked in the driveway. It didn't look as though it had moved since I'd cruised by hours earlier.

On one side of 404 there was a small vacant lot, overgrown with weeds and littered with junk, apparently the neighborhood dumping ground. On the other side, separated by approximately thirty feet of dirt and dying vegetation, was number 406 Webster. It was a single-story cracker box, only marginally more well cared for than the place I was about to break into.

A window on the side of 406 faced the yard. My greatest danger—on the outside, at any rate—was that someone in 406 might pass the window and see me opening the hatchlike cellar door into 404.

Crouched in the darkness beside my objective, I waited. And listened . . .

The street was quiet. Not even a radio or TV playing near enough to hear.

The glowing dial on my watch told me it was ten minutes after two A.M. I'd calculated that by this hour, Ray

Wilson should be in deepest sleep, and most likely to be caught unawares. At least, that was the plan.

I crept to the cellar hatch, stepping cautiously, keeping my breathing shallow and silent. My eyes were becoming accustomed to the darkness so that I could make out the shapes of objects, if not details.

There was a rusty padlock on the hatch. Damn! I would have to use the lock pick on a door after all. But as I ran my fingers over the rough metal I realized that the lock wasn't locked. Maybe there was too much rust, or Ray Wilson forgot to press the arm into the mechanism. I didn't care why. The only thing that mattered was that I would be able to get into the cellar.

I ran my fingers all the way around the cellar door and found no other obstacle. Without making a sound, I removed the padlock from the metal strap of the hasp and placed it on the ground. Grasping the edge of the wood with both hands, I eased the door up an inch.

Creak . . .

I stood still, and silently counted to sixty.

Nothing stirred on Webster Street, but I couldn't risk more noise from a corroded hinge. I would have given a thousand dollars for a can of WD 40, but when you don't have what you need, you improvise.

Holding the door in place with one hand, I used an old photographer's trick that Ian had taught me years ago in Africa. Before digital cameras, it was something we did to clean 35-mm negatives for printing when we had to work fast and under primitive conditions, without luxuries like dust-free cloths. I took my thumb and index finger and rubbed them on either side of my nostrils, making "nose grease," then massaged my homemade lubricant into the hinges. It took four applications, and I'd had to add some saliva, but it worked. I could open the door hatch, without it creaking, far enough so that I could squeeze inside.

Lying flat along the edge of the opening, with the cellar's

cover resting on my back, I managed to pull the flashlight from my waistband, point it into the blackness below, and press the switch.

The narrow tunnel of light showed me that I was staring into what had once been a storage cellar for coal. There were still a few black lumps of the anthracite scattered along the floor. This hatch had been used for delivery of the coal; the chute was still in place. A truck would back up to the hatch and dump the coal down the chute and into the cellar, to be burned in a furnace and keep the place warm during harsh Ohio winters.

There was nothing near the opening that I could use to descend into the cellar, so I maneuvered my legs and rear onto the chute and started to slide. It was filthy, but that old chute saved me from having to jump down a good ten feet and chance breaking an ankle. In the unlikely event that I began to make a habit of breaking and entering, I'd be sure to bring a rappelling rope and hook, just in case.

At the end of the chute, I landed on the cellar floor with a thump. Not too loud, but I switched off the flashlight, crouched into the damp darkness and listened.

No sound from above.

While I counted slowly to 120, I tried to keep my breathing shallow because of the basement's unpleasant stench. It smelled of rats.

Like the odor from a hostile skunk, the stink of rats is unmistakable, and impossible to forget. I hadn't encountered that smell since Walter rescued me twenty-four years ago, but I recognized it instantly. This time the experience was different, because I was different. Tonight I was repelled, but I wasn't afraid. At least, I wasn't afraid of the four-legged vermin on Webster Street.

After two minutes with no sound of movement from above, I stood up, clicked on the flashlight again, and examined the contents of the basement. There was an ancient furnace with the door hanging half off, several sagging cardboard boxes without tops. Newspapers and old clothes spilled out of them. In front of the boxes was a wooden kitchen chair. It lay on its side, with one of the back legs broken off.

Tipped up against a wall, I saw the frame of a single bed. Carefully, quietly, I pulled it down to rest on its four legs.

The bed had no mattress, only the metal frame and coiled springs. I reached into my left-hand pocket for the roll of duct tape. Assuming that I survived my first encounter with Ray Wilson this morning, I wanted to be ready for the second.

With as little sound as possible, I tore strips of tape from the roll into twelve-inch lengths and attached several strips to each of the four corners of the bed.

When I finished the preparations, I turned away—and accidentally kicked an empty gasoline can. My misstep sent it rattling and banging across the basement's concrete floor. To my ears, it sounded as loud as a clash of cymbals.

I heard movement upstairs in the house. The flesh on the back of my neck prickled with fear.

Chapter 39

I DUCKED BEHIND the furnace and pressed my back against the wall as footsteps shuffled across the floor above my head. They were coming from the left, from the back of the little house. I guessed that was where his bedroom was, and that the noise had awakened him.

Bad news for me. I'd wanted to catch him while he was asleep.

At the top of the stairs, the doorknob turned. The door *screeched* open and a man croaked out a stream of curses. His voice was hoarse and raspy. Even though I hadn't heard it for twenty-four years, I recognized that voice. A chill knifed through me. Not more than twenty feet away stood the man from my nightmares.

A light switch clicked on, and the center of the basement was illuminated by a weak bulb dangling from the ceiling on a frayed cord. It cut a few inches into the shadows outside its light radius, but it didn't touch the darkness behind the furnace.

He spewed more curses, followed by the word "rats."

He thought the noise had been caused by the reeking, four-legged residents of the cellar, and not by a two-legged invader. The noise hadn't made him suspicious. That was vital, if I was going to succeed in what I had driven more than four hundred miles to do.

I couldn't see him from where I was, but I didn't hear any footsteps descending. Another tense moment, then the light was switched off and the cellar door closed.

Still in my hiding place, I waited and listened until I heard shambling footsteps, going away. But this time they were moving right, toward the front of the house. He was not returning to bed.

The sounds of movement stopped. When I was sure it was safe, I turned on my flashlight and came out from behind the furnace. The first thing my beam caught was two glowing red eyes, staring at me. I gasped. But the rat must have been more frightened of me than I was of him, because he scurried away into a hiding place of his own.

Taking a few deep breaths slowed my racing pulse.

I moved the flashlight around until I found the broken kitchen chair. It was old, and constructed from solid wood. I picked up the detached back leg and hefted it. Used as a cudgel, it was heavy enough to do some damage, if that became necessary. I didn't want to discharge my 9-mm pistol upstairs and chance waking up neighbors who might call the police. The Glock 19 isn't a popgun.

Before I went upstairs, I had to find something that would quiet those door hinges. Swinging the light along the shelves on the wall, I examined the usual tools and jars found in practically every cellar and garage, looking for WD 40. There wasn't any, but I did find a dirty old oilcan. Taking it down, I shook it. There was a little oil inside. Not much, but maybe just enough.

With the chair leg clamped under my arm and the oilcan in my hand, I crept up the stairs. I was careful to place my feet on the opposite sides of each plank, to avoid the noise made when a person puts a foot in the middle of an old wooden step. I couldn't risk having him hear a creak on the stairs because that was a sound a rat could not have made.

For a moment, it was like being back in Africa with Ian, sneaking through the bush to get wildlife pictures. It's not true that stepping on a twig will spook an animal, because that's a sound that other animals can make. Nothing alarming about that. I had to learn to cradle my cameras in my arms and against my chest in a way that kept metal from touching metal. A metallic *clink* was one sound no animal could make. It could send a herd into a stampede, or frighten away a lone creature we'd spent hours tracking.

At the top of the stairs I pressed an ear against the crack, and listened.

He was coughing, the kind of deep, wheezing cough that seemed to heave up from the soles of his feet. That was definitely coming from the direction of the living room. When the coughing subsided, I heard voices.

My heart sank at the thought that he wasn't alone, but as my hearing grew more acute, I realized that he'd only turned on the TV. Fervently, I hoped that the set was placed so that his back was to the basement door.

In the darkness, I used my fingers to trace a path to the noisy hinges. I shook drops of oil onto them. In a few seconds, the can was empty.

I put the oilcan down at the far edge of the top step and . . . very carefully . . . turned the handle on the basement door.

An inch at a time, I eased the door open. Thanks to the precious oil, there was only a tiny squeak, and it was drowned out by the soundtrack laughter coming from the television set. I stood still against the door on the cellar side for a few seconds, then, hefting the broken chair leg, I stepped into the house.

I was in a small kitchen. Shapes of a stove and sink and

refrigerator were faintly visible, courtesy of a feeble night-light plugged into an outlet on the back wall.

Through the half-opened door to the living room, I made out the shape of a big chair with a high, rounded back. Probably a recliner. It faced a TV set which was spilling light around it.

Before my mind processed the fact that I didn't see the top of a head in that chair, an arm shot out and caught me around the throat. He *had* realized someone was in the cellar. Like a wary animal used to being hunted, he'd lurked in the darkness, waiting to spring at whoever appeared.

The chair leg and flashlight clattered to the floor as I tried to pry his arm away, but his other hand was clamped around his wrist. It was like pulling at cement. With the side of his head pressed against mine, I was forced to breathe the foul alcoholic fumes coming from his mouth. His forearm was squeezing my neck so hard I was afraid he'd crush my larynx!

Exploding with primal fury, I twisted my torso, trying to jerk him off balance. The hand that anchored his wrist slipped just enough for me to make one desperate maneuver. I torpedoed my left elbow into his chest so hard I heard a rib crack! It broke his grip. Reverberation from the blow I landed sent a spike of pain up into my shoulder, but I was so crazed by the rush of adrenaline that it barely registered.

He uttered a sharp, wounded grunt, then straightened up and grabbed at me again. Using a self-defense action that Matt Phoenix had taught me, I rammed the heel of my right hand up under his nose. His head snapped backward and blood spurted from his nostrils. With a gurgling cry, he fell to the floor, hit his head . . . and lay still.

Standing over him, pointing the pistol at one of his knees, and taking air in deep gasps, my mind began to clear. The bright red veil of madness dissolved from in front of my eyes.

I stared down at the crumpled figure on the floor.

He had seemed so much bigger when I was small.

That was my first thought. My second was, *Dear God, please don't let me have killed him!*

After giving him a kick in the side, sharp enough to prove he really was unconscious and not faking, I knelt down and felt at the base of his throat for a pulse.

There was a beat. He was alive.

I switched on the light at the top of the cellar stairs, shoved the flashlight into my pocket, and picked up the broken chair leg. Clasping the weapon beneath one arm, I used both hands to grab Ray Wilson by the collar of his shirt. One step at a time, I dragged him down into his rat-infested basement.

Chapter 40

RAY WILSON STIRRED, and awoke to find his mouth shut with duct tape and his body spread-eagled. His wrists and ankles were fastened securely—very securely—to the four edges of the metal bed.

And then he saw me standing over him, with a pair of needle-nose pliers in one hand and a Glock 19 in the other.

Wilson's eyes popped wide open. He struggled to speak and struggled against his bonds. I let him go at it until the effort exhausted him. When he realized it was futile, he stopped trying to wrench himself free.

"That's better." Frightening people wasn't something I was used to doing, so I imitated a scary character I'd created for the kidnapping-of-Jillian storyline we did a couple of years ago. In a menacing tone, I said, "Now you understand that you can't get away."

Guttural sounds from his throat.

"Are you asking what I'm going to do to you? You're helpless and alone. I can do any terrible thing. Unless you give me what I want, this will not be a pleasant experience."

He began struggling again. I leaned in close and waved the Glock in front of his face. He stopped moving.

I had taken away his shoes while he was unconscious. His feet were dirty, and about as revolting as feet could be, but I made myself do it because it was important that he feel completely vulnerable.

Moving down to the end of the bed, to his exposed soles, I trailed the barrel of the pistol from his heel up to his toes. His body began to tremble.

Straightening, I told him, "I'm not going to shoot you . . . yet. I want something from you. If you don't give it to me, in a little while you'll be begging for a bullet in the head."

I had to steel myself so that I wouldn't gag on the next bit of business I'd planned. Waving the pliers in front of him, I moved next to his midsection and pointed the nasty-looking implement down toward the zipper on his pants.

A primitive gurgle of terror came from deep in his throat as I grasped the metal tab with the tip of the pliers and started to pull the zipper down.

"It won't do any good to try to scream. No one can hear you." Before I'd undone his pants more than an inch—I hadn't planned to go more than *two* inches—he wet himself.

Suddenly an awful stench assailed my nostrils. He had done more than simply urinate.

Ewww, gross! Revolting. He's soiled himself, and I have to smell it. The good news is that he's probably ready to talk now, and I hadn't given him so much as a pinch with the pliers. Of course, his nose looks broken, and I heard one of his ribs crack in our struggle, but he started that fight. I'd never intended to make him bleed. My plan was to surprise him while he was asleep and force him downstairs by poking the Glock in his back.

I admit that years ago I'd fantasized about hurting him physically, but I knew that I would never have been able to do it, except in self-defense. I'd suffered at his hands, but it hadn't turned me into someone who could inflict physical pain on purpose. Bluffing was my game. It was time to see if my bluff would win the pot.

"You've got information I want."

He shook his head violently.

Tears rolled down his sallow, sunken cheeks, coursing through the rough stubble of beard. Just as I remembered, his shoulders were wide, but below his short-sleeved shirt, I saw that his flesh was loose, and creped with age. Beneath his tan cotton trousers, his legs looked thin, but there was a roll of flab around his waist. He'd lost most of his greasy brown hair. In spite of some changes in his appearance, I had not a fraction of a doubt that this miserable, weeping coward was the man from whom Walter had rescued me.

"You have one way out of this situation, and that's to tell me what I want to know."

He stopped moving and stared up at me, a flicker of hope in his eyes.

"Think of this encounter of ours as a TV game show. You give me the right answers—and you'll win your life." I let that sink in, then added, "But if you lie to me . . ." I snapped the tips of the pliers together a few times and was satisfied to see him flinch.

"I believe we understand each other well enough to start the game." I ejected the clip from my pistol and showed it to him. "See. Full magazine. Fifteen rounds. If I have to shoot you, I'm going to start with your knees." I snapped the clip back into the Glock.

"I'm going to take the tape off your mouth so you can talk, but if you lie, or try to scream, I'll shoot you in the knees. You'll be in terrible agony, but you'll still be able to talk. Tell the truth, or you'll never be able to walk again. It's your choice."

Keeping the Glock aimed at his knees, I leaned down and ripped the tape from his mouth. He licked his lips, swallowed several times, and gulped in air. But he didn't yell.

"What do you want to know?" His voice was a hoarse whisper.

"Twenty-four years ago, in Downsville, West Virginia, the sheriff found a little girl in the back of your van."

He stared at me, wide-eyed. His lips moved, but no sound came out. I think he guessed who I was. Fresh tears glistened in his eyes. Fresh fear.

"Who was that child?"

"I don't know."

"Wrong answer." I aimed the Glock at his right kneecap.

"No—don't! What I mean—I never knew her real name. I got the kid from the mother."

Muscles in my stomach clenched, but I ignored the sudden ache. "Tell me," I said. Those words came out of my mouth, but the voice sounded like that of a stranger.

"She was a real good-looking hooker—" The expression on my face must have frightened him, because he started to talk faster, explaining, "I mean, she wasn't *exactly* a hooker, but she was dancing in a strip club, out in Los Angeles. Sometimes she did . . . ah . . . private dances . . . in one of the back rooms. She had a heavy accent, said her name was Soya, that she'd come over from Russia to get married . . ."

The story I got in bits and pieces was that the Russian woman told Wilson she was dancing in that place to earn money because she had a child to take care of. A little girl, three years old . . .

"The guy she married—an American—picked her out of a kind of catalogue with pictures of Russian gals who wanted to marry an American and live in the U.S. She said he was mean to her, an' when she had the baby, he didn't believe it was his. She said he beat her and threatened to kill them both. One day she couldn't take it anymore, took the kid, an' ran away . . .''

Wilson said that Soya and her child lived in a room in the motel near the strip club. She told him she gave the little girl a pill to make her sleep while she was working. But it was getting too hard for Soya to take care of her.

"She said she wanted to get shed of the kid so she could go somewhere an' make an 'American life' for herself—that was her words: 'American life.' She asked me if I knew a couple who were good people an' wanted a kid."

The pain in my stomach was getting worse. Cold perspiration was breaking out on my skull and dampening my hair, but I forced him to keep on with the story.

"I saw a chance to make a buck an' told her that in America, good couples wouldn't just take any kid—they had to get money, too. She said she could pay two hundred dollars. Swore that was all she had. I told her I knew somebody nice who might take the kid for two hundred, but I had to get a look at the goods—in case something was wrong with it. She let me come to her room to see for myself. I looked. The kid was asleep. So pretty . . . I told her I'd see what kind of a deal I could make for her. Next night I came back, told her I had a great couple—young but they couldn't have any kids of their own. I showed her a picture of them. It was a picture I took out of a wallet, the kind they sell in drugstores. She was a dumb foreigner, didn't know the difference. I said this couple, they wanted the girl right away because they were moving to . . . ah, someplace, I forgot where I said. After work that night, she gave me the two hundred an' the kid. She was packing a little bag when I left, so I guess she was getting out."

"What was her full name?"

"All she told me was Soya—wouldn't say any more. She was scared."

"What did she call—what was the child's name?"

"Something Russian. Sounded like E-cat-arena."

Ekaterina. That was a Russian name; the American form of it was Katherine. I knew that from the *What to Name the Baby* book most writers owned. "Go on," I said.

"There weren't no couple. I took the kid—*you*, I guess—while you was asleep. When you woke up, I told you your mom was dead. You cried a lot, then you stopped. I got you food. You stayed real quiet. We lived in my van, washed up at gas stations. I made sure you always brushed your teeth. We traveled around. I stole some cars and sold 'em. When my van broke down an' I couldn't get it fixed, I copped another one, switched plates. But then we got stopped by that fat guy sheriff in West Virginia. I knew the jig was up, an' I ran."

"What made the woman confide in *you*, turn her child over to *you*?"

"She said it was 'cause I was polite—didn't try to grab at her. Said I seemed like a gentleman."

It took a monumental effort to keep from retching. I knew what kind of a "gentleman" this creep really was.

I MADE HIM go over the story again and again, to be certain what he told me was consistent. We'd been at it for several hours and the details had remained constant.

In spite of the rustling of rats in the shadows, and the horrible stench from his body waste, I wanted more.

"Tell me about Soya."

"Aww, come on," he whined. "I only saw her twice, an' it was long time ago."

I gestured with the Glock. "Describe her again."

He shook his head as though trying to rattle loose a long-forgotten image. "Good body. 'Course she hadda have that—bein' a stripper an' all. Sort of dark blonde hair, cut real short. Made me think of a cartoon—Peter Pan. When she danced she wore a long red wig."

"Eye color?"

"I tole you before, I don' remember eyes! They weren't brown—that's all I can say."

Before I could ask another question, I heard a sound coming from the floor above us.

Footsteps!

My heart started doing acrobatics in my chest!

Chapter 41

WILSON HEARD THE footsteps, too. He opened his mouth to yell, but I waved the Glock at him and whatever sound he was going to make died in his throat.

What now? Bobby said Wilson lived alone!

At the top of the stairs, the cellar door banged open.

My hand tightened around the Glock. Of course I wouldn't shoot the intruder. My hope was to throw a sufficient scare into the person so I could get away without being arrested.

I had a good reason—if not the right—to unlawfully detain the man who knew where I came from. There was no moral argument I could make for holding a stranger just because he wandered into the cellar, but nevertheless I was going to have to take another prisoner.

The cuffs of a man's trousers and a pair of heavy black shoes appeared on the top step. The legs started to descend . . .

Before I could order the man to stop and raise his hands,

he leaned forward, into the circle of light from the hanging bulb.

"Come up and talk to me."

I didn't know I'd been holding my breath until I let it out with a whoosh of relief.

"What are you doing here?" I asked Walter Maysfield.

"I guessed where you were going." He jerked a thumb backward. "Upstairs."

When Wilson realized that this new person was not going to rescue him, he let loose another stream of curses. I retaped his mouth.

After checking to be sure that the strips holding him to the bed were still too taut for escape, I followed Walter up into the kitchen.

The room was long and narrow. Curling linoleum on the floor was sticky beneath my shoes, and looked as though it had never felt the touch of a mop. The sink was rust-stained. Dishes encrusted with bits of food were piled on the counter next to it. A pair of cabinets had front panels with missing knobs. Opposite the sink was an old refrigerator that was making a sound like the rough idling of an ancient car. The place was so filthy I was sure a thousand roaches lurked just out of sight.

It surprised me to see early morning light coming through the dirty window. Down in that cellar, I'd lost track of time.

Facing Walter, I said, "You knew what I was up to, and you didn't try to stop me?"

He shook his head. "Somebody wanting to find their parents—that's a pretty basic drive. Wasn't my place to keep you from it, but I wasn't going to let you do something foolish."

I gave him a weak laugh. "Too late for that."

"No, it isn't. The bastard's still alive."

A new worry hit me. "Magic! What about—"

"Don't worry. After you left this morning, I called

Nancy. Told her I had an emergency. She came over to stay with him until one of us gets back." He gave my shoulder a comforting pat. "I think of that little guy as sort of my 'grand-cat.'"

When Bobby located him, Walter was a widower without children. Now we'd become a kind of little family. I had treasured friends, but never having had a family, I was just beginning to realize how much I'd missed. The family scenes I'd written for the show were created out of my imagination, and a ton of wishful thinking.

Walter leaned his back against the refrigerator. The pressure of his weight partially muffled the noise. In the near quiet, I realized how exhausted I was, both emotionally and physically. I hadn't been to bed for more than twenty-four hours, and I'd had little sleep before that. Menacing Ray Wilson was much harder on me than I had supposed. He actually *believed* that I would torture him with pliers. I had gambled on that—and won the gamble—but now I was fighting to keep from crying with the strain, and from revulsion at what I'd been driven to do.

I looked up to see Walter studying me.

"You all right?" he asked.

"Yes," I lied.

"Did you get the information you wanted out of him?"

"Some of it. He swears it's all he knows. He was so frightened, I think he was telling the truth."

I recounted the story Ray Wilson had told me. As it unfolded, Walter reached out and encased one of my hands in his big paws.

Walter's solid, bearlike presence helped me get through the telling. By the time I finished, my throat was so dry I could hardly swallow. Not wanting to sip from a glass Wilson had used, I ran water in the sink, caught some in my cupped palms, and splashed the cool liquid into my mouth. When I'd had enough and straightened up, Walter gave me a clean handkerchief from his jacket pocket to dry my hands.

Walter pursed his lips in thought. "Now I know why there wasn't any missing child report made on you."

"Because I wasn't *missing*—she paid to get rid of me."

"Sounds like your mom was in a bad spot. Scared. In a strange country. You should be thankful she didn't kill you—she could have done. Housecats are better mothers than some human females. But this one paid money to give you a chance."

"And look what that turned out to be," I said sharply.

"Yeah, she made a big mistake, but you grew up an' made a good life for yourself." Walter's tone was stern. He wasn't going to let me fall into a trap of self-pity.

"You're right. I have no right to be bitter about the woman who gave me up. I'm alive, and I survived that . . . thing . . . in the basement." I couldn't bring myself to voice my next thought: I wonder what became of *her*. I think Walter knew what was in my head.

I looked away, unable to deal with that yet.

Mercifully, he changed the subject. Tapping the floor with the toe of his shoe, he asked, "What did you plan to do with our friend down there after he talked?"

"Make an anonymous call to the police, let them know he was tied up in his cellar, and suggest they check for outstanding warrants."

Walter pulled back one lapel on his jacket and indicated the folded papers stuck in a pocket. "Got a warrant," he said. "It's to bring Mr. Wilson back to Downsville on the stolen car charge."

Amazed, I asked, "How did you manage that?"

"Was a long time ago, but I still got some friends in Downsville law enforcement. An' a couple judges who remember me fondly. I convinced one of them to issue the car theft warrant. Won't hold up more'n a day at most, but by then I hope we'll have something else."

"A *stolen car* warrant?" My energy came back with a rush of anger. "What about what he did to me?"

Walter grimaced. "The statute of limitations has run out on your case. I have an idea how we can get him for good, but you gotta help me."

"You saw the scene in the basement. Whatever it takes, I'll do."

"My friends in Downsville got official pals here in Ohio. I found out Wilson was arrested for indecent exposure at a schoolyard three months ago. He claimed he was drunk an' just takin' a leak—excuse the expression. They should've tossed his tail in jail, but he's on probation. Thanks to my friends talkin' to their friends, some Ohio cops are gonna search here this morning. I want us to search it first—now—to make sure they don't miss anything."

"Let's get started." I began to move toward the living room. "You take the bedroom."

"Not so quick," Walter said. "You haven't heard what I'm suggestin' you do."

That stopped me. "What?"

"We'll take Wilson to Downsville. They'll put him on ice until Ohio takes him back on the probation violation." He paused for a moment, seeming to be reluctant to go on.

"Walter, what do you want to say?"

"How would you feel 'bout telling what happened to you—what he did. You got a big job in TV now. That makes you a celebrity. If you talk about your experience, maybe other girls—ones he's done stuff to recently— maybe they'll have the courage to come forward. If one of 'em does, then we can lock him up for a long time."

"Maybe he hasn't harmed anyone else."

"There's always another victim with these guys," Walter said. "They don't stop until they're put away, or dead. I'd prefer him dead, but I'm not a killer."

My stomach muscles clenched painfully to think that a world of strangers, and my friends, would learn about . . . that time in my life. Nancy and Penny and Matt. Tommy and Betty, the cast and crew of *Love*. I couldn't help wondering if they'd look at me the same way after they knew. Would I have that label stuck on me for life: child victim?

At the same time, I knew I couldn't live with myself if I let fear stop me from doing something that might help put Wilson in prison.

"Will you?" he asked.

I didn't want to talk right at that moment, so I just nodded.

Walter smiled. "Good girl. I'm proud of you." He pulled two sets of latex investigator's gloves out of a pocket and handed a pair to me. "Let's get to lookin'."

Chapter 42

"WE WON'T REMOVE anything that's evidence," Walter said as we pulled on the latex gloves. "We'll leave it for the Ohio cops to find."

"Got it." I was grateful to have an act to perform that would keep my mind off Walter's plan. I began to search the kitchen as Walter headed for the bedroom.

After ten minutes, I hadn't found anything that could put Wilson in jail, but I did learn two things about him: he must have lived mostly on dry cereal—he had five boxes of different brands on a high shelf—and he had a low standard of cleanliness. The few plates and saucers in his cabinets were dirty. Cups and glasses were stained from whatever they'd contained. There were no detergents, only a bar of soap in a slimy puddle next to the sink. Underneath the sink was half a roll of the cheapest paper towels, but there were no cleansers or sponges. A couple of rags were stuffed into holes in the walls that had probably been made by rats.

I maneuvered the refrigerator away from the wall far enough to peer behind it. Nothing hidden there, but the movement sent a wave of cockroaches scurrying across the floor. Walter came into the kitchen as I was rocking the refrigerator back into place.

I asked him if he'd found anything.

"Under the mattress," he said. "Underwear."

"What kind?"

"A child's." The disgusted expression on his face warned me not to pursue the subject.

I didn't want to. Instead, I asked, "Did you check the bathroom?"

He snorted. "A lady wouldn't want to use it, but there was nothing we're after."

"I haven't had any luck here, either."

"One room left," Walter said, heading for the front of the house.

Ray Wilson's living room was furnished with a sagging old brown couch, a wing chair with upholstery so stained and threadbare that he might have found the thing set out on the street for trash collection. A small wooden bookcase held bottles of liquor in place of books. An imitation leather recliner faced a big-screen television set.

"That TV's the most expensive thing in the house," Walter said. "Three thousand dollars, at least."

On an upended wooden apple crate next to Wilson's top-of-the-line home theater was a combination DVD and VHS player. Stacked beside the player was a two-foot high pile of movies. Walter and I went through them quickly, taking each from its box. They were major studio films, ranging from current pictures all the way back to some made in the 1930s. Every one of them starred young girls.

"It makes me sick to think of that pervert watching movies made innocently, for families," I said.

Walter grunted. "But it's not illegal to have things you can buy in any video store."

We looked behind and beneath the cushions on the couch and the chair, and tipped them up to see if anything was hidden underneath. I found thick balls of dust, some candy wrappers—and a well-thumbed catalogue of children's clothing. My stomach lurched as I thought of him staring at the pictures of child models, but having it wasn't illegal.

While Walter righted the furniture and put the cushions back, I moved the liquor bottles. Nothing behind them. Walter examined light fixtures while I tested the floor-boards to see if any were loose. We looked at each other and shook our heads: nothing.

Finally, we stood in the middle of the living room, staring at each other in frustration.

"The underwear isn't going to be enough to get Wilson locked up," Walter said.

"I have the feeling I've missed something, but I can't think what." I closed my eyes, visualizing the rooms we'd searched. "Something's off . . ." Then it hit me and I opened my eyes. "Come on."

I led Walter back to the kitchen and indicated the high shelf next to the stove.

"Who has five boxes of cereal at the same time?" Stretching, I reached for the nearest one. The moment it was in my hands, I knew the box didn't contain cereal. The top was folded in, to look unopened, but when I turned it upside down, two videotapes slipped out of the box.

"These aren't professional recordings," I said.

Walter reached over my head for the next box and looked inside. "More tapes."

None of the five boxes held cereal.

"No titles," Walter said. "Just some numbers on the labels."

"Dates? Or a code?"

Walter shrugged. "Can't tell at a glance, an' we don't have time to figure it out. Let the cops do that." He set the boxes on the counter, took a tape into the living room, inserted it into the VHS slot, and pushed Play.

With the first crudely lighted images, I knew what we had found: homemade child pornography. Revolted, I turned my back on the set.

A long minute or two later, Walter turned it off and removed the tape. "He filmed himself with a little girl. That's enough for an arrest, at least."

"What do you mean, 'at least'?"

"A sleazy defense attorney might get him off, saying it was all playacting. The lighting's so bad they could claim the kid wasn't a real kid, but a midget."

"That's ridiculous!"

"Juries have done crazy things. Judges, too. Trouble is, most good people find it hard to believe that somebody who looks normal could do sick things to children. We'll still need a real young person to stand up an' tell what he did."

I knew Walter was right. Making an official report of my story might be the only way to get someone else to speak up. As I thought about what lay ahead, a cold lump of dread began forming in my chest.

Chapter 43

AFTER RETURNING THE cereal boxes to the shelf where we'd found them, Walter and I went back down to the cellar. While I held the pistol on Wilson, Walter ripped the tape from his mouth. He took the folded papers out of his pocket and showed them to our prisoner.

"Raymond E. Wilson, I have here a warrant for your arrest issued by the city of Downsville, West Virginia, and am duly authorized to escort you to the police station in Belle Valley, Ohio. There you will be held, to await extradition back to Downsville. Do you understand?"

I moved in, holding the Glock close enough to Wilson's head to discourage any attempt to escape as Walter yanked the tape strips first from around his ankles, and then from his wrists.

"They gonna let me go, once I tell 'em what that bitch did to me."

"I didn't see her do anything." The tapes were off. "Get up," Walter snapped.

Wilson struggled to stand; he was stiff and sore from his hours bound to the bed frame. "You found me tied up. I sure as hell didn't do that to myself." Wilson massaged his wrists and rubbed his ankles together, restoring circulation.

"When I arrived to take you into custody, you were in your living room, watching television," Walter said blandly.

"That's a damn lie!"

"Who do you think anybody's gonna believe—a scumbag like you, or a thirty-year lawman like me?"

"Okay, fatso," Wilson snarled, pointing to his swollen, blood-encrusted nose. "The cops will know I didn't do this."

"No, *I* did," Walter said. "You resisted arrest, and attacked me. I defended myself, using the force necessary to subdue you. Now, upstairs. March."

In the kitchen, Walter stripped off the latex gloves and asked for the Glock. I gave it to him, removed my own pair of gloves, and also gave those to Walter. He stuck them in his pocket. Indicating Wilson, Walter said, "I'll get him cleaned up."

While Walter was making Wilson scrub himself clean in the shower, I used paper towels and water from the sink to wash up as best I could. I got the dirt off my face and hands, but my shirt and pants were filthy from sliding down the coal chute.

Walter brought Wilson back into the kitchen and handed me the Glock. Our prisoner was dressed in fresh clothes. I kept the pistol on Wilson while Walter fastened his wrists behind his back with handcuffs.

"Where did you get those?" I asked.

"Borrowed 'em from my friends in Downsville, when I picked up the warrant."

Walter took the pistol back and prodded Wilson toward the front door.

"Take a look outside," Walter said.

I opened the door and surveyed the street in both direc-
tions. Webster was deserted at the moment. "Eight o'clock
Saturday morning. The neighbors must be sleeping in,"
I said.

Walter took Wilson to his rental car, put him in the rear,
and snarled, "I'll shoot your miserable head off it you even
reach for a door handle." Keeping Wilson in sight, Walter
drew me to the far side of the vehicle and lowered his
voice. "How did you get here?"

I told him about buying the Skylark that was in the motel parking lot, about my pregnancy disguise, and the false
name and I.D.

"Clever," he said. "What are you going to do with the
car?"

"My original plan was to drive it back to New York City
and leave it unlocked in a bad neighborhood."

Walter smiled with approval. "Where it would be
stripped down to the axle in about ten minutes."

"I was going to take the subway home, but now that
you're here I'd like us to stick together."

"Yes. Is there anything in the motel room that could
identify you?" he asked.

I shook my head. "The tote bag with the disguise is in
the trunk. I paid in cash for two nights."

"Go get your car. Throw the contents of your bag into
several different Dumpsters. Do you know where the police station is?"

"I saw it yesterday afternoon, while I was exploring the
town."

"Park the car a couple blocks away from there an' leave
it for the car thieves. Walk to the station an' join me." He
aimed a critical frown at my dirty clothes. "Do you have
something else to wear?"

"Just the maternity dress."

"If you show up at the station looking like that, it might

make somebody think Wilson's telling the truth about you keeping him in the cellar."

I looked at my watch. "I'll find a store and buy a new top and slacks, then I'll ditch these clothes."

"One more thing. When you give your statement about my finding you with Wilson, and what he did, leave out details about your mother."

"What do you mean?"

"Just say Wilson said your mom was dead—that's true, that's what he told you. If the woman's still alive an' reads about this, then she might show up someday. But fakes wanting money could come forward, too, telling the story Wilson gave you. A DNA test will expose a phony, but that takes a while. I don't want your hopes raised an' then crushed."

I didn't know how I felt about the possibility of meeting my mother someday, or even how I felt about *her*. It was too soon to sort out my emotions.

Instead of talking about that now, before I was ready, I gestured toward the back of Wilson's head, which was visible through the rear window. "He'll probably tell the story," I said, "to defend himself against a kidnapping charge."

Walter shook his head. "He won't say anything."

"But how can you be certain?"

"Because I'm going to tell him that if he does, I'll make sure the guys in jail with him know he's a child molester. If he shuts up, I won't."

"How can you keep other inmates from finding out what he is?"

"I can't." Walter's tone was wry. "I'm only promising him that *I* won't tell."

Unspoken between us was the knowledge that Ray Wilson was not going to have it easy, for whatever time he was locked up.

With our plans made for meeting at the police station,

Walter climbed behind the steering wheel and drove off with his prisoner.

The street was still empty of people, and no cars had gone by since we came out onto the sidewalk. I took a deep breath of fresh morning air and started retracing my steps to the motel.

At the corner of Webster and Cook, a Belle Valley P.D. patrol car passed me. It was cruising quietly, without excess speed or use of the siren. I knelt down, pretending to retie my shoelace, and watched it stop in front of 404 Webster. A husky young police officer in uniform was behind the wheel. In the passenger seat was a middle-aged bald man wearing a tan suit. They got out of the car and headed for Wilson's front door.

I stood up with feigned casualness and turned onto Cook Street, increasing my pace as soon as I was out of sight of the Belle Valley P.D.

BY THE TIME I had bought new clothes, got rid of the disguise and my grubby slacks and shirt, abandoned the Skylark, and reached the Belle Valley Police Department, Walter greeted me with the news that the search of Ray Wilson's house had produced videotapes showing Wilson molesting children. "The guys here have been spot-checking and fast-forwarding through them, but the tape quality is real bad, and there's no sound. It's gonna be hard to make a case."

"So, without corroborating testimony from at least one of his victims, Wilson might go free." I was stating the obvious. The police would publicize Wilson's arrest, and ask victims to come forward, but given the level of humiliation and shame likely to be felt by families, it could be that no one would. Many adult women refuse to report sexual assault, fearing that admitting to having been raped would taint them. I understood that fear; I had it myself, but I couldn't let it stop me from what I had to do. Absent names of Wilson's victims, it was up to me to try to inspire somebody to come out of hiding and file charges against him.

Walter believed that, even though I worked offscreen, my connection to *Love of My Life* made me at least a minor celebrity, and therefore of media interest. Reluctantly, I'd had to agree with him. It seemed that any show business connection appealed to the press. Every time a crime was committed by someone who worked for a famous actor, currently or in the past—even if it was in a menial job— news accounts and broadcasts about the event began by mentioning the actor. If a second cousin of the man who serviced Mel Gibson's cars was arrested, that report would lead with Mel Gibson's name. Perhaps my speaking up about having been a victim of Ray Wilson would make it a little easier for someone else to admit it. With all of my heart, I hoped so.

After I told my story privately to Captain Don Anderson of the Belle Valley Police Department, he called for a video camera and a stenographer. When everything was in place, I sat down to face the lens. Under Captain Anderson's methodical questioning, I recounted, in painful detail, my time in Ray Wilson's power. While it was difficult, to my surprise, I discovered that there was also a degree of freedom in the telling. I felt as though I was being relieved of a heavy burden.

The ugly part of my story ended with my rescue by Sheriff Walter Maysfield.

Telling Captain Anderson that I was checking out of my motel and would be there soon, Walter had made his own statement before I arrived. He described how he had discovered me, and included information regarding the stolen van, about finding Ray Wilson's fingerprints in the vehicle, and Walter's unsuccessful attempts to capture the man. Years later Wilson was traced to Belle Valley by a private detective that I had hired.

Although Captain Anderson already knew the answer, for the sake of the official record, he asked me, "Why did you go to the trouble and expense of looking for Wilson? You must have known the statute of limitations on your case had run out."

"I wanted to learn where I came from, and how I ended up with him."

"What did you find out?"

"Not much. When I was a little girl, he told me my mother was dead. This morning, when Sheriff Maysfield and I confronted him, he said that she gave me to him, but swore that was all he knew about her, that she didn't tell him her name." A partial truth. "The most important reason I came here is that I wanted to try to stop him from hurting other children."

WE WERE SITTING in Captain Anderson's office, in straight-back wooden chairs next to the captain's desk, waiting to read and sign our statements. Walter had tipped his chair against the wall as he thumbed through a stack of "wanted" circulars. I was perched at the edge of my seat, replaying in my mind every word Ray Wilson had told me about the woman who gave birth to me. I was sure Wilson believed the story, but was it true? Had she lied to him? Did I want to find out?

I looked around, hoping for something to distract me from thinking about it. Unlike New York's Twentieth Precinct, which seemed to be busy around the clock, on this Saturday morning, there were only two police officers visible from where I sat, and no public enemies. One officer was filling out a form, and the other was reading a magazine and drinking from a tall Styrofoam cup. Coffee! I realized how much I would give at that moment for a cup of coffee—even police-station coffee.

My cell phone rang, interrupting my craving. Instantly,

I felt my spine stiffen with apprehension. The people in my life had promised not to call me this weekend unless it was an emergency.

"Hello?"

"Sorry to interrupt your vacation, honey." It was Matt. "There's something I have to tell you." His tone was somber. It wasn't going to be good news.

I clenched the pen in my hand so hard it bit into the flesh of my palm. "What's happened?"

"An actor on your show—Jay Garwood. He's been shot," Matt said.

Chapter 44

MY HEART POUNDED with fear. "Is he alive?" I asked.

Walter brought the front legs of his chair back down to the floor, scooted it closer to mine, and leaned forward. "What happened?"

"Jay Garwood's been shot," I whispered.

"Who are you talking to?" Matt asked.

"Walter."

"Maysfield's with you at a *spa*? Where exactly are you?"

"I'll explain when we get back. Tell me—is Jay alive?"

"Just barely."

I nodded at Walter and mouthed "yes."

Walter leaned back, his face creased in thought.

"Garwood's at St. Vincent's Hospital, on West Twelfth Street," Matt said. "He's critical."

"What happened?"

"At five o'clock this morning Garwood was about to go jogging, but he was shot as he came out of his apartment."

"His apartment? Jay lives on West Eleventh Street. That's not in the Twentieth Precinct. How did you and G. G. get the case?"

"We didn't. The shooting took place in the Tenth. Manhattan South. Penny heard about it on the radio half an hour ago. She knows Garwood was an actor on your show so she told me. I called the Tenth and got the details—more than what's been released in news reports. Garwood would have died from his wound, but he got lucky. A cabdriver was parked up the street, having a smoke. He heard the shot, saw him fall, and got a glimpse of someone running away. It was still too dark for the driver to be able to describe the assailant."

"Was it a mugging?" I asked that question, even though my instincts told me this was absolutely *not* a random street crime.

"We don't think so," Matt said. "Garwood had forty dollars on him, and was wearing a gold Rolex. The shooter didn't take anything—just plugged him in the gut and ran."

"Jay was shot in the stomach?" I shuddered. "Oh, Lord, that would have been a horrible way to die."

"It wouldn't be where I'd want to be shot, that's for sure. The assailant was close enough to Garwood to have hit him in the head and killed him instantly," Matt said. "Artie Wallace, the lead detective on the case, believes this shooting was personal, that whoever did it wanted Garwood to suffer before he bled out. I think he's right."

"Matt, you and G. G. should be on this case, too. I'm sure it's connected to the death of Veronica Rose. Jay Garwood had been going out with her. First Veronica is murdered, and then a couple of weeks later Jay is almost killed, too. You can't tell me you think that's a *coincidence*?"

"No, I don't," Matt said. "G. G. and I are going down to the Tenth to compare notes with Artie Wallace and his partner."

I looked up to see Walter moving out into the main

room. He was speaking quietly into his cell phone as he walked.

"Morgan, are you there?"

"Oh, yes, I'm sorry. I was distracted for a moment. Look—Jay is close to his ex-wife. Her name is Loretta Garwood. She lives on West Ninth with their fifteen-year-old daughter, Annie. Somebody should let her know—"

"She and the girl are at St. Vincent's now. Mrs. Garwood's name was in his wallet, listed as the person to notify in case of an emergency. Artie hightailed it right over to her apartment to see her himself. Just in case."

"In case of what?" But before the question was completely out of my mouth I realized what Matt was saying. "You mean, in case she wasn't at home that early in the morning? Or in case she opened the door with a smoking gun in her hand? Does he think Loretta shot him?"

"It's a possibility. When somebody is murdered, or almost, it's more likely the killer was a so-called loved one than a stranger."

"I think that detective is wrong this time."

"Oh, really? Then what's your theory?"

"I don't have one," I admitted. *Yet.*

"Let the professionals work the case. Stay out of it."

"That's pretty arrogant," I said hotly.

"I don't want you arrested for obstruction of justice—I'd miss the trouble you cause me." Before I could respond, Matt added, "Okay, I've told you all I know about the Garwood attack. Now you tell me the truth about where you are, and what you and Sherlock's father are doing."

"Not on the phone. I'll explain when we get home."

"When will that be?" I heard impatience in his tone.

"Hey." I lowered my voice. "Just because we've slept together, doesn't mean you can start dictating where I go and what I do. And with whom."

"Walter Maysfield is *living* with you. I'd be jealous as hell if he wasn't a hundred years old."

"He's seventy-two. Haven't you heard: seventy is the new fifty. One day I'll tell you what a wonderful friend he was to me when I was a child, and growing up."

"Make it soon. I'd like to know something about you— before the day we met eight months ago."

I tried to steer him away from that subject with a joke. "Has it been only eight months? Seems longer."

"We met October ninth of last year, at Metropolitan Hospital, on the seventh floor. Your boss at the network had been struck by a hit-and-run driver. G. G. and I were investigating."

In contrast to my attempt at humor, his tone was serious. His detailed memory of that night surprised me. I didn't know what to say, so I made light of it by asking, "What was I wearing?"

"Something baggy, too big. You didn't dress very attractively back then, but I liked your face."

"I don't remember anything at all about you," I lied. "G. G. was the one I thought was sexy."

That made him laugh, and soon we said warm goodbyes.

When Walter saw that I'd finished my call, he came back.

"You can catch a Jet Blue flight out of Pittsburgh that'll get you back to New York by one o'clock this afternoon."

"Pittsburgh?"

"It's the nearest big city, 'bout fifty miles away. I'll drive you, then come back here to make sure Wilson stays in custody 'til we can nail him with a bigger charge than just possession of those tapes."

AS SOON AS we got in Walter's rental car to drive to Pittsburgh, I phoned Tommy Zenos. I was pretty sure that he hadn't heard the news about Jay, because on Friday nights Tommy played in a poker game that lasted until dawn, and then he slept until the late afternoon on Saturdays. He said it was the weekly therapy that kept him sane. I didn't bother to dial his landline, because he would have turned that off to sleep, but I knew he always kept one of his two cell phones on. His father and I were the only people who had that number.

"Hello . . . ?" He sounded barely conscious.

"Tommy, this is Morgan. Wake up, please. It's important."

He cleared his throat. I pictured him sitting up and shaking his head to clear it. He did that when he'd had too many late nights and fell asleep on his side of our partner's desk. "I'm . . . 'kay. I'm okay. What's the matter?"

I told Tommy that Jay had been shot, and was in critical condition at St. Vincent's. "The police are investigating, but they don't yet know who did it. I'll be back in the city in a few hours. Now this is what you need to do—are you completely awake?"

"Yes." His voice sounded stronger. "Is Jay going to be all right?"

"I don't know. He's in a fine hospital, and we'll make sure he gets everything he needs."

I heard Tommy gasp. "Oh, no! What about the *show*?"

"You've got to find an actor to replace Jay in the role temporarily," I said. "Because of the current storyline, there's no way I can redo the schedule to tape around him until he recovers." *If* he recovers, was my unspoken thought.

"Right. Right. I'll get somebody who looks enough like Jay to keep the transition from being jarring, and we'll have the announcer say, 'The role of Evan Duran is being played temporarily by . . . whoever.'"

Hearing the energy in his voice, I knew I couldn't have given him a better assignment. Tommy, whose fears and insecurities displayed themselves in myriad ways—from his addiction to chocolate to his string of broken engagements—was brilliant at two aspects of the television business: making deals and casting.

"Jay isn't scheduled to tape this coming week until Wednesday," I said. "As soon as you find the right actor, hire our best coach to help the substitute Evan give us the character nuances we need in the part. Can the budget handle that extra expense?"

"We have more than enough in my secret fund," Tommy said proudly. He'd amassed a financial cushion by slightly inflating each item in the budget we submitted yearly to the network. What we didn't use for production, Tommy put away to cover unexpected problems, so we wouldn't have to ask for extra money. Because of his economic sleight of hand, Tommy had earned *Love of My Life* the best reputation in the business for fiscal responsibility.

A few months ago, when I discovered what Tommy was doing, he had said, "We're not taking anything for ourselves. I'm just fighting a kind of guerrilla war against the bean counters." My admiration for him rose at that moment. I realized again that there was more to my co-executive producer than the nail-biting buffoon some people thought him to be. That was his protective coloration; jungle animals used it to survive.

Tommy asked, "When I find the candidates for Evan Duran, do you want to see tapes before we hire one?"

"Not necessary. You've got the Midas touch when it comes to picking actors."

Besides, I'm going to be busy trying to figure out who shot Jay Garwood.

Chapter 45

"YOU'RE A MESS," Matt said, surprising me by standing at the end of the Jet Blue tunnel as I stepped foot into the terminal at JFK.

"What are you doing up here, beyond the security checkpoints?"

"I flashed the badge," Matt said. "I didn't want to risk missing you in the crowd."

Walter had managed to get me to Pittsburgh in time to catch the Jet Blue flight to New York City. In the ten minutes I had between buying the ticket and boarding the airbus, I'd called Matt to tell him when I'd be home. He'd asked what flight I was taking, but I hadn't expected him to meet me. I didn't even want to see him until after I'd had a bath, shampooed my hair, brushed my teeth, and put on clean clothes. Glancing at myself in the plane's bathroom mirror before landing, I realized I looked even worse than the time I'd fallen into Lake Victoria, and Ian had had to pull me out before the crocodiles got to me. Of course, then

I didn't have the dark circles under my eyes from having gone almost forty-eight hours without sleep.

Matt stared over my head at the other deplaning passengers. "Where's Maysfield?"

"He's staying in Ohio for a few days."

"Doing what?"

"It's a long story," I said. "And before I share it with you, I want to clean up. Tell me about Jay Garwood. What's his condition?"

"Still critical. He's in a coma."

As we made our way toward the street exit through the swarm of travelers arriving and departing, I asked, "Do the doctors say what Jay's chances of recovery are?"

"About fifty-fifty. The odds would be a lot worse if he wasn't in such good physical shape. His wife told Artie that Garwood went running at five o'clock every morning, no matter what the weather was like."

That was an interesting bit of information. It started me thinking. "If Loretta Garwood knew his schedule, I wonder who else did," I said.

"We're investigating that. 'We' means official law enforcement, so don't try to help. Did you check your bag?"

"No bag." Patting a pocket of the camouflage print jacket I'd purchased that morning—in the first place in Belle Valley I'd found open, an Army-Navy surplus store— I added, "All I have with me is my wallet." The wallet with my own identification in it. I'd gotten rid of the Charlotte Brown driver's license, along with my disguise, the pliers, duct tape, flashlight, and lock pick.

Out on the sidewalk, I saw Matt's NYPD Crown Victoria parked in the passenger loading zone, with an OFFICIAL BUSINESS sign clipped to the sun visor. He opened the passenger door for me and I got in. Sinking back against the seat, I realized that not only was I exhausted, but just about every part of my body ached. Before we were out of JFK and onto the highway, I was sound asleep.

Matt woke me when he slowed to a stop in front of the Dakota. I opened my eyes to see Jim, the new daytime security man, start toward the car. Matt waved him away, and Jim retreated into his kiosk.

"Wash off the dust of Ohio and take a nap. How would you feel about my coming over for dinner? I'll bring it."

"I'd like that," I said. "Chinese?"

"You got it. Seven o'clock?"

"Perfect."

Matt leaned over and kissed me on the forehead, then reached past me to open the car door. Just as I was starting to climb out, he touched my hand. With a smile, he asked, "Are you sure Maysfield will be in Ohio? We'll be alone?"

I knew what he was really asking. "We'll be as alone as we were in Boston," I said.

The thought of being in Matt's arms tonight made my pulse tingle with anticipation.

AS SOON AS I opened the door to my apartment, Magic bounded down the hall to greet me. He leapt into my arms, rubbed the top of his head under my chin, and then climbed up onto my shoulder, where he draped himself around my neck like a scarf and started to purr.

"Morgan?" Nancy came out of the kitchen, wiping her hands on a paper towel.

"I'm so glad to be home," I said.

She stopped abruptly and stared at me. "*Where* was that spa—in a coal mine?"

I managed a weak laugh. "You don't know how close you are."

A few minutes later, Nancy and I were sitting at the kitchen table with a plate of Oreo cookies between us. Over steaming mugs of coffee, and with Magic curled up in my lap, I told Nancy the truth about my childhood, about

Ray Wilson, and all that I had done—and learned—in the Ohio coal cellar.

As she listened, tears rolled down Nancy's cheeks. She reached across the table and gripped my hand in silent, loving support.

And for the first time since Ian died almost six years ago, I cried, too.

Chapter 46

AFTER BATHING, SHAMPOOING my hair, brushing and
flossing my teeth, coating my nails with fresh clear polish,
and taking a two-hour nap beside Magic, I got up and put
on the pale blue silk robe Nancy gave me for my birthday
last year. (Or what had been guess-timated as my birthday;
I had no idea on which day I actually had been born.) Because I usually slept in oversized T-shirts of Bruce Lee or
the New York Knicks, I'd thought of this elegant robe as
too "nice" to wear. Until tonight.

An hour before Matt was due, I gave Magic his dinner
and settled at the kitchen table with one of the white legal
pads I used to work out plotlines for *Love*. But what I
needed it for this evening had nothing to do with the show.
I was trying to use my plotting experience to spot a link between the murder of Veronica Rose and the attempted murder of Jay Garwood. If I could, I was sure it would be the
missing piece of information that would clear Nancy.

At least the prosecutors wouldn't be able to charge her with the assault on Jay. Nancy had told me that she couldn't sleep last night, so from four A.M. to after seven, she was at my computer, ordering Christmas presents online, using her credit cards. The times of those transactions were electronically embedded, and thus could be confirmed. This year, I wasn't going to tease Nancy about being so compulsively efficient that she habitually completed her Christmas shopping list well before Labor Day.

Flattening the white legal pad on the table, I used a large box of Sweet'N Low to draw a straight line down the middle, from top to bottom, dividing the page into two columns. I headed the left-hand side "Facts," and the right-hand side "Questions."

Under "Facts," I listed:

1. Veronica Rose was struck fatally with a paint can in her empty apartment.
2. Nancy Cummings discovered Veronica's body.
3. Didi discovered Nancy kneeling over the body.
4. Didi claims her mother and father were reconciling.
5. Prosecutors contend Nancy murdered Veronica out of jealousy.
6. Nancy and Veronica had verbal fights in front of witnesses.
7. In Boston, Veronica had had affairs with other women's husbands.
8. None of those men or women was in New York at time of the murder.
9. Jay Garwood hinted that he and Veronica were going to be married.
10. Didi became hysterical at mention of Garwood's name.
11. Arnold prevented me from talking to Didi.
12. Someone tried to kill Jay Garwood.

On the "Questions" side of the page, I wrote:

1. Why was Veronica Rose killed?
2. Why did someone try to kill Jay Garwood?
3. Who would want to kill *both* Veronica and Jay?
4. Why was Didi's reaction to Jay's name so violent?
5. Why won't Arnold let me question Didi?
6. Did one of the "Boston Five" (Laura and George Reynolds, Gloria and Ralph Hartley, or Cathy Chatsworth) hire a killer?
7. Which alibis are solid?

The Boston Five scored highest here. Not only did Bobby Novello check out their whereabouts at the time of Veronica's death, but they were thoroughly investigated by the Boston private detective firm Bobby employed to work with him, and also by the separate agency hired by Nancy's attorney, Kent Wayne. After exhaustive tracing of movements and travel records, they were united in the conclusion that none of those five people was in New York—nor even in a city nearby—when Veronica was killed. No connection had been found linking any of the Boston Five to a professional assassin.

From what I'd learned of their social circle, infidelity was a kind of indoor sport. The emotional havoc Veronica's romantic greed caused was probably painful, but as much as they all played around, it didn't seem as though their passions ran deep enough to commit murder. Besides, why would any of them have wanted Jay Garwood dead? It was unlikely that Veronica's Boston group knew Jay, but I made a note to call Bobby tomorrow and have him see if he and his Merry Men could find any connection between either Reynolds, Hartley, or Cathy Chatsworth to Jay.

As for the other suspects on my personal list: Jay Garwood's alibi is that he was with his ex-wife and their daughter, Annie. Loretta and Annie Garwood confirmed his story. But they *might* lie for him.

Arnold Rose's alibi is that he was with a client. The client confirmed it. However, time of death cannot be calculated scientifically down to the minute, so Arnold *might* have been able to kill her before he left their apartment building. Playing devil's advocate, I had to admit that possibility crashed on the rocky shores of motive. Even if Arnold had been *able* to kill Veronica in time to keep his appointment, *why* would he have murdered her? I had no answer to that.

Unfortunately, nothing we'd learned so far was a help to Nancy. She was the only person confirmed to have been on the scene around the time of Veronica's death. According to the prosecutor's theory of the case, Nancy was the one person who had both motive and opportunity. The only thing wrong with that theory was that Nancy is innocent. But how can we prove it?

More questions:

8. Was Veronica going to choose Jay or Arnold? (My guess was Arnold.)
9. Did the loser (Jay) kill her? (Unlikely. Disappointment is a weak motive.)
10. If Arnold murdered her, what was his motive? (I'm back to that again.)

Carefully reading both columns, my conclusion was that the three most important questions were 1. *Why* was Veronica killed; 2. *Why* was Jay almost murdered; and 3. Who would want *both* of them dead?

Loretta Garwood? That was possible, but when Walter and I talked to her, she gave the impression of having a good relationship with her ex-husband. I didn't think it was an act. Besides, if she had wanted to get back together with

Jay—once he was making good money again—she had the chance before Jay met Veronica Rose.

Loretta might have killed Jay, or Veronica, but why both of them? I just couldn't see her as a killer. It's true that she knew Jay's jogging schedule, but I was sure she couldn't have gotten into Veronica's security building without being announced. The police hadn't discovered anyone, other than Nancy, who had come to see Veronica that day.

As though my mind was stuck in an endless loop, I came back to Arnold Rose. But it didn't make sense that Arnold would murder Veronica when he was sending signals that he was reconciling with her. He'd made a point of explaining his ex to me, of describing her need for attention. He knew about her affairs. It seemed unlikely that he would have killed her just because she was dating Jay. A man with Arnold's ego couldn't have thought that Jay—a supporting actor on Daytime TV—was serious competition. Even if Arnold had regarded Jay as an obstacle to reconciliation with Veronica, he would more likely have paid Jay to back off, or frightened him away.

As a criminal defense attorney, Arnold would know how to hire a hit man to kill Veronica, but I couldn't picture him putting himself in the power of someone who might betray him one day, perhaps in dealing with the law for a lesser charge if the hit man—or, not to succumb to gender stereotyping, the hit woman—was arrested for another crime.

The single most important person in the world to Arnold is Didi. I found it hard to believe that he would do anything to damage his relationship with his daughter.

Didi . . . I put the pad down and thought about her.

Although she was only twelve years old, Didi Rose was one of the most manipulative people I'd ever met. A few months ago she'd tried to destroy her father's romance with Nancy by faking an injury for which Nancy was blamed. I knew that children killed, but Didi wanted her parents back together, so why would she have murdered her mother?

As I stared at what I'd written in the two columns, a new thought came knocking at my frontal lobes. Could there be *two* killers? One who murdered Veronica, and another who tried to kill Jay?

As quickly as it appeared, I swatted that idea away. While I've created quite a few unlikely scenarios for the show—they're great fun to write and for fans to watch— this "two killer" theory was too implausible, even for me. It had to be that one person committed both crimes.

When Jay awakens from his coma, he might be able to tell us who shot him. I refused to believe that Jay wouldn't survive. When I'd called St. Vincent's earlier to check on Jay's condition, Dr. Henry Lyons told me he was still critical. "Until he regains consciousness," Dr. Lyons had said, "we can't tell what he's able to remember, or if he'll have any long-term problems."

The doorbell rang. I looked at the wall clock and realized I'd lost track of time. It was seven P.M.

Matt's here. I'd told the reception desk I was expecting him. My heartbeat raced as I hurried to the front door to let him in.

Chapter 47

OPENING THE DOOR, I saw Matt smiling at me. He was carrying a bag of Chinese takeout in one hand and a bottle of wine under his arm. I moved back so that he could enter. As he stepped into the hallway, I took the bag and bottle from him, stooped enough to set them on the floor, and straightened up. Immediately, he drew me into his arms. My heart started to thud in my chest.

We kissed until I was breathless. Just as our lips parted an inch, I felt something soft brush my bare ankle. I looked down to see Magic easing his face into the bag of Chinese food.

Matt saw it too and laughed. "Do you let him eat Chinese?"

"No. He has his own veterinarian-approved menu, and it doesn't include cashew chicken, beef with snow peas, and pork fried rice."

Denied his new culinary experience, Magic scampered away from us in a huff. We took the food and the wine into the kitchen and put them down on the table. Matt touched my hand, sending little electric tingles all through my body.

"Are you hungry?" he asked softly.

"Not for Chinese food . . ."

He kissed me again. When we came up for air, I led Matt into my bedroom. He shut the door, hooked his fingers into the belt of my robe, and drew me to him. Gently, he untied the silk cord, opened the robe, and cupped my breasts in his hands. So full of desire I thought I might burst, I fumbled at the buttons on his dark blue shirt. In spite of my nervousness, in seconds I had the shirt open. Our arms went around each other, skin touching skin. Our lips parted, and our tongues began to explore . . .

As Matt slipped out of the rest of his clothes, I lay back on the bed.

We were so desperate for each other that it was over quickly, but a few minutes later, we began to kiss and caress again. This time our lovemaking was long and leisurely. After an hour of the most glorious sensations, we collapsed in each other's arms, totally spent.

Smiling, Matt whispered, "I think you're going to kill me."

"It'll be the perfect crime." I gave him the lightest little kiss on his chest. "Now, what about some Chinese food?"

"Do you have a crane here, to hoist me up out of this bed?"

DRESSED AGAIN, HAND in hand, we ambled into the kitchen—and discovered that while Matt and I were in the bedroom with the door closed, Magic had been busy.

"Oh, no!"

The bag from the Chinese restaurant was tipped over onto the table. Two of the cartons were open, with the contents scattered. A shallow lake of sauce had pooled in the middle of the tabletop, soaking the bottom of the legal pad on which I'd been working before Matt arrived. Magic crouched on one side of this jumbled buffet, chewing contentedly on a thin slice of beef. Little paw prints, coated in brown Chinese sauce, charted Magic's course across my white pages.

Matt grabbed paper towels from the roll beside the sink. I picked Magic up and relocated him to the floor. "Naughty cat," I said.

Together, Matt and I began to clean up the mess.

Holding paper towels beneath it, I moved the dripping bag over to the plastic drain board. Taking out the little packets of fortune cookies, soy sauce, and two pairs of chopsticks, I said, "There are two intact cartons." I took them out and opened the tops. "Hmmm, cashew chicken and white rice. Plenty for dinner."

"I'm glad that cat doesn't like Merlot," Matt said. "Or maybe he just couldn't open the bottle. Where's your corkscrew?"

I took it out of the drawer beside the stove, handed it to him, and transferred our food into ceramic dishes, to heat for a few seconds in the microwave.

"I don't care what the so-called rules say—I like red wine with chicken."

"I know you do." Matt smiled at me as he worked the cork out of the bottle.

Magic jumped up onto the stool below the wall phone and began to groom his whiskers.

Pouring the dark ruby wine for us, Matt nodded toward Magic. "If a cat can look smug, that one does. He must have forgotten he used to be homeless."

"I don't think anyone ever forgets that." I looked into Magic's green eyes and thought, *We have a bond, little guy.* I knew that soon I'd have to tell Matt about it. But not tonight.

* * *

WE WERE COMFORTABLY full and having coffee when the phone rang. It was the line connected to the Dakota's front desk.

Matt lifted one eyebrow and joked, "Do you have a late date?"

I quipped right back, "Of course I do, but he's an hour early."

Puzzled, I got up and crossed to the wall phone. "Hello?"

"Mrs. Tyler?" It was the gravelly voice of Frank, the night security man. "Somebody down here wants to see you. He's pretty upset."

"Give me that phone!" I heard a man in the background, and he sounded furious. I recognized that voice.

"Frank? Let me speak to him."

I heard a growl, an expletive, and a *clank*. I pictured the phone being snatched across the desk.

"Morgan!"

"Yes, Arnold. What's the matter?"

"I demand to see Didi!"

"Didi?"

"Don't try to tell me she's not up there with you!" I heard what sounded like a fist smacked angrily onto the top of the reception desk.

"She's not here, Arnold."

"I don't believe you!"

"Then come up and see for yourself."

"Tell this ape you're giving me permission."

Arnold mumbled something, and Frank came back on the line. "What do you want me to do, Mrs. Tyler?"

"Let him come upstairs. Mr. Rose has visited before— he knows which apartment it is." I replaced the phone on the wall hook and turned to Matt. "You better put your shoes on. We're about to have company."

"I heard," he said, getting up and heading back toward the bedroom. I followed, to grab something to wear other than this thin silk robe.

By the time Arnold started jabbing at the doorbell, I'd pulled on sweatpants and a loose shirt. Matt was wearing socks, shoes, and his sports jacket, but a glance in the bedroom mirror at the two of us told me that we still looked like we'd been doing exactly what we had been doing.

The moment I opened the front door, Arnold barged in past me, without even saying hello. He saw Matt sitting in the living room and jerked to a stop.

"Phoenix—how long have you been here?"

"Long enough to know Morgan's not hiding your daughter." Matt stood up. "If I were you, I'd start behaving myself." His spoke in his strong-arm-of-the-law tone.

Suddenly, Arnold seemed to fold into himself, deflating like one of the big balloons after a Macy's Thanksgiving Day parade. He sank into the wing chair next to the sofa. "She's gone," he said.

He looked haggard, and seemed so genuinely upset that I sat on the edge of the sofa and reached out to touch his hand in sympathy. "What happened?"

"I don't know," he said. His features twisted in pain. Or fear. "She hasn't made any friends in New York yet. She likes you—so I thought perhaps she'd come here."

"No. I haven't seen her, or heard from her." I looked up at Matt. His arms were folded across his chest as he watched Arnold.

Matt asked, "How long has she been gone?"

"I saw her at six. She said she wanted to take a nap before dinner. That was unusual, but she's been through so much . . . When I went to wake her, she wasn't in her room, or anywhere in the apartment."

Matt looked at his watch. "It's ten o'clock. Could she have gone out to a movie, without telling you?"

Arnold shook his head. From the grim set of Matt's lips, I could see that he didn't believe it either.

"Did she take anything with her—clothes, a suitcase?"

"I'm not sure. I looked in her closet. She has a lot of

clothes. I didn't see any empty hangers. Her set of luggage was there."

"Matt, Didi's only twelve. Alone in this city—" I didn't want to finish the sentence. "Isn't there something you can do to find her?"

"Do you have a picture?" Matt asked.

Arnold took his wallet out of an inside pocket of his jacket and removed a photo of Didi. Smiling, her lovely large brown eyes shining with confidence. This was Didi before her mother's death.

"She cut her hair," Arnold said softly. As though talking to himself, he added, "She couldn't have been kidnapped. I was in the apartment, in my den. The housekeeper was in the kitchen. It's a secure building. We didn't have any visitors . . . She's gone. She left me."

Matt persuaded Arnold to come with him to the station house, to report Didi as a runaway. The Arnold Rose who left with Matt looked twenty years older than the man who'd rudely brushed past me at the front door a short time earlier.

After they left, I called Nancy. I didn't think Didi would go there, but I'd hoped Nancy might have an idea. She didn't.

"Didi doesn't go to school—she has tutors—so she doesn't have classmates," Nancy said. "According to Arnold, she doesn't like her teachers very much, so I can't see her running off to one of them. Her entire world revolves around her riding competitions."

Suddenly I remembered the tough-as-rawhide little woman who used yellow headbands to hold back her iron gray hair. "Mrs. Woodburn, the woman who owns the stable where Didi works out. Do you have any idea where she lives?"

"She has an apartment on the top floor of the Woodburn Academy," Nancy said. "Arnold mentioned that a few months ago—he couldn't fathom how she could stand the smell of horses twenty-four hours a day. Didi might go there. That stable was practically her second home. Are you going to call Arnold?"

"No. I'm going to make a surprise visit to Mrs. Woodburn."

"Good luck," Nancy said. "If she's there, I hope Didi will talk to you."

Before I left the Dakota, I changed into slacks, a tank top, and a cotton jacket. My last act was to slip the small digital recorder I used to dictate story notes into the side pocket of the jacket.

Chapter 48

IT WAS NEARLY eleven o'clock when I got out of the cab at the corner of Amsterdam Avenue and Eighty-fifth Street, half a block south of the Woodburn Academy. I would have called Matt to tell him where I thought Didi might be, but Arnold was with him, and I wanted to talk to Didi before Arnold could stop me.

The street was pretty quiet. Some vehicle traffic, but the majority of the cars I saw were snug in their precious parking spaces. The few businesses on the block were closed for the night. I passed a trio of teenage girls, giggling, their arms linked. They were talking about a boy named Jerry and didn't seem to notice me.

Most of the wide, three-story building that housed the Woodburn Academy was dark, but light shone through the slats of two shuttered windows on the top floor. Cautiously, I made my way across the front of the building, looking for an entrance that would lead to the residence above the stables. I found it on the north side: a small alcove with an unmarked door. Easy to miss unless someone was looking for it.

I tried the door, but it was locked. There was enough illumination from the street lamp at the corner of Amsterdam and Eighty-sixth to see a button just below a wall speaker. I pressed it, heard a faint buzz from deep inside, and waited. No response. I pushed the buzzer again, holding my finger against it longer this time. Another moment, and a woman's raspy voice came through the speaker.

"Who the hell is it?" Her tone was not welcoming.

"Morgan Tyler, a friend of Didi's. I need to see you, Mrs. Woodburn."

"We're not open. Come back tomorrow."

"This is urgent. I'm not going away until I speak to you. Please let me come up, just for a few minutes."

"No. Go away."

I made a calculated bluff. "Didi Rose is missing. I think she's with you. If you don't let me talk to her, I'll tell the police you kidnapped Didi."

She muttered a word the nuns told me not to say. Ever. Two seconds of silence, then the door buzzed open.

Narrow wooden stairs led up to the living quarters. I took them two at a time.

Mrs. Woodburn stood in the doorway, waiting for me. She was in a long terry cloth zip-up robe and fuzzy slippers instead of jeans and riding boots, but her hair was still held back from her face by a yellow headband.

"I did not kidnap Didi." She was keeping her voice low, but there was an angry snap in her tone. "No matter how much Mr. Rose pays me to let her ride, I didn't sign on for *this*."

She stepped back to let me into her living room. It was decorated like a tack room, with bridles and harnesses on the walls, along with dozens of photographs from horse shows. At the far end of the room, next to a closed door, stood a display case that held an assortment of award plaques, first-place ribbons, and a few engraved silver prize cups that could use a polish. A painting of a handsome black horse hung above a gas fireplace.

To me, the most interesting thing in the room was the big leather couch beneath the window. Interesting, because it was made up like a bed, with sheets, a blanket, and a pillow. I guessed Mrs. Woodburn was sleeping here.

Copies of *Young Rider* magazine covered the coffee table in front of the couch. On top of one issue was a short glass half full of amber liquid. I was close enough to Mrs. Woodburn to catch a faint whiff of liquor on her breath.

"Where's Didi?" I asked.

Mrs. Woodburn nodded toward the closed door. "I gave her the bedroom. She got here about four hours ago, just after I closed up. Crying so hard she could barely see. I said I wanted to call her father, but that just made her more hysterical. I gave her a glass of milk—she wouldn't eat anything—and then I tried to persuade her to go to sleep. She said she would, and she was quiet for a while, but a few minutes ago I heard her turn the bedroom TV on. I was trying to figure out what to do, when you came, accusing me of kidnapping."

"I apologize for that, Mrs. Woodburn. May I see her?"

My reluctant hostess waved one hand in a go-ahead gesture.

I knocked lightly on the door, waited a few seconds. Knocked a little harder, to be heard over the sound of a television show. No response. I opened the door.

Carrying on the horse-world theme, Mrs. Woodburn's bedroom was decorated like a bunkhouse—or what I imagined a bunkhouse looked like from the old western movies I'd seen. A simple wooden bed with a bright blanket folded at the bottom of it. Walls covered with photos of horses and people standing beside or riding horses. A bedside lamp made from a carved statue of a horse. A bureau. Only two objects didn't belong in this decor: a big-screen TV set, and the slender figure lying on the bed, with the sheet pulled up to her neck. Didi's face was buried in a pillow.

I closed the door and moved within a few feet of the bed.

"Didi. It's Morgan. I'm here to help you."

"Nobody can help me." Her voice was partially muffled by the pillow, but her words were clear enough to understand.

"I think I can, if you'll let me." She didn't reply, but at least she didn't scream and order me away. I sat down on the edge of the bed, careful to keep at least a foot of space between us, so as not to crowd her. "Didi, your dad came to see me tonight. He's very worried about you."

She sat up and turned toward me. Her eyes were red and swollen from hours of crying. "I want to go far away, but I don't have enough money to buy a ticket. You could get a ticket for me—I'll pay you back. I can't go home—Daddy's going to hate me!"

"Oh, Didi, he couldn't possibly hate you. He adores you."

"He won't love me when he finds out what I did." The tears started again, filling her eyes and rolling down her pale cheeks.

There was something else in Didi's eyes: guilt. When I reached out to comfort her, she threw herself into my arms, sobbing against my chest. I stroked her hair, murmuring words meant to soothe. Slowly, the gasping sobs that made her thin shoulders tremble began to subside.

"Tell me, Didi. You'll feel so much better when you share it with me. And I promise I will help you."

She drew her head away from my chest and rubbed her running nose with the back of one hand. Keeping an arm still around her, I reached over and plucked several tissues from the box on the bedside table. I gave them to her and she blew her nose.

While Didi was wiping and blowing her nose, a picture

began to form in my mind. It was an ugly picture, but the fragments of it that I'd seen up to this moment at last fit together into a coherent whole. If my guess was right, it would save Nancy's life, but it would devastate Didi's.

I took some more tissues and dabbed gently at Didi's wet cheeks. "You told a lie, didn't you, sweetie?"

Staring down at her fingers twisting the sheet, she nodded.

"About Jay Garwood, wasn't it?"

Still unwilling to look at me, she nodded again.

"Is he dead?" Her voice was so low I could barely hear it, and she sounded closer to age five than to twelve.

"No," I said. "He's in the hospital, but he's going to be all right." I made my voice strong, to sound sure, even though this answer was more my hope than the truth.

She responded to my words by lifting her head to look at me. "He wasn't killed? He was just *injured*. That's not so bad . . . When somebody injures somebody, they just have to pay money for it, right?"

"That's true a lot of the time," I said, to encourage her to go on. Now I was sure I knew what had happened, but she had to tell me the details. Turning slightly away from her, pretending to reach for another tissue, I slipped my right hand into the pocket of my jacket and turned on the little tape recorder.

"When one person injures another, often the problem can be solved by settling some money on the one who's hurt."

"Then the person wouldn't have to go to jail?" Her voice was full of hope.

"Your father is a brilliant attorney," I said. "He knows how to make deals that are fair to everyone."

She sighed, as though a terrible burden had been lifted from her shoulders.

"Did you lie to your dad? Did you tell him something about Jay that wasn't true?"

"Yes," she admitted. "I didn't want anyone to get hurt, but I wanted Daddy to live with Mummy and me again." She swallowed, but went on. "I told Daddy that Jay . . . tried to . . . you know . . . *kiss* me."

"But he didn't."

She shook her head. "No. But Daddy got *soo* mad! He went running out. I think he was going to see Jay, to tell him not to come near us again. A little while later, Millie— that's our housekeeper—asked me to go downstairs and ask Mummy what time she wanted her to serve dinner." Her eyes began to fill with tears again. "But when I got there, Nancy had killed Mummy. I never got to tell her . . ." She couldn't finish. Her breath started to come in little gasps.

I cradled her in my arms until her breathing normalized. When she was calm again, I said softly, "So your daddy hurt Jay, because of what you told him."

"Yes. I woke up really early this morning. Daddy was coming home. He didn't see me, but I saw him putting his gun back in the safe. Then later it was on TV that Jay had been shot and I just knew that's where Daddy had been. But it's going to be all right, because Jay didn't die, and Daddy will pay him."

"When Jay is better, I think things can be worked out. What you need to do right now is get some rest. Do you think you can sleep?"

She nodded. "Will you tell Daddy, about what I did? Tell him I did it so he could be happy with us. We'd be a family again . . ." Her eyes were starting to close. "Morgan, can you turn off the light, but leave the TV on?"

"Sure. I'll come back in the morning. We'll have breakfast together, and make some plans."

I'm not sure she heard me; she might already have fallen asleep. I turned the recorder off.

Leaving the academy building, I turned south. The

Twentieth Precinct was less than four blocks away, on West Eighty-second. Matt and Arnold were probably still there.

I hadn't gone more than a few feet when I was grabbed from behind and a hand was clapped over my mouth.

Chapter 49

HE DRAGGED ME into the dark alley between buildings on the south side of the riding academy. Shoving me hard against the wall, my brow mashed into the rough brick, he hissed in my ear. "I'm going to take my hand away, but if you scream, I'll kill you. Understand?"

I stopped struggling, stood still, and gave him what little bit of a nod I could manage. He had me pinned so forcefully I could barely move my head.

Still keeping my face and body pressed against the alley wall, his hand came away from my mouth. Before I could take a deep breath, I heard a *click*, and felt the cold steel muzzle of a pistol against my cheek.

I didn't have to turn around to see who was holding a weapon on me. "Why are you doing this, Arnold?"

"You phoned Didi, and lured her away. You put her up there, with that horse woman."

"No, Arnold, I didn't call her." I turned around but kept my back to the brick wall. If I had to launch myself at him, to keep him from shooting me, it would be better to have something to push off from. "Didi ran away by herself. After you and Matt left the Dakota, I got the idea she might come here."

It was pretty dark, but there was just enough light from the three-quarter moon and from the streetlight just past the mouth of the alley for me to see Arnold's face. His features were a portrait of anguish. Beads of sweat dotted his high forehead, but his hand holding the pistol on me was steady. I had no doubt that if I made a wrong move, or said the wrong thing, he would kill me.

I leaned against the wall, my hands at my sides, and kept my tone gentle. Nonthreatening. "Didi's in a terrible state," I said. "She knows that you tried to kill Jay Garwood, and she's hysterical because she feels guilty about it."

"Guilty? That's ridiculous! She didn't do anything wrong. It was that bastard—"

"No, Arnold. She feels guilty because she lied to you about Jay."

"What are you saying?" His voice was tense. Arnold was so smart, I think he suspected what I was about to say, but was fighting comprehension.

"Didi told you Jay tried to do something to her, but he didn't. She said that because she wanted you to stop him from seeing Veronica. She thought you'd just scare him away."

"No! That's not true—she wouldn't lie to me."

"Arnold, she's done it before. Remember back a few months ago, when she had her riding accident? You thought it was because Nancy was careless in tightening the girth, but that wasn't true. Didi held her arm inside the strap so that it couldn't be tightened properly and so would slip while she was riding. She fell off that horse on purpose, so that you'd blame Nancy and break up with her."

Arnold shook his head furiously. "Ridiculous! If that

were true, Nancy would have told me. We had a terrible fight. I said awful things—accused her of deliberately trying to hurt my daughter. She wouldn't have taken that if what you're saying—"

"Nancy refused to tell you the truth, and wouldn't let me, because she said it would break your heart to think Didi would do something like that. Nancy took the blame because she loved you." *That turned out to be a big mistake,* I thought, but I kept those words to myself.

I could see that Arnold was shaken by what I'd told him. The pistol's barrel was still pointed at my heart, but his mind had turned inward, processing what he'd heard. I took a chance on his divided attention, eased my right hand into my pocket, and turned on the little tape recorder.

"Didi saw you come home early this morning," I said. "She saw you put the pistol back in your safe. This afternoon, when she heard that someone shot Jay Garwood, she realized you were the one, and she knew it was her fault. When I told her that Jay was alive, not dead, she broke down and told me what made her run away."

"No! No . . ."

"I knew Nancy didn't murder Veronica, so I've been trying to figure out who did. I didn't seriously consider you, because you didn't have a motive. But now I know my mistake was in using the wrong *verb.* Of course you wouldn't have *murdered* Veronica—but you killed her, probably by accident. You thought she'd exposed Didi to a child molester, so you hit her in a fit of rage, with the nearest object handy. I'm sure you didn't mean to kill her—you lost your head for that one terrible instant. Then, realizing she was dead, you panicked and left the building to keep the appointment with your client. You didn't know Nancy was coming to see Veronica, or that Nancy would be discovered with the body and charged with murder. You wouldn't have deliberately framed Nancy, would you?"

"No." Arnold's voice was a croak of pain. He took a

deep breath and swallowed before he went on. "That lawyer I wanted her to hire—Cynthia, the one I trained—I was really going to mastermind Nancy's defense, behind the scenes. I would have done anything to save her from prison."

"Anything except *confess*," I said, angry that he'd made Nancy suffer.

"I had to think of Didi. Her mother was . . . gone. I couldn't let her lose her father, too." Arnold began to look a little unsteady on his feet. "It's so hot." He lowered the pistol, but just a couple of inches; the barrel was still aimed at my kill zone.

"Arnold, you look sick," I said.

"I've got to sit down. Have to think . . ." He brought the gun back up and gestured with it. "We'll go to my car."

The last thing I wanted to do was get into a car with a distraught killer holding a 9-mm automatic, but I was sure that if I tried to run, he'd shoot me. Even in his current confused state, he was bigger and stronger than I, and armed. And desperate. I couldn't hope to overpower him. All things considered, I decided to do what he wanted. At the very least, cooperating would buy me some time. Silently, I swore at myself for leaving the apartment in such a hurry I forgot to take the little canister of Mace I usually carried when I went out alone at night.

With Arnold holding the pistol against my side in such a way that no one passing us on the sidewalk could see what he was doing, he directed me forward and around the corner to his big silver Lincoln. He pressed the button on the car key, which turned off the burglar alarm and unlocked the doors. Bizarrely, even now he played the courtly gentleman and opened the passenger door for me.

"Get in, lean forward, and put your hands flat on the dashboard," he said. "I don't want to shoot you, but I will if you scream, or try to run."

I did as I was commanded.

As he climbed in behind the wheel, I said, "I'm cooperating, Arnold. I want to talk to you." He settled his bulk and closed his door, but kept the weapon pointed at me.

I said, "This position is getting uncomfortable."

"All right," he said. "Lean back against the seat and lock your fingers together. Rest your clasped hands in your lap."

I followed instructions.

He turned the key in the ignition. The motor came to life. He let it idle. "It's hot outside. I need air-conditioning so I can think," he said.

His needing to think was good for me. Clearly, his internal "jury" was still deliberating my fate.

Jury. That thought inspired a tactic I could take with him. "Arnold, you went a little crazy because you thought your daughter had been molested. Veronica's death was just an accident. No jury would convict you."

He kept the gun on me. "What about my shooting Garwood? That wasn't in the heat of the moment. I'd charted his habits, found out about his five A.M. jogging routine, and I lay in wait for him."

"But you didn't *kill* him," I said. "You could have—you could have aimed at his head or his chest—but instead you fired to hurt him, to make him suffer. Isn't that right?"

"Wrong. I fully intended to kill him, but I wanted him to die in as much pain as possible, because of what he . . . Oh, God!" Arnold's face contorted in horror. It was as though *finally* the full realization struck him that what he had done was based on a child's lie. He whispered, "Didi . . . she'll never get over knowing . . ."

Didi was his weakness. I hammered on that. "You can protect Didi. Let's go to the District Attorney. You'll explain what happened, and make a deal. You can say you *thought* Jay had been inappropriate with Didi—you don't need to say she told you that he had. If you confess, and plea-bargain, there won't be a criminal trial. She won't have to testify about what she did. You'll spare her a terrible ordeal. And you can probably make a deal with Jay for no civil trial. He'd only sue you for *money*, compensation for what he's going through. If you're willing to pay, I'll make him understand that he's better off agreeing to a settlement instead of waiting years to get to court, and paying a lawyer."

We sat in silence. Arnold had set the air conditioner on high. While he was thinking, the temperature in the vehicle got lower and lower. I began to shiver, but I wasn't sure whether it was from the cold or from the fear that I wouldn't leave this car alive.

Well, I wasn't going to just sit here and wait to die. Carefully, I unlocked my fingers and slid my right hand over toward the passenger door. Keeping my body straight, moving only that one hand, I explored the door until I grasped the handle.

At that moment Arnold heaved a deep sigh. I stiffened. He'd made up his mind and was going to do—something. With a little groan, he transferred the pistol to his left hand, turned the key again, and started the car.

My hand gripped the door handle. If I had to, I'd jump, risking minor injuries to stay alive. "Arnold, where are we going?"

"To the police station," he said.

Traffic was light. The Twentieth Precinct was only three blocks away. We were in front of the entrance in a couple of minutes.

Arnold stopped the car, but didn't turn off the engine. "Get out."

"You can pull into that spot next to the cruiser," I said.

"Open your door and get out." His voice was without inflection. The voice of a robot. At this moment, he seemed even more frightening than he had been back in the alley. I wasn't going to argue with him.

I opened the door, swung my right leg out onto the street. Suddenly, I felt a powerful shove in the middle of my back. I went tumbling out of the car, onto the cement. My left shoulder thudded against the curb.

The uniformed officer at the entrance yelled, "Hey! Stop!" as Arnold floored the accelerator and zoomed away. The Lincoln's taillights, glowing like two red eyes, disappeared as the car screeched around the next corner.

"Are you okay, miss?" asked the police officer as he helped me to stand.

My shoulder hurt where it collided with the curb, my left knee was skinned and the fabric covering it shredded, but when I reached into my right-hand pocket and pulled out the unharmed little tape recorder, I said, "I'm fine, but I need to see Detective Phoenix right away."

Chapter 50

THE VOICE QUALITY on the tape recording was excellent. Copies were made and sent over to the office of the District Attorney. A warrant for Arnold's apprehension was drawn up, signed, and an all points bulletin alert broadcast to law enforcement personnel in the tristate area, warning that Arnold Rose should be considered "armed and dangerous."

As soon as Matt and G. G. listened to the tape and began the warrant process, I phoned Nancy, to tell her what had happened, and that she was no longer in danger of going to prison. She would have her life back, and be able to resume her career.

Although profoundly relieved that her ordeal was over, Nancy couldn't take pleasure in Arnold's situation; there was a time not long ago when she'd thought she was in love with him.

One thing about this resolution worried me. I asked Nancy, "What's going to happen to Didi, without either of her parents? She can't stay on with Mrs. Woodburn."

"Arnold has a sister in Maryland," Nancy said. "Carol Grant. I've met her a few times. She's a lovely woman, with a nice husband who's a public affairs officer in the Navy. They have a ten-year-old daughter. Didi could probably live with them. I think I should phone Carol now, and tell her what's happened. I'd hate to have her hear about this on the news."

Ten minutes later, my cell rang. "I just talked to Arnold's sister," Nancy said. "She'll be at Mrs. Woodburn's door by the time Didi wakes up tomorrow."

IT WAS NEARLY four in the morning, and G. G. had finally gone home to bed. Only four men and women on the midnight to eight A.M. shift were at their desks, doing paperwork. I'd never been in the squad room when it was this quiet.

Matt and I were having sandwiches and coffee at his desk when Matt's phone rang. He picked it up, listened, said "good" a couple of times, then thanked whoever called and hung up. He looked up at me, grinning. "They got Rose at JFK. He's claiming he doesn't know who he is, or how he got there. He didn't have a weapon on him."

"What's this 'I don't know who I am' business? Is he going to try an insanity defense?"

Matt shrugged. "That's up to him, or his lawyer. We're done here. I'll take you home."

I crumpled up the last of my sandwich and the wrapper and tossed it into Matt's trashcan. "Will you stay over with me?"

"Only if you promise not to get frisky until I've had a few hours sleep," he said.

"I promise."

As we exited the precinct house, out into the predawn air, I asked playfully, "Does a promise count if I kept my fingers crossed?"

As it turned out, we were both too tired to get frisky. I slept in the circle of Matt's arms, and Magic slept on top of Matt.

Hours later, when we awakened, I knew the time had come to tell Matt what I'd been keeping from him. At any moment, the media would have my story. I didn't want Matt to learn about me that way.

I turned around in his arms, to face him. He brushed the hair out of my eyes.

"I must look a mess," I said.

He smiled sleepily. "My kind of mess."

"Matt, there's something you don't know about me . . ."

"There's a lot I don't know. I figured out months ago that there was something important you were keeping to yourself. It made me a little crazy that you wouldn't let me really get to know you, but I haven't pushed. I wanted you tell me about it when you were ready."

"I am now . . ."

I told Matt everything—about Ray Wilson, about Walter rescuing me from him, and giving me his last name. I told him what I *hadn't* known until Bobby found Walter retired in Florida: that Walter had arranged for my safety and my schooling. I even told Matt how and why I went to Belle Valley, what I did to make Ray Wilson tell me where I came from. I described the interview Walter and I did with the Ohio police, and that I'd told them they could go public with my story, in the hope it would encourage other people who had been hurt by Wilson to come forward and testify against him.

From time to time during my story, I felt Matt's muscles clench, but he listened without interrupting. He just held me, and gently stroked my back. When I finally stopped talking, he tightened his arms around me and whispered, "I'm so sorry you had to go through that."

"I survived, and so many people have gone through a lot worse. There's one more thing I have to tell you, and if it makes a difference, I'll understand." I felt Matt tense. "Because of . . . an injury . . . when I was little, I can't have children."

Matt was quiet for a few seconds, and then he eased himself into a sitting position. "Are you sure about that? Doctors make mistakes."

I sat up, too, and shook my head. "There's no mistake. Most people want children. You should know before we . . . before we get too serious."

Matt said softly, "I've been serious about you for a long time."

"But you didn't know about this. It must matter to you."

"I guess I thought I'd have kids someday, but it hasn't been something I've ever focused on. I've seen enough awful things in my job to know there aren't any guarantees in life."

"What are you saying?"

"That you're more important to me than any woman I've ever known," he said. "I'm a lucky guy."

We lay down again, and fell asleep in each other's arms.

BECAUSE OF MY connection to a hit television show, my story did get into the media. All over the media.

My friends and coworkers were kind, supportive, and nonintrusive. I saw sympathy in their eyes, but they didn't ask any questions.

At the office, Betty fielded calls from reporters who wanted interviews. I didn't give any. TV magazine shows called, wanting me to guest on camera. I refused. I didn't want attention; I wanted Ray Wilson to be locked up for the rest of his life.

Walter had been in Ohio for five days when he called with the news I'd been waiting for: after reading about me, a mother had come forward with her young daughter to testify that Ray Wilson had molested the girl in a park restroom. At last, there was evidence recent enough to bring him to trial.

Wilson never got to trial. While he was in the jailhouse shower, someone stabbed him to death with the sharpened handle of a metal spoon. The police went through the motions of an investigation, but Walter said they didn't try very hard to find Wilson's killer.

Jay Garwood recovered from being shot by Arnold Rose, and became a celebrity because of it. I reworked his storyline slightly, so that he could come back to the show without slowing his healing. He immediately asked Tommy for a raise, based on his belief that the publicity about him was bringing many new viewers to the show. It was true that our ratings were up. Tommy agreed to a modest increase, and said he would consider more when Jay's current contract expired.

Nancy decided to use vacation time she'd accrued and take a month off before she went back to work at the law firm. "Chet's invited me to go to Vienna and Prague with him. Maybe even Bratislava. He needs to study some recently declassified World War Two archives for his book. We'll be traveling just as *friends*. Separate rooms. I insisted on paying for my own plane tickets and hotel bills. What do you think?"

"I think you should at least let him pay for dinner when you two go out," I joked. "Seriously, that trip is a wonderful idea." The enthusiasm in my voice was genuine. "After all you've been through, you need a radical change of scene. I predict you two will have a great time together. Besides, as you mentioned once, he's tall enough so you can wear high heels with him."

"Thank you," she said. "What do you want me to bring you back from Europe?"

"Anything—as long as it's made of chocolate."

That night, while Matt and I were having dinner, he said, "I've been thinking about your mother."

"So have I."

"She left you twenty-seven years ago. It's likely she's no longer alive."

"More than likely—it's probable."

Matt reached across the table and took my hand. "Are you going to look for her?"

"I don't know . . ." I said. And that was the truth.

GET CLUED IN

Ever wonder how to find out about all the latest Berkley Prime Crime and Signet mysteries?

berkleysignetmysteries.com

- *See what's new*
- *Find author appearances*
- *Win fantastic prizes*
- *Get reading recommendations*
- *Sign up for the mystery newsletter*
- *Chat with authors and other fans*
- *Read interviews with authors you love*

MYSTERY SOLVED.